THE HOUSE OF WOMEN

THE HOUSE OF WOMEN

Chaim Bermant

ST. MARTIN'S PRESS
NEW YORK

THE HOUSE OF WOMEN. Copyright © 1983 by Chaim Bermant.
All rights reserved. Printed in the United States of America.
No part of this book may be used or reproduced in any
manner whatsoever without written permission except in the
case of brief quotations embodied in critical articles or reviews.
For information, address St. Martin's Press, 175 Fifth Avenue,
New York, N.Y. 10010.

Library of Congress Cataloging in Publication Data

Bermant, Chaim, 1929—
　The house of women.

　I. Title.
PR6052.E63H6　1983　　　823'.914　　　83-2925
ISBN 0-312-39306-7

Published in Great Britain by George Weidenfeld &
Nicolson Limited

First U.S. Edition

10 9 8 7 6 5 4 3 2 1

Contents

1 The House of Women 1
2 Dark Age 16
3 Life with Stevie 27
4 The Second Coming 40
5 The Candidate 56
6 Otto 71
7 Vesta 94
8 Kept Woman 115
9 Grace 134
10 Woman of Letters 144
11 Rustic Idyll 159
12 Atonement 174
13 Prodigal Daughter 194
14 A Woman for all Seasons 214
15 Ladies in Retirement 235

1
The House of Women

Father wanted a small family, but he also wanted an heir, and he had four daughters and two wives before he eventually had a son.

He was not, he said, adverse to daughters as such, but his grandfather had had four sons, his father two and he felt obliged to have at least one – 'a replacement', as he called him – to keep his branch of the family going, especially as other branches had faded out of their own accord. His family name was Courlander. Two of his uncles had changed their name to Lander, and a third to Lancer, which was perhaps just as well, for apparently none of them had brought particular credit to the family, and in any case two of them had died without issue. Father's own brother Willie was a bachelor, and therefore the full burden of perpetuating the line fell on him, and he approached it with a gravity which he did not display in other walks of life and which must have borne heavily on poor mummy.

Father had a younger sister called Stevie, and in 1931 or 1932, when she was eighteen, she was sent to Berlin to perfect her German and there became friendly with Thea, a banker's daughter. Thea later came to England to study, spent three years at Cambridge and stayed frequently with my grandparents. She was tall and slender, with great, soulful eyes, and a severe, rather manly hairstyle. All her photographs show her to be a rather handsome young woman. None show her smiling, and I could never understand the basis of her relationship with Stevie, who was large and genial, even if she rarely had anything to be genial about. In time she also became friendly with father, who was rather like Stevie in appearance and build, and not unlike her in temperament. He was at that time in the family metal business.

He had never wanted to be a businessman, but grew up in an age when sons did what was expected of them, and he was expected, like his older brother, Willie, to work in the business. Stevie believed that he had proposed to Thea because it was likewise expected of him.

'She was of good family – which is to say she was rich – of good appearance, and with a good education. I am not really sure if your father wanted her as a wife, but *his* father wanted her as a daughter-in-law. The proposal, when it came, was totally unexpected, and poor Thea said to me: "So you think he is serious, I can never tell with you English." But he was perfectly serious and they married shortly before the war. It was a desolate little affair.'

I remember studying the wedding group as a child, trying to work out who was who – they had all changed so much in the seven or eight intervening years. There was grandpa, small and thin with a bushy moustache and large ears, his head to the side, looking rather pleased with himself; grandma, her mouth taut with disapproval, her glasses glinting in a half-hearted attempt at a smile; Uncle Willie, tall thin, with a long nose, thin black moustache, and ill-fitting jacket, his head held up high, with a slightly quizzical look, as if something was happening which he could not quite fathom; Callum, the best man, heavy-shouldered, with deep-set, blue eyes, his face flushed, his mouth open as if he was still drawing breath from some mighty exertion; father, baring a fine set of teeth in a smile which made him look fierce rather than amiable, and poor, white-faced mummy, holding on to his arm as a drunk might hold on to a lamp-post, and looking like an angel on a tombstone. Only Stevie, with her large, lustrous eyes, looked wholesome, human and alive.

There were no relatives from mummy's side of the family, which struck me as odd and, being a precocious and inquisitive little horror, I often pressed father about it; but he was not very forthcoming, and even Stevie, who was usually frank and open about almost everything, seemed reluctant to talk about it. When I asked grandma she got rather impatient (as she often did). 'Not everyone is fortunate enough to have parents and family, you know. She was an orphan,' which, indeed, was the simple truth of the matter, but at that time I associated orphans with distant days and poverty, and poverty was not something which I could readily associate with my family. The full, unhappy truth was to emerge later and it explained many of the things which had mystified me about my mother.

Father had hardly settled down to married life, when the war broke out and he joined the army. He was thirty by then and, according to Stevie, he hadn't even waited to be called up, but used the war as an excuse to snatch at his freedom. Stevie, I should perhaps add, nearly always spoke of marriage as a form of incarceration, but it is true that the photos we have of father as a soldier make him look slimmer, younger, happier, more alert, than he ever seemed in civilian dress. But that may have been because in the first year of the war he was in the same unit as Callum, and this may have given him the cheerful air of a boy among boys. Callum himself was a professional soldier. He and father were at Harrow together, and they then toured the world together; but when Callum went on to Sandhurst, father went on to Oxford. The war, therefore, was something of a reunion, and like most Englishmen, father enjoyed an easier, or at least chummier, relationship with men than with women.

Leave, to judge from the number of his children, could not have been all that infrequent. When we asked him about his war experience, he would say: 'Barely heard the sound of fire, dear child. It was all very boring.' Still, we would see him from time to time at ceremonial occasions with a breastful of medals, which, he insisted, 'were all for being somewhere or other, and not for doing anything special'. He was commissioned early in the war and according to Stevie, he was a lieutenant when Vesta was born, a captain when I was born and a major by the time

Vida appeared. 'I think they gave him a pip per child,' she said. 'If only he had remained in uniform till Rocky came along he might have been a colonel.' Uncle Willie, who had served with valour and who had received the Military Cross during the Burma campaign, rose only to the rank of captain. 'Very unfair,' said father, 'but that's how the world is, unfair – and the army is even worse than the world.'

Willie not only received the MC in Burma, but numerous bullet wounds and cyclical malaria as well, and one could tell the seasons by the onset of his attacks.

'People who haven't fought against the Japs don't know what war is,' he would say, with extravagant frequency. 'Tough, fearless, indestructable – never give in. You could outshoot a Jap, but man for man you could never outfight him. They'll rule the world one day – the Japs.'

Vesta was born in 1940 and everyone who was around at the time spoke of her as the most exquisite infant they had ever seen. There is a photograph taken of mother and her which looks like a Botticelli.

I was born some fourteen months later and there is no similar photo of mother and me. The war had by then been raging for two years and we were living in the country, so that it may have been more difficult to get to a photographer, but the main reason I think lay in the fact that I was a distinctly unbeautiful child and, according to Stevie, father's first words when he set eyes on me (I was by then over a year old) were: 'What a lovely little ugly duckling.' The ugly ducklings of lore eventually became swans, but I stayed as I was and became known in the family as Ducks, and Ducks I have remained from that day even unto this (and as my actual name is Henrietta, I am much happier with Ducks).

Vida was born in 1943. Father must by then have reconciled himself to the thought that he might never have a son, and called her Davida, after his maternal grandfather to whom he had been very attached. Davida was quickly corrupted to Vida, which is an awkward name to carry through English life, and especially an English public school, and she soon became variously known as VD, Syphilis, Pox and Clap, and for a time, and of her own accord, she assumed the name of Alice, but she liked Vida and reverted to it once she left school.

Vida, like Vesta, was a beautiful child and, like her, became a beautiful woman; but there was always something vaguely ethereal about Vesta, who was grey-eyed, with a greyish tinge to her blonde hair, and a greyish touch to her personality, whereas Vida was a pocket version of Stevie, dark-haired, dark-eyed, full-mouthed (with a little too much chin), earthy. One could not imagine Vesta, for all her attractions, inspiring anything as sordid as lust, whereas Vida rarely inspired anything else, which did not mean that she was promiscuous, for unlike her aunt and her sisters (or at least some of them) she kept her passions under firm control.

And then came Rachelle, or Rocky, as we called her, which, in the event, proved a not inappropriate name, and if Vesta was the most beautiful among us, Rocky was the most attractive. 'When I see Vesta,' one of her admirers told us, 'I hear organ music playing in the distance.' Rocky inspired the sound of jazz. We were rather tall, but Rocky was petite, mercurial, with bright, green eyes flecked with brown, high cheek-bones, snub nose, freckles, and when she smiled, or even when she talked, small dimples appeared everywhere, in her cheeks, by her mouth, under her eyes. She sparkled like a diamond, and could be as hard as one.

Grandpa had what he called a 'cottage', though it was in fact a fairly substantial house with a large garden in a small village in Essex, and mummy moved there shortly after Vesta was born. Grandma was her only companion and they didn't get on all that well. 'Your mummy', Stevie explained, 'was used to servants. There were none to be had in wartime and she therefore turned to your grandma for help, and she, for her part, was not used to being regarded as a servant, and in any case, as you know, she is a rather firm little woman. "There's a war on," she would say, "and we must all learn to cope." ' Grandpa finally saved the situation by getting Mrs Evans, the elderly widow of a former employee, to come out and act as housekeeper, but that too brought its own complications. Mummy was in the habit of taking long walks by herself in the dark. Mrs Evans also noticed that the bedside table was stacked with foreign-looking books and she sometimes overheard her speaking on the telephone in German, and finally became convinced that she was a German spy. She told the police, and the village constable came round on his bicycle to investigate and followed mummy on some of her walks, and did find something mysterious in the fact that she took such walks without even the need to exercise a dog, but finally reached the conclusion that 'she's not a spy – just batty'.

Shortly after I was born, Stevie, who was in the Woman's Auxiliary Air Force, was posted to a base not far from us and joined the household several nights a week and most weekends. Things should have become more cheerful, but it was then that mother had the first of her breakdowns.

'I think it might have come earlier,' said Stevie, 'but she waited till I was around for a sympathetic presence.'

My earliest memory of mummy was at a Victory Day party, when I was nearly four. It was in a large house, I can't remember whose. There was a lot of music and noise, and balloons and paper streamers, and we were all laughing and singing, when mummy, for no reason at all, burst into tears and ran out of the room, and Stevie ran after her. Father came home on compassionate leave, but in fact never went back to the army. We returned to London, but mother said the London air did not agree with her. We rented a large house in the country.

Mrs Evans came to live with us, but she couldn't cope with both the house and the children, and father brought in a governess, a tall, handsome woman called Tilly, who, at first sight, we found rather severe and intimidating, which was perhaps why he had brought her in. A few months later grandpa died. I was six or seven at the time. I hadn't seen all that much of him and remembered him as a rather worried-looking little man whose clothes seemed very old-fashioned and too large for him. He had been staying with us at the time and died in his sleep and I was surprised at the number of cars which turned up for his funeral, and not only cars, but buses, all crowded with people. His father – an immigrant from Germany – had established a small metal business which he had built up into a considerable enterprise, including an engineering workshop which employed nearly two hundred people, and his entire workforce had turned up for the funeral.

Grandpa living had been a silent, shadowy figure, and grandpa dead was so little different from grandpa alive that his passing hardly affected us, but we were soon to be affected in other ways.

Shortly after Rocky was born, mummy was taken ill. We were never told the nature of the illness, but she stopped speaking, spent most of her time in bed and, in fact, from that time onwards I cannot remember seeing her fully dressed. Father, according to Stevie, was also under strain, but if he was he didn't show it. Mummy seemed to be wasting away, whereas father seemed to be growing in size. 'People do when they're under strain,' said Stevie, 'they eat more, they drink more.'

Then one day mummy was taken to hospital and months passed before we were allowed a visit. We had seen her in hospital before, after Rocky was born, but it had been cheerful then. The place had been full of flowers, and happy groups of visiting relatives, and pretty young nurses in crisp aprons, but this place, a large mansion in large grounds, was different. Visitors were few, the nurses seemed elderly and frumpish and there were many dimly-lit corridors. Mummy sat upright in bed, with sunken eyes, looking very white and frail and saying nothing. I'm not sure if she even recognized us. Father tried to sound cheerful and chatted away endlessly all the time we were there, but her face remained expressionless. That was the last time we saw her, and she died a few weeks later. She had by then been transferred to another hospital. The snows were so bad that the tyres of the hearse had to be fitted with chains to get to the crematorium for the funeral.

'We're orphans now, you know,' said Vesta in her low voice. There it was, that word again, and again it didn't fit, for the orphans we read about all seemed to have sad, cramped lives. It wasn't like that at all with us. In fact things became rather lively. There was something of a war of succession between grandma and Tilly on who should be in charge of the house. Father, I suppose, could have settled it, but he didn't like to intervene in such matters and in any case he was often away on business. Whenever Tilly would give an order, grandma would give a counter-order and vice versa, and as Mrs Evans tended to side with grandma we felt, out of fairness, that we should side with Tilly.

'It wasn't really a matter of who was boss,' Stevie later explained. 'Mother was afraid that as long as Tilly was around your father might marry her. I tried to tell her that her fears were groundless and that your father was too much of a snob.'

Perhaps Stevie came to have the same fear, for Vesta and I noticed that whenever father was home, Stevie somehow contrived to bring one of her friends with her for a meal, or sometimes for a night or a weekend. Vesta and I, certainly, would have been perfectly content with Tilly as a new mother. She was fair-haired, with slanting grey eyes which made her look a bit like a vixen, and a brisk, cheerful, no-nonsense personality, and had no difficulty in putting anyone, except possibly grandma, in place.

'She's just the sort of woman father needs,' said Vesta, which was a rather precocious utterance for a child of nine, and I was not quite precocious enough to know what she meant by it (I don't think she was either).

The fact is that though Tilly was virtually a mother to us, we knew very little about her (if it comes to that, we hadn't known all that much about our actual mother), and she was something of a mystery woman. She never spoke about herself or her family, did not seem to have any private life, and appeared to have sprung ready-made out of the ground. I had a habit of intercepting the postman as he came up the drive in the mornings and I noticed that she received letters from Leeds, all written in the same slightly childish hand, usually about once a fortnight, but sometimes in rapid succession, and when I handed them to her she did not have the look of a person receiving good news. I shared a room with Vida and she woke me in the middle of the night once to tell me she could hear the sound of sobbing. I couldn't hear a thing, but she had ears like a wolf-hound and I got out of bed, tiptoed out into the passage and stood outside Tilly's room, listening. There was no mistaking the sound. She was crying her heart out. Both Vida and I watched her carefully at breakfast the next morning, but she was her usual perky, bright-eyed self, which is more than we were, and if she had suffered some deep misfortune, she showed no sign of it. We told Vesta about it and she said, 'She's probably in love,' which left me a little mystified. 'Aren't people in love supposed to be happy?' I asked. 'Yes,' she said, 'if everything goes well, but things usually don't.' But I was still mystified, for if she was in love, who could she be in love with?

'Haven't you got eyes?' said Vesta. 'Father.'

'*Father*?'

'Father!'

I was eight or nine by then, and thought I knew what love was, but I was under the impression that it affected only people of a certain age and in certain circumstances. The idea that anyone could fall in love with a man of forty with four children struck me as vaguely absurd.

But then I noticed that Aunt Stevie was falling in and out of love with all sorts of people, of all different ages, though to my eyes, at least, she seemed to be of a fairly advanced age herself.

She was, in fact, about five years younger than father, tall with a good figure, a slightly large face, and large, luminous eyes which were slightly, ever so slightly, off centre, but which somehow, to my eyes at least, added to her attractions. She had a beautiful voice and laugh and a gay personality, and for as a long as I can remember her, she was surrounded by men. I remember one in particular, called Derek, because he looked like Gregory Peck and I asked her if she was going to marry him. 'It's not up to me, my love,' she said, 'women were not made to woo. You had better ask him.' Which is exactly what I did, and that, for the time being at least, was the last I or Aunt Stevie saw of him.

And then came Nick. I didn't care much for Nick, partly because she seemed to care too much for him, and he treated her in a casual off-hand way. At mealtimes she would sit with her food untouched, feasting on him with such ravenous eyes that one half-expected bits of him to come away, but he seemed quite oblivious to her adoration. He was tall and lean, with sunken cheeks, grey eyes and prematurely grey hair, parted at the side and a slight scar across his forehead. I don't know if he was younger than her for, in spite of his grey hair, he was extremely boyish in appearance and looked younger. He was a doctor and had a slight whiff of ether about him which made him seem even cooler than he was. Stevie was a something or other at the BBC and, as far as we knew, not particularly well off, but she showered him with presents: gold cigarette case, gold lighter, cufflinks made out of Roman gold coins.

'I don't think he'll marry her,' said Vesta, 'he's a cad,' which was strong language coming from Vesta, though I wasn't quite sure what being a cad had to do with marrying or not marrying people, for I was already then beginning to read books in which women, to their eventual distress, were marrying cads right and left. I thought that if he was, indeed, a cad, it was better that he should keep his distance, but I couldn't see quite how that could be arranged for, apart from anything else, he was also on good terms with father and Tilly.

I asked Stevie the by now, inevitable question: was she going to marry him? And she said, 'I don't know, Ducks. I don't like to think about it. These things never seem to last, but it's heaven while they do.' And her eyes seemed to fill up, but she immediately brightened and added: 'But it's not only people who marry who live happily ever after, you know.' They didn't marry, but watching them left me with a fairly clear idea of what love was, and whatever it was, it was not something which affected Tilly. Yet I couldn't understand why so lively and attractive a woman didn't have a whole column of men at her heels and one evening I asked her straight out if she had a boyfriend.

'That, Ducks, is a very personal question. It's all right in a small child, but you're getting too old for that.'

'I don't see why. It wouldn't bother me if someone asked if I had a boyfriend – not that I have.'

'But I'm much older than you and, if I haven't, I might find it embarrassing to say no.'

'And if you have?'

'I might prefer to keep quiet about it.'

And I concluded that she did have a boyfriend and that she preferred for some reason to keep quiet about it. But why?

'She might be married,' said Vesta.

'Married? Where's her husband? And besides, if she has a husband, why does she need a boyfriend?'

'Wives sometimes don't get on with their husbands and live apart,' said Vesta, which did not strike me as a satisfactory answer.

There was only one way of settling the issue. I had seen a play on television, a sordid love story, in which a wife intercepted her husband's letters and steamed them open. I decided to do the same, and half-scalded myself in the process; but as soon as it was done, I rushed upstairs and locked myself in the bathroom to read it. I turned it this way and that, that way and this, but couldn't make out a word. It wasn't in English, or German, which I might have understood, or Latin or French, which I would have recognized, or any other language I had come across. I half-feared, from the sort of handwriting on the envelope, that it might be foreign, but I wasn't prepared for this. Vesta might have known what it was, but I hesitated to ask her because she was so proper and would have been so scandalized by the thought that I had actually opened someone else's letter that she would probably refuse even to look at it, but I had to ask someone or burst. She was scandalized and gave me a long lecture and warned me that if I went on in this way I would end up on the gallows, which, at that moment, I would have regarded as a small price to learn the contents of that letter. She did, however, look at it and said it was Hebrew.

'But how could it be?'

'That's neither your business nor mine.'

'Do you mean she's Jewish?'

'What if she is? We're Jewish – sort of.'

'But do you mean she's Jewish Jewish – Jewish proper?'

'That's none of your business.'

Our Jewishness was a source of bother to us as children, if only because it touched upon an area of uncertainty, and because it set us slightly apart from almost everyone else we knew.

In a way being set apart was in itself not a bad thing. We went to a very posh prep school, which set us apart for a start, and within the school others were set apart by the fact that they were the children of well-known parents. One little girl, for example, was the daughter of an earl, another was the daughter of a Cabinet Minister, a third was the step-daughter of a film-star – which was, to our eyes, perhaps the greatest distinction of all – so that being Jewish in itself might not have bothered us, and might, indeed, have been a source of pride, if we had known for a fact that we were, but it was not the sort of fact on which our elders cared to elaborate.

It was Vesta who first raised the question. Somebody in her class had said she was Jewish – not by way of reproach, but almost in deference, during Bible class. Tilly was the first person she approached and she proved to be unusually evasive. 'I think you had better ask your father.' Father wasn't about, so she asked grandma, who wanted to know why she wanted to know. 'Because somebody in class said I was,' said Vesta. 'Then tell them to mind their own business,' said grandma. But once

Vesta got her teeth into a subject she did not let go easily. She waited till father got back, and asked him.

'Yes,' he said, 'I daresay we are.'

'What does that mean?'

'Well I should imagine non-Jews regard us as Jewish.'

Later Stevie mentioned that she had been baited at school because she was Jewish (and father retorted: 'You weren't baited because you were Jewish, you were baited because you were obnoxious'). We certainly hadn't been brought up to think of ourselves as Jews, or anything else for that matter. We never set foot in synagogue except for the occasional wedding, but then we occasionally found ourselves in church for the same reason, in fact more than occasionally, for father would always attend the church parade on Remembrance Sunday with all his medals and we would all go to the annual carol service. We also celebrated Christmas, with a Christmas dinner and Christmas presents, and, of course, a Christmas tree, so that if it came to religious observance, we were perhaps more Christian than Jewish. I suppose if someone had stopped father and asked him straight out if he was a Jew, he would have said yes, but it was no more relevant – indeed a great deal less relevant – than the fact that he was getting thin on top. We were in fact pagans, with a sentimental feeling for religion if only because we were safely distanced from it. When the steeple of the local church was blown down during a storm one night, father, of all people, became treasurer of the Church Restoration Fund, and our garden was the venue for an annual fête in aid of parish charities. The discovery that Tilly was so Jewish as to receive letters in Hebrew, therefore, had an oddly unsettling effect on me, which may simply have been due to guilt feelings about opening her letter in the first place. Yet guilt should make one contrite; whereas my feelings were directed against her rather than myself. I had done something unforgivable and could not forgive her for it. I felt that there was something rather devious about her. She had never actually *denied* she was Jewish, and had merely fallen in with the family habit of leaving the subject unmentioned, but at least we in the family had never received actual letters in Hebrew. She was the real thing, and had kept it a dark secret. I was sure it was this rather than the fact that she was Jewish which had affected my attitude to her, but from then on I felt she was not to be trusted.

There then came a dramatic chain of events which – possibly because of subconscious guilt-feelings – I somehow associated with that unfortunate letter.

Once Tilly had settled in and had become accepted, we regarded her as a permanent fixture in our lives. Mrs Evans we knew was a servant, and she might leave, as servants so often did; grandma was old and might go the way of grandpa; but Tilly, we thought, was forever, and we could not imagine her having a life apart from us, or even wanting to. One morning, however, she called us together and, in the casual tone she might have used to announce that she was arranging an outing to a local museum, told us that she was leaving.

We exchanged looks of stunned disbelief and she had to repeat herself before it sunk in. I was the first to find my voice, and it was quivering:

'How long for?'

'For good, I'm afraid.'

'Do you mean forever and ever?' asked Rocky.

'Well, I might come on a visit, but otherwise it's goodbye Tilly.'

'But why?'

'Many reasons which I needn't go into now, but in any case you're big girls. You don't need a governess. You're nearly eleven, Vesta, and even Rocky is nearly five. Mrs Evans and your grandma should manage between them.'

The curious thing was that I was as shocked and upset by the announcement as the others, and that night, like the others, I cried myself to sleep. It was the greatest trauma of our young lives, and far more painful than the death of mummy. We hadn't seen all that much of mummy while she was alive, and she had always seemed rather distant and slightly disembodied, while Tilly was the one constant element to our existence. We felt not only shocked, but betrayed. How could she *want* to leave us? It was perhaps this feeling which made the parting, when it finally did come, rather easier than it might have been, but it still wasn't easy. She hugged and kissed each of us in turn, and I had the feeling – or did I imagine it? – that she hesitated a little when it came to my turn, and, even in my distress, I couldn't help fixing her with a glance which told her: 'It's all right, your secret is safe with me.'

2
Dark Age

We would have missed Tilly in any circumstances, but the fact that she was replaced by grandma made us miss her doubly, for we could not help comparing the two. Grandma was a nice but sombre old woman and her regime tended to have a dampening effect on our spirits (Vesta didn't mind her, but then her spirits were always damp). She was as strict as Tilly, but we knew where we were with Tilly and if we did something wrong she took us aside there and then and put us right in words of one syllable, ending with the words: 'Is that clear?'

'Yes, Tilly.'

'Are you sure it's clear?'

'I'm sure.'

'Then let's have no more of this nonsense.'

Grandma, on the other hand, merely sulked to show her displeasure and, as we were never really certain what we had done wrong in the first place, we rarely did anything to put it right, so that her sulks became more or less permanent and she became a different person once she took charge.

In Tilly's time we used to go into London every two or three weeks, usually on a Saturday, and visit Uncle Willie, who had a flat off Kensington High Street. It was not, I suppose, a small flat, but everything seemed small compared to our house with its long corridors and gloomy alcoves, and dark corners and its servants' quarters, and its outhouses and hot-houses. Actually, one had the feeling that the whole place was slightly overheated, I don't mean physically, for the central heating was never adequate to deal with its vacant spaces, but because of the general atmosphere of preciousness, induced partly by its inmates and partly by the antique furniture and expensive bric-à-brac with which father liked to surround himself. The house had belonged to a well-known local family which believed there was no future for the country gentleman in 'socialist England' and had emigrated to Rhodesia. The house, which had the rather odd name of 'West Wynds', and its contents came on the market in the late forties and father bought it for what he called 'a song', though what was a song to father was grand opera to anyone else. I envied those of my friends who lived in smaller houses in which one could run around without fear of grazing a Louis xv commode, or demolishing an ormolu clock, and I used to cherish our visits to London, which I regarded as an excursion into the real world. We would often go shopping, then to a theatre matinée and finally to the Hyde Park Hotel for tea. On Sunday mornings we would go for walks in Kensington Gardens or Holland Park, but our great treat was a visit to Stevie. She lived near Regent's Park and, if Willie's flat seemed small, Stevie's seemed tiny, and consisted of a bed-sitting room (with the bed piled high with teddy bears and pandas), a bathroom and a kitchen which was hardly more than a cupboard and which was lined with spice jars as a library is lined with books. The place always smelt of garlic, eau-de-Cologne and wine, which is not in itself a pleasant mixture, but we loved it because it brought Stevie to mind, and we adored Stevie. She prepared us a lunch of chops and chips, which we drank down with gallons of fizz. She sometimes looked rather pale and wan, and was less communicative than usual, which suggested that she was having difficulties with her young men, who seemed to be growing younger as she was growing older, though, young or old, none of them seemed to last.

One black Sunday whilst Tilly was still with us she 'phoned to say she was unwell and wouldn't be able to have us round to lunch. We ate in an hotel instead, and then went boating in the park, but on the way home we came across Stevie by herself, in dark glasses, her face blotchy and swollen. She didn't notice us till we were upon her, and turned as if she was about to run, but Vesta took her hand, and she broke down and cried. It was the unhappiest moment of my young life. When she took off her glasses to wipe her eyes, we noticed that one was bruised and the other swollen and shut. Fortunately Tilly was in conversation with someone else at that moment and had not witnessed the scene, which could only have lasted a minute, and we kept our secret to ourselves. When we got home, however, I felt I had to mention it to father, but all he could say was, 'Poor cow. She'll never learn.'

Once Tilly was gone our visits to London almost stopped. Grandma felt too old to take us and Uncle Willie too feeble to entertain us, and I suspect that Stevie had grown too tired of our (or at least of my) inquisitiveness.

The next few years were something of a dark age. I was an avid reader and all my reading had suggested that if people were unhappy it was due to some great misfortune, like death, famine or plague, or the machinations of the wicked, wicked uncles, aunts, step-mothers, witches and the like, but I discovered that one could be made unhappy by people who were good, or even very good.

Grandma looked like everyone's picture of a model grandmother, small, white-haired, with gold-rimmed glasses and, although she must have been seventy by then, she was restless and hardworking. We didn't know when she rose in the morning, for she was always up and about by the time we came down for breakfast, and she was still busy with something or other by the time we went to bed, and for all I know she never went to sleep at all. She also ate very little – no meat, no fish, a few vegetables, some black bread – and drank a great deal of water, and I suppose what made us think she was good was the fact that she seemed to get very little out of life, for we were brought up to associate self-indulgence with wickedness and self-denial with virtue.

But whether good, or merely abstemious, she made us miserable. We were discouraged from laughing loudly, or, indeed laughing at all, from raising our voices, or running around. She discontinued our birthday parties, which she thought were a waste of time and money, and, in any case, she thought we were too old for them, and as we no longer invited friends to parties, we were no longer invited back.

Rocky, who was the most high-spirited, suffered the most, and suggested one evening: 'Let's drown her in the village pond, and you can blame it all on me. They can't touch me, I'm far too young.' She was seven at the time. I wondered what she might be up to by the time she was ten.

What added to our misery was the suspicion that we were getting poorer, which didn't mean to say that we had actually become poor. The poor talked about money, we didn't, but we definitely became conscious of the fact that there was less of it about. The shops had suddenly begun to fill after the years of post-war austerity. There were more things to buy, but we seemed to have less money to buy them with. We used to be taken to and from school by a local car-hire firm, but suddenly all that changed and we had to come and go by bus, which at first we regarded as something of an adventure, but we wearied of it, especially in the winter, when we had to leave home while it was still dark, and it was dark again by the time we got back. In the summer, while Tilly was around, we used to take a rather grand house by the coast in Devon. Now we took something cramped and musty, which wasn't even near the beach, on the Isle of Wight.

We also noticed that when things went well, father was away for short periods at a time, and when they didn't go so well he was away for rather longer. Now he was away so often and for so long that we hardly saw anything of him, and when he did appear, his face was white and pouchy, and his manner uncommunicative, and he was short with everyone, even his mother.

The conviction that we were growing poorer carried with it one source of hope. We all presumed that, in common with most of our friends in prep school, we would all be going on to boarding-school, and what worried me was the thought that Vesta would be leaving home a year before me and, for a dreadful twelve months, I would be reduced to the company of my two younger sisters. I had never considered Vesta an ideal companion. She was far too proper for my tastes and regarded any order from an elder, however unreasonable, as law. She also had an eternal air of melancholy which hung over her like a private little cloud and I had often felt tempted to take her by the shoulders and shake her out of it. I also knew that she for her part regarded me as loud, coarse and unruly, but she was well read, thoughtful and full of improbable bits of wisdom, and there was a lot to be learnt from her company, whereas Vida and Rocky were still in their giggly phase, and it didn't look as if they would ever grow out of it. I had made no friends in the school itself whom I might see after school hours, for it had a very wide catchment area, and we were the only pupils from our village.

But poverty or no poverty, there was no reprieve, and Vesta went on to boarding-school. It was, I suppose, a question of priority, and it was unthinkable that any of us should do anything else. If father had had to sell the house to pay for the school fees, he would no doubt have done so.

The company of Vida and Rocky was even more dreadful than I had anticipated. They were full of little secrets, private code-words and private jokes, and there were times when I turned even to grandma for conversation.

It's amazing whom you can become friends with when you're friendless. We became quite chummy and, after Vida and Rocky were in bed, she told me our whole family history, a subject on which everyone had been so reticent that I began to have fantasies that we were an illegitimate branch of some great ducal – perhaps even royal – house. I was aware if only from our name, that we had some continental connections, but then the Continent abounded with dukes and princelings. Grandma robbed me of my fantasies, but she was at pains to emphasize that, she at least, came from good stock and was descended from a 'very old family'. Her father, a solicitor, was also an accomplished linguist and had many foreigners among his clients, including my great-grandfather, who was a German immigrant. Her father helped to set him up in business, not only in the sense that he prepared the necessary legal papers, but lent him money, which is how she eventually met grandpa. It was, she said, just over fifty years since they married, and at first everything went well; they had three beautiful children, their business prospered. Then the First World War broke out and the skies fell in.

'It was terrible,' she said, 'terrible. The name of the company was immediately changed from Courlander to Lander, and his two older brothers changed their names to Lander and Lancer, but your grandfather, who was the youngest and who had been to an English public school, felt it was a little like sailing under false colours, and he insisted on staying Courlander. Willie and your father, who were by then at school, had a terrible time of it, and the whole business nearly collapsed. I dare say it would have collapsed if my father hadn't helped them. Grandpa and his brothers were hardly on speaking terms, and eventually, with the help of my father, he bought them out. In the end he did very well, but for a time it was touch and go.'

As our relationship developed she told me about her private aggravations, and she felt aggrieved about everybody. Stevie, she said, had had the best of everything – the best governesses, the best schools – but she was a disappointment.

'One expects a girl of good family to marry early. She's now nearly forty and it doesn't look as if she'll marry at all, and, given her way of life, that's hardly surprising.' She would not be drawn on what she meant by 'her way of life'.

She had many complaints about father. He had taken his degree at Oxford and had eaten his dinners at Lincoln's Inn, but did not stay on to be called to the Bar. 'That's his trouble, he's good at starting things, but not at finishing them.' She also thought he had made an unfortunate marriage. 'Your mother was very pleasant to look at, but very poorly and not really in a fit state to marry or raise a family. I suppose it was our fault in a way, for we gave him every encouragement, but that was before she had her first breakdown. She was otherwise a very fine young woman, good family, a Cambridge graduate, an accomplished pianist, but unstable. She shouldn't have been allowed to marry.'

Uncle Willie, she said, had spent all his life missing chances. 'He could have married a lovely girl from a very fine family, but could never make up his mind. When he became an army officer, I kept asking myself, how can a man like that give orders if he doesn't know his own mind. Then he caught this dreadful disease. He wasn't a particularly young man when he went in, but he was an old man when he came out, poor boy. I'm not really sure if he's in a fit state to look after the company, and your father, I'm sorry to say, is not as helpful as he should be.'

'He seems to be working very hard,' I said.

'He *seems* to be working very hard, but that's because he's always travelling, but if you ask me he likes to travel if only to get away from his responsibilities. And he does have expensive tastes. If I didn't keep a careful eye on household bills, I daren't think where we would be. I wish he'd get married.'

I sat up at that, for Stevie had mentioned more than once that grandma was afraid that he might do just that, and I put the point to her, though not in those exact words. She answered quite crossly.

'Don't be absurd, child. Of course I want him to marry, both for his own sake and for yours, only he can't be relied upon to make a sensible match. In a way it's fortunate that he's not as well off as he used to be, otherwise he'd be at the mercy of the first vixen he met.'

I once, in a thoughtless moment, asked if she thought he should have married Tilly, and she gave me a disapproving look but did not answer, as if to say: 'That's a preposterous question even from a twelve year old.' Tilly was a topic on which she would not be drawn.

My exchanges with grandma were curiously one-sided, for she never asked me questions about myself, about what I thought, what I read, what I did. Though I was not (or I thought I wasn't) egocentric, there was a lot going on inside me at this time and I needed a listener, which is, I suppose, why I began keeping a diary. The entries, even at this distance, do not make exciting reading:

Saturday 10 October 1953
Uncle Willie to lunch. He had expected to see father and was cross to find him away. We said he was in America. He said he couldn't be, not in America, and that he was expected for an important meeting in London first thing on Monday morning. He sulked throughout the meal, and kept throwing out words like 'unreliable', 'irresponsible'. He wore a baggy old suit. His moustache covers his lips and it billows when he speaks. Mrs Evans mistook him for the gardener. Stevie came to tea. Surprised to find Willie. The two have never got on and didn't have much to say to each other. V. and R. served up some fairy cakes they had just baked. Dreadful. Grandma didn't touch hers. Probably afraid it was poisoned. Willie returned to London by train, Stevie by car. She didn't even give him a lift to the station.

Sunday 11 October
Rained all day. Roast mutton for lunch, followed by stewed fruit and custard. Stewed fruit tasteless, custard lumpy. Ugh. Grandma moved slowly, as if in pain, and white-faced. Kept snapping at everybody all morning and lay down after lunch. 'Do you think she might pop off?' asked R. hopefully. Father arrived as I was getting ready for bed. Rushed downstairs to greet him, and *he* snapped at me. 'Why aren't you in bed?' 'Because I wanted to say hullo to you,' I said. 'Hullo,' he said. 'Now go back to bed.' What's the matter with everybody? If this goes on I'll leave home.

Monday 12 October
Rose early, but father already gone. No sign of grandma. Unlike her to lie in. We tiptoe into her room. She's fast asleep and breathing heavily. 'Now's our chance,' says R., 'let's put a pillow over her face.' I send her and V. off to school, and I

wait till Mrs Evans comes. By the time we're back grandma is on her feet again. Father 'phoned to say not to wait for him for dinner. During dinner he 'phoned again to say he was staying over in London. Feeling of crisis in the air. No one says a word to us, least of all grandma. Don't suppose anybody tells her anything either.

Thursday 15 October
Long letter from Vesta. She's miserable at school. Thought she would be. Been there five weeks, and the longer she's there the worse it gets. The building reminds her of the hospital in which mummy died, the girls are noisy, and there isn't a quiet corner in the place. I write back to say that if it's any consolation to her, I am miserable at home. Hardly see father.

Saturday 17 October
Woke about two in the morning with stomach cramps. On the way to toilet, notice light from downstairs room reflected on lawn. Burglars? Hesitate. Curiosity gets the better of me. Tiptoe downstairs. Hear father's voice coming from study, no one else. He's either talking to himself, or on 'phone, loudly. Either he's angry or it's a bad line. Cramps get worse and rush to toilet. Don't touch breakfast, nor much lunch either. At tea R. offers me slice of her home-made apple flan. I throw it at her. Father in study all morning working on papers, leaves early in afternoon to catch plane for Germany. Ask grandma what he's doing in Germany. 'Heaven only knows,' she says. At supper V. says she's going to be a nun. 'Finish your haddock first,' grandma tells her. Rained all day. It's raining now.

Sunday 18 October
Rain. Stomach still bothering me, wonder if it's anything to do with the weather. R. says I might be pregnant. At breakfast V. has my egg and R. my bacon. Grandma asks me to pin-point pain. I say it's all over the place. 'That's all right then,' she says, and tells me to go to bed with hot-water bottle. Afraid of missing Stevie who's due for lunch. Pain gets worse, and I go to bed. Stevie arrives and finds me in tears. 'Is it your stomach?' she says. 'No,' I say, 'wouldn't mind the stomach, I'm just feeling miserable,' and she throws her arms round

me and breaks down herself. I'm so astounded I forget my misery and my pain. I wipe her eyes, blow her nose and ask what's the matter. She says it's nothing and makes me promise not to tell anyone – and especially not grandma – that she'd been crying. Feel better by afternoon. Rain stops and Stevie and I walk to village. Air cold and raw, ground marshy. No one about. She tells me I've nothing to be miserable about, that I have a wonderful father, that I'm very clever, and that I can look forward to a rich, full and happy life. And I ask her if she didn't have a wonderful father. 'Oh yes,' she says, 'he was wonderful.' And wasn't she clever herself? 'Oh yes, very. I went to university on a scholarship.' And we walk on saying nothing. Look at myself in mirror for a long time before going to bed. Everyone compliments me on being clever, no one on my looks. Is that a way of telling me I'm ugly?

Then came a red-letter day, and I mean red.

Monday 19 October
Shortly after lessons begin I have odd feeling I'm leaking. Try to ignore it, but it doesn't stop. I ask permission to leave room, rush out to the toilet and find I'm dripping blood. Oh good, I think, I'm dying, but don't like idea of being found dead in lav. In the meantime dripping stops and I go back to class, but on the way Beak sees me and calls me into her room. Wonder what I've done this time. She asks me to turn round. 'Oh dear,' she says, 'we are messy, aren't we – and precocious. I suppose you know what's happened. I think this calls for a hot cup of tea, don't you?' And it's only then that she tells me I've had a period. Vesta had been given a little booklet about it at her school, which I had read and had had a good giggle over, but I didn't think it had anything to do with me, or at least someone of my age. In any case, I liked the thought that I was dying. She drives me home and tells me it's only the second time that's happened in the history of the school. Grandma takes me to doctor. He says congratulations, as if I've won a prize.

Tuesday 20 October
Father home. Looks pleased with himself, and gifts for all. Book-mark for me, Bavarian peasant costumes for V. and R. They tear off clothes and get into them there and then, and are all over father. Look at grandma and him to see if she's passed

on my secret. Don't think she has. I kept it dark. Look at myself closely in mirror before going to bed. Like the idea of being able to be pregnant, but not half as attractive as idea of being dead.

And then an entry which, though I didn't know it, was to have important consequences for us all and which was to cause a suspension of further entries for years to come:

Saturday 24 October
After much nagging from V. and R. father agrees to take us on 'magical, mystery tour'. Just then, 'phone goes. Father full of exclamations. 'God! Good God! Good heavens! When? How?' When he's finished he sits down with odd look on his face. 'Bad news?' I ask. 'Depends,' he says. Anyhow it's bad news for us and magical mystery tour is off. An hour later we hear all about it on radio. Tony Roscoe, Callum's older brother, killed in riding accident . . .

3
Life with Stevie

At that time Callum was hardly more than a name to us. We knew that he had been father's best friend and best man at his wedding. Stevie had also confessed to having had a schoolgirl crush on him, but then she had had crushes on everybody, and I was a little surprised that she didn't look more crushed.

He was a professional soldier whose career had almost come to an abrupt end in the early years of the war, when he was torpedoed in the South Atlantic. He was one of the few survivors and spent over a week in an open boat in shark-infested waters before being picked up, more dead than alive. He had suffered what he thought was a minor injury to his arm when the ship blew up, but it got progressively worse while he was in the water.

'It was the worst part of the whole experience,' he said. 'It got red and swollen like a great big Bologna sausage and stank to high heaven. I would have dumped it overboard if I could, in fact the chaps in the boat threatened to dump me overboard, especially as rations were getting short.'

His arm was amputated shortly after he was landed in Cape Town and in the course of his convalescence he met a volunteer nurse: 'Small woman, black hair, gap-toothed, slant-eyed. Thought she was Chinese. Turned out to be Jewish. So there you are, not only lost an arm, but found a wife.' She was called Sophie and was the only daughter of a Lithuanian Jew, who had come out to South Africa as a gold prospector and eventually became a mining magnate.

Callum's grandfather, 'a wop wine merchant', as he

called him, had received a baronetcy 'for sucking up to the old queen', and acquired a large estate near the Cambridge–Essex border, about twelve miles from 'West Wynds'.

Callum once dropped in while Tilly was still with us. Stevie was also there with a woman friend, and sitting down to dinner he counted no less than ten females round the table (including us four). 'Good God,' he said to father, 'a bloody house of women. You'll turn into a woman yourself living among that lot', and looking at him at that moment I felt that there was something in what Callum said.

He left the army after the war and settled in South Africa, and appears to have spent most of his time playing polo. He liked South Africa, 'Beautiful country, marvellous climate, great opportunites,' and urged father to settle there. As the years went by father saw less and less of him. 'England's become such a piffling little place,' he said. 'If it wasn't for Epsom and Newmarket, it wouldn't be worth while setting foot there.'

But the death of his older brother changed everything. He was now heir both to the title and the family estate.

'We'll have to come back,' he told father at the funeral. 'Sophie can't wait to be lady of the manor.' She didn't have to wait long.

The second baronet died suddenly in the course of his Christmas dinner and Callum and Sophie moved into Roscoe House, as the family seat was known, early in the new year.

Callum always called the place St Pancras, for it was built during the last phase of the Gothic revival and, with its turrets and towers and battlements, it did bear a distinct likeness to St Pancras station; the first time I saw it I half-expected to see railway lines stretching out from the back.

The house was not open to the public, and the second baronet, who was an elderly recluse, did not care for visitors at all, public or private. We were taken for a furtive tour of the place during one of the rare occasions that he was away. But now, with Callum installed as the third baronet, we were able to examine it at leisure and were duly impressed. We merely had a large house, Callum had a stately one; seeing him in his riding-boots by the huge fireplace in the great hall, under a portrait of the first baronet, I felt, even at the tender age of thirteen, the first intimations of the fact that I was a woman. I don't know if it was the title – Sir Callum Roscoe, Bart – or the setting, or the man himself which affected me more, but I took in the scene not only with my eyes, but with my whole body, and felt that I would retain a vivid picture of that particular scene for the rest of my days.

He and Sophie had two children of about my age, Robin and Grace. They were twins and not so much unidentical as opposites. Robin was tall, thin, pale-faced and pensive, though with gleaming white teeth and a smile which could light up a room. Grace was red-haired, green-eyed, of robust build and robust temperament, with slightly over-large teeth and full, almost negroid, lips. In a way she was almost ugly, but she sparkled and was so exuberant that she gave an impression of noise even when she was silent, which she rarely was. She was to quieten and slim down, and to become my most intimate friend; at first, however, I found her insufferable – as did everybody else – but I sought out her company on every possible pretext as a means of being near her father.

I loved everything about him. His voice was hoarse and husky, his face flushed with globules of sweat on his forehead, as if ever in the midst of great exertions. A loose, blond lock flopped over his eyes, which were bloodshot and pouchy, but he was the first man that I was aware of as a man. His very disability – though he never treated it as such – seemed to add to his manliness, and he only had to glance in my direction for a delicious sensation of warmth to spread through my body. I was murderously jealous of Sophie.

I couldn't quite understand the basis of his friendship with father. Father was so mild and languid as to be almost comatose, whereas Callum seemed to rage with energy, always active, on the move, on the go, fast horses, fast cars and – I suspected – fast women. In spite of his handicap he played polo, golf and tennis, and went in for steeple-chasing and swimming, whereas father did not always seem disposed to summon up sufficient energy to breathe, though he would indulge in an occasional game of tennis.

If I was to sum up father in a sentence, it would be Callum without the fire, for they were fairly similar in colouring and build, though father's hair was sparser and darker, while Callum's bulk was firmer. Father went up and down in size. I used to think he would go lean when things were going badly and fat when they were going well, but Stevie explained that it was the other way about. When he was under stress, he would eat and drink compulsively and neglect his appearance; when they were going well he would take himself in hand and slim down. But even when slimmed down there was something faintly flabby about him. He had a soft voice and rather retiring manner, whereas there was something thrusting and aggressive about Callum. One felt like sounding the retreat when he entered a room. I couldn't quite square his manner with the fact that he was of Italian origin. There was nothing remotely Italianate about him, and he reminded one rather of a beserk John Bull.

The fact that he was father's best friend may have suggested that this was simply the attraction of opposites, but while such attractions are commonplace in marriage, they are uncommon among friends. I gradually came to reassess my impressions of both and to realize that the one was not as aggressive as he seemed, nor the other as retiring, and that both were consciously, or unconsciously, acting out predetermined roles.

Yet I sometimes wondered if their friendship was genuine, for Callum had a habit of referring to father as 'the Jew boy'. I once asked him why and he said: 'A habit I picked up at Harrow. That's what everybody called him.'

Stevie had mixed feelings about Callum and suspected that he hated Jews.

'But how can he?' I asked. 'His wife's Jewish.'

'So is her money, so what? You should hear him talk about his father-in-law, "the old Jew boy", "Shylock" and worse, and to his face, and the old boy laps it up with glee.'

'It's all rather odd,' I said, 'because Robin is circumcised.'

'Most upper-class English boys are. But in any case, how do you know?'

'Grace told me.'

Callum's father-in-law, a dapper little figure with thick glasses and a white pointed beard and bright dancing eyes, was, I think, the first openly Jewish Jew I met, which is to say, pork dishes were not served while he was in residence, and he celebrated Passover, or at least the first night thereof, in the traditional Jewish manner. Callum and his family would travel to South Africa every year for the occasion. 'I'd do anything to be out of this country in the spring,' said Callum, 'even turn Jew for a week.' He quite enjoyed the rituals, he said, 'and the festive food, but I couldn't take the wine. I thought it would be pepped up with good Christian blood, but not a bit of it, it was like bloody syrup, couldn't touch it.'

The splendours of the Roscoe establishment made ours look small, shabby and ramshackle, and father often spoke of the possibility of buying a farm.

'You couldn't afford it, dear boy,' said Callum. 'Unless you want to grub away like a peasant, farming costs the earth. I can tell you I would have had to give all this up if I hadn't married Sophie. You can't accumulate capital, you can't even inherit it. Nowadays you can only make money the hard way. You've got to marry it. Find yourself an heiress.'

I was amazed that father could talk of buying anything, for 'West Wynds' was falling apart. It was doing so by gradual, almost imperceptible degrees, but Vesta, who was only home every three or four months, could see it all at a glance and she was convinced that the family was living far beyond its means. I was due to join her at Hellenslea in September, but she said it would be wrong of us to allow father to make sacrifices which he couldn't really afford when we could get a perfectly sound education in the local grammar school. She had, by then, begun to like the place and admitted that she would be sorry to leave, but she didn't feel she had any option.

I had the same feelings and I suggested that she take the matter up with father.

'No,' she said, 'you do it.'

'Why me? You're the oldest.'

'You have a more direct way.'

I wasn't sure if I had the more direct way, but I did have ulterior motives. At 'West Wynds' I was only twelve miles from Callum; at boarding-school I would be eighty miles from him, and I agreed to approach father at the first suitable opportunity, which was not all that easy to find, for he was now away more than ever.

'Poor Willie is near the end of his tether,' grandma kept muttering, 'everything's being left to him. Everything.' But I was determined, and late one night, when I heard his car pull into the drive, I jumped out of bed, put on my dressing-gown, and was waiting for him as he entered. I had just begun to use curlers, so I couldn't have been a pretty sight, and he looked as if he might turn and flee.

'Good God, why aren't you in bed? Don't you know what time it is?'

'You don't seem to be around at any other time, and I wanted to talk to you.'

'Can't it wait till the morning?'

'No, it can't.'

He was taken aback by my tone. So, as a matter of fact, was I.

'Has something happened to upset you?'

'No, nothing has, or rather nothing new. I'm upset because it's almost impossible to talk to you. You either aren't here, or if you are here you're busy, or tired. You seem to have time for everybody except us.'

'Come on,' he said, leading me by the hand into the kitchen, 'let's have a cup of tea, but be quiet about it. I wouldn't like to have the lot of you on top of me at this time of the night.' But I wanted to get the matter off my chest there and then.

'The tea can wait,' I said.

'No it can't. I've been travelling for the last twelve hours and feel entitled to some refreshment. You, young lady, have the makings of a shrew. I don't mind if you're going to bully your husband, but you're not going to start by bullying me. Now what is it?'

'I have the feeling that we can't really afford to live here, and that you can't afford to send us to boarding-school.'

'You too?'

'Why, has anybody else spoken to you about it?'

'Vida, Rocky, everybody. They complained that I'd put them to shame by arriving on speech day in my old Wolseley, while all the other parents came in Rolls or Bentleys, or in spanking new Rovers. Well, I happen to like my Wolseley.'

'But can you really afford to send us to Hellenslea?'

'I daresay if I'd had to pay for it out of my own pocket I might have had to think about it, but it's all paid for out of a family trust established by your grandfather. Any other questions?'

I had a great many, but his answer had taken the wind right out of my sails.

'Do you, do you have to use the money for school fees?'

'You do, that's why one has trusts, to make sure that one complies with the wish of the testator, so that if you have any thought that I can use the money to buy myself a Rolls, you can forget about it. The places are booked and they're paid for, not only for you, but also, if I'm not mistaken, for your children.'

'But supposing we hate the school?'

'Then you might be sent to another, and if you hate the other, you will go to a third, but to boarding-school you will go, and the sooner the better. But in the meantime, to bed.'

My *démarche* did have one important effect. It opened father's eyes to the fact that he had some budding adults in his family who were less than satisfied with the way they were being treated; now, when he was in town, he made greater efforts to be back home in time for dinner and to talk to us over meals. The conversation did not flow too freely, for I, at least, was conscious of the effort he was making, and, in any case, much of it was dominated by tittle-tattle from Vida and Rocky. One evening, however, a little to my surprise, he invited me to join him on a walk. The day had been hot and humid, but towards evening there was a spectacular downpour and the air was rich with the smell of moist earth.

I put my arm in his and he said: 'You're almost as tall as I am. At this rate you'll be eight foot by the time you're fully grown.'

'I am fully grown,' I said, 'or nearly so.'

'You make it sound as if it's something to complain about.'

'In a way it is. I feel bored with everything, bored with school, bored with "West Wynds", bored with Vida and Rocky, bored –'

'That's part of growing up.'

'But good Lord, how long does it go on for?'

'You'll be going on to Helenslea in another few months. You're a bright girl and it's a good school, so the competition'll be stiffer. You'll make new friends. Good God, if you're bored already at thirteen, how will you come to regard life at thirty?'

'I've asked myself the same question. Up to about a year ago there seemed to be something new to look forward to every day, but now one day seems as empty as the next and all I can see ahead is more of the same.'

'Well I can promise you this. There are dramatic changes in store. I don't want to talk about them now because there's many a slip etcetera. I'm not sure if everybody in the family will be happy with them, but whatever lies ahead, it won't be more of the same.'

And he was as good as his word, but I cannot imagine that the events which followed were the ones he had in mind.

Grandma and the rest of us were at supper one evening,

when we heard the noise of crashing crockery coming from the kitchen. We all rushed to see what had happened, and found Mrs Evans sprawled on the floor with the crockery dresser on top of her and broken dishes all about here. She had apparently felt dizzy, grabbed at the dresser to steady herself, and had brought it down on top of her. A doctor and ambulance were quickly on the scene, but she was dead. A minute later grandma collapsed. Both the doctor and ambulance were still with us, and they removed the dead Mrs Evans and the still breathing form of grandma in the same vehicle. Half an hour later she too was dead and I found myself in charge of the household. It was my proudest moment and I think I acquitted myself with aplomb.

The doctor summoned his wife to look after us, but I didn't really think it was necessary. In fact the greatest shock of the evening came, not from the two deaths, but from something else. Father was in New York and had left the telephone number of his hotel where he could be contacted in case of emergency. I rang the number and a woman answered. I recognized the voice at once. It was Tilly.

Grandma's funeral was a curious affair. The day was sunny and warm. Everyone was in black, but a stylish black, and with every flower bed in the crematorium ablaze with colour, the occasion felt more like a garden party.

One doesn't really know how many relatives one has till one drops dead, and there were quite a number of people there whom I only vaguely recognized and who didn't recognize me at all. Grandma was from a sizeable clan of fairly well-heeled but nondescript people, and I had the impression that one of the reasons we lived in the country was that father was anxious to get away, and stay away, from them.

I had half-expected Tilly to be there, but she didn't turn up, and I dare say a crematorium is not the best place to unveil a paramour.

The thought of that 'phone call weighed heavily upon

me all the time. Tilly hadn't identified herself, but there was no mistaking that voice – metallic, sonorous and slightly nasal – and I almost blurted out there and then: 'Is that Tilly?' When father returned the next day, I sought an appropriate moment to ask if it was Tilly who had answered the 'phone, but on reflection I felt that, if he didn't want to volunteer the information, I had no business to ask. I didn't mention it to a soul till Vesta arrived, and she said:

'Tilly? It couldn't have been Tilly.'

'Why not?'

'Because I can't imagine it, that's all. And don't forget, grandma and poor Mrs Evans had just died within an hour of each other, and you were in a state of shock.'

'I was *not* in a state of shock,' I almost shouted.

'The thing about being in a state of shock is that you can be so shocked that you don't know it, and you could have imagined it.'

Vesta seemed to have a reservoir of all sorts of arcane information and, whenever she chose to draw on it, I felt ill-equipped to argue.

Once grandma was safely reduced to ashes I thought that Tilly's second coming was imminent, but instead we had a sort of Regency period. As we were on our own and father had to go abroad again, Stevie felt obliged to take a few weeks off to look after us; by the time they were over, even Rocky was wishing that grandma would rise from the dead. It is one thing to have a cherished aunt whom one sees sporadically for a few hours at a time, and quite another to have her installed *in loco parentis*. It nearly brought a permanent end to our friendship. She was like grandma writ large, except that where grandma sulked quietly, she sulked explosively, and we were never certain what would bring on her tirades, or what could stop them.

There was a brief honeymoon period while we were still numb with shock, when she was like a fairy godmother, preparing special dishes, telling amusing stories, playing games, and then, suddenly, for no apparent reason, she turned into a wicked witch.

We usually came home from school at about five and found a snack waiting, which saw us through until dinner. One day we came home and the snack wasn't there. We went into the kitchen and made ourselves something to eat, when we were startled by a cry from the doorway. There she was, with fists on her hips, her eyes blazing.

'What the hell do you think you're doing? Who asked you to come in here . . . Look at the mess . . .'

There was, indeed, something of a mess, but nothing which we couldn't have cleared up in a minute, but she didn't give us a chance to and stood there raging till she was out of breath.

'You spoilt brats. Do you have to stuff yourselves every waking minute? How do you expect me to get dinner ready when there's such a mess in the kitchen? I've got half a mind to send you to bed right now without a meal . . .' And from then on she could rarely talk to us in a normal tone of voice. I could understand her bawling at Vida and Rocky – I often did the same – but there was no need to bawl at me. I assumed from the way she pounced on the 'phone every time it rang, that she was waiting for a call which never came and that her love life was not all it should be which, all things considered, wasn't surprising.

One evening, after one of us had been guilty of some small misdemeanour – I wasn't even sure which of us was the guilty party, and what we were guilty of – she sent us upstairs to bed without supper. Vida and Rocky went up meekly, and perhaps even thankfully, for her cooking was eccentric so that missing a meal was no penance – but I had had about enough, and I said to her:

'Do you mean me as well?'

'Yes,' she bawled, 'you as well.'

'I'm hungry,' I said in a calm, matter-of-fact voice, 'and if you don't want to give me anything to eat, I'll make it myself.'

I thought (hoped?) she might explode, but instead, after looking at me in silence for a moment, she broke down into a paroxysm of tears. I spent the rest of the evening making her cups of tea and comforting her.

'I don't know what's happening to me,' she sobbed. 'I'm not normally like this, honestly I'm not. I suppose it's mummy's death. We weren't very close, or I thought we weren't, but it's meant more to me than I imagined, the terrible suddenness of it. I was such a disappointment to her and poor daddy. You must all hate me, I don't blame you, I hate myself. I wish I was dead . . .'

The next morning she looked dizzy and drugged and could hardly stand on her feet. I more or less ordered her back to bed and stayed off school for the rest of the week to take charge of the household. Vida and Rocky looked at me with new eyes, did as they were told and were quick about it. I did the ordering and the cooking, as well as any of the cleaning left unfinished by our daily help, and rather enjoyed it. The only burden on my spirit was Stevie, who staggered round like a bloated ghost, wringing her hands and telling me that she didn't know what to do with herself. She was afraid to go back to London and face anyone, and besides she didn't see how she could leave us on our own. I ached to tell her that if I managed with her, I would manage without, but even I couldn't be so cruel. What worried me most was the battery of pills and capsules by her bedside. I was afraid she would take an overdose, and the first thing I did when I woke in the morning was to rush into her room to see if she was still alive, which she was, just. I was going to ask her why she didn't see a doctor, but obviously, to judge from all those pills, she had been seeing too many.

'It's the wretched holidays,' she said. 'I'm all right when I'm at work – or I usually am – but they gave me a month's compassionate leave. Damn then and their compassion.'

The day father was due back she managed to compose herself sufficiently to look fairly normal, but even so he was troubled by her appearance and asked if we had been a handful.

'No, no,' she assured him, 'they were no problem,' which was more than could have been said for her.

The following week we got a new housekeeper, Mrs Donelly, a brisk, plump, amiable woman, who, apart from anything else, was a good cook. We all became very fond of her, and Vida said to me: 'Now I know what it's like to have a mother,' and Rocky said: 'If only daddy would marry her, we'd all live happily ever after.'

Callum stopped by for a meal one day and regarded both the woman and her cuisine with approval. As soon as she was out of the room, he leant over to father and, in a whisper which could have been heard two rooms away, he said: 'You're on to a good thing you old dog, where did you find her?'

'Do you think Mrs Donelly could be father's girlfriend?' Vida asked me in her lisping voice. She was eleven and I wondered if I should tell her about Tilly.

In the event I didn't have to. Shortly after Vesta came home for the summer holidays, father brought us together in the drawing-room for a family conference. Such conferences were rare and they were only summoned for the most momentous occasions. I was in one armchair, Vesta in another, and the two others on the sofa, while father stood, with his back to the fireplace, a gold watch-chain across his well-cut waistcoat (he must have been about the last man in England to wear such a watch), a hand on his lapel as if about to make a speech. The others sat bolt upright, their faces tensed. I alone was relaxed, perfectly certain as to what was coming.

Father cleared his throat and began:

'I think you will be interested to know that I am minded to remarry.' At which the two younger ones errupted with elation, and father had to calm them down before he could continue.

'I know you've all been missing a certain party; life at "West Wynds" hasn't been quite the same since she's been away. I have also been missing her, and I'm sure you'll be delighted to know that she's coming back as your mother.'

'Congratulations,' I said.

The rest were too stunned to say anything.

4
The Second Coming

It was, I suppose, something which could only have happened over grandma's dead body.

I wasn't at all happy about it and felt as if I had inherited grandma's antipathies to Tilly, though I may have harboured them ever since the discovery that she was Jewish. As I have said before, though there was nothing in our way of life to suggest we were Jews, we never tried to hide the fact, whereas Tilly, who was Jewish enough to have received letters in Hebrew, had stayed under our roof for nearly six years without once drawing attention to the fact, and harboured it, indeed, as if it was a dark secret. Had she been saving the fact until she was mistress of the household and in a position to convert us all to Judaism? Would we have to go to synagogue every week and eat kosher? (I wasn't quite sure what the word implied, but I was fairly sure that it wasn't my sort of thing.)

There were changes ahead, but our conversion to Judaism was, for the time being at least, not one of them.

After father came down from Oxford, he had spent a few years working in the family firm with no great enthusiasm and no great success. He had hoped to branch out on his own after the war, but the early death of his father forced him to reconsider his plans, especially as the company had grown considerably during the war and was short of senior personnel. Even then he planned to disengage himself after a few years, sell his share of the company and join some former army colleagues in an overseas venture. He was never specific as to what exactly the venture would be, but in the immediate post-war years, everything at home seemed dismal and everything abroad seemed promising. He was thirty-six when the war finished. Soon he was in his forties and too caught up in the operations of the company to disengage himself and start afresh. By then its fortunes were declining and it would have looked as if he was leaving a sinking ship, though in retrospect it was clear that it would have been better both for him and the company if he had left.

Willie had taken over as chairman, and father's principal function was that of sales manager. He liked to travel, had numerous overseas connections and seemed the ideal man for the job, but his approach was too gentlemanly. He was the practitioner of a soft sell, so soft as to be wet.

All this I was to learn much later. Business matters were never discussed in our presence, but even as children we felt a certain degree of strain had entered into the previously happy relationship between father and Willie, which we ascribed to business difficulties. I happened to pick up the 'phone extension once and overheard Willie talking to father, high-pitched and angry, and using the sort of language I had never associated with any member of my family.

'What the hell do you think you were doing in America – having a holiday? You spent more than you earned. Do you always have to stay in the Plaza? When the hell . . .'

We also, as I have already said, had intimations that money was not as plentiful as it used to be. We were aware that we were very much poorer than the Roscoes, but then so was the whole world. As time passed, however, it gradually dawned on us that a good part of the world was richer than us. The fact in itself didn't worry me, and I was moved more by curiosity than concern.

Then everything changed. Roof-tiles, which had been descending like autumn leaves with every wind, were replaced; broken gates were mended; the drive, which was full of pot-holes and weeds, was resurfaced, and, most ominous of all, father sold his Wolseley and bought a Rover.

A few days later he brought us together to inform us that

he had acquired a farm of some six hundred acres whose lands backed on to us, and that he was retiring from business to devote himself to farming, 'something that I've wanted to do all my life'.

Vesta looked solemn and troubled, but then she usually did. The younger girls clasped their hands with elation. I think that they fancied the place was about to be converted into an adventure playground with their own private zoo. I recalled the conversation father had had with Callum about the costs of farming and asked if it wouldn't be very expensive.

'Very expensive indeed,' he said. 'The farm is in a run-down condition. Buildings, machinery, plant, have all been neglected and I also intend to acquire some new livestock. It'll cost a fortune.'

'Are we going to be as rich as the Roscoes?' chirped in Rocky.

'No, my dear, we shall probably be as poor as mice.'

'Can I look after the cows?' asked Vida.

'By all means. When you're home on holiday I shall be expecting you all to give a hand, though, strictly speaking, the livestock will be Tilly's department.'

'This is going to be fun,' said Rocky, bouncing up and down with excitement.

There was an unspoken house rule that we did not discuss money, for father felt the subject was 'vulgar and tedious', but on the other hand I kept wondering how he would pay for it all. Could grandma have left that much? Was Tilly an heiress? If so, what had she been doing as a governess? And now that the subject had been broached, I felt entitled to take it further.

'Where's the money coming from?' I asked.

He looked at me over the top of his glasses – which he donned only on special occasions – for a moment, and said: 'That's an impertinent question, don't you think?' – which brought the meeting to a close.

There were many sides to father, of which this – Papa Pompous – was the one I liked least, partly because it was cold and distant, and partly because it was an assumed *persona* which I felt, or at least hoped, bore no relation to the real self. It may have been a *persona* – Major Courlander – which he had assumed in the army and which he resuscitated from time to time as occasion required, as if he had told himself: 'Now, my good man, you've been the amiable, easy-going duffer for far too long, and it's about time you took yourself in hand.' I sometimes wished – especially as I grew older – that father was a little firmer, not as part of a rehearsed act. What specially irked me at that particular moment was the feeling that my question was perfectly justified and that if there had been a transformation in the family's fortunes, we, the children, had a right to know. As a matter of fact, I felt the question should have come from Vesta. She, however, thought father was right, but then she believed that everyone in authority was right and that authorities were there to be obeyed.

Stevie, to my surprise, was as much in the dark as we were. 'I know he sold his share of the business to Willie, but that couldn't have brought him more than fourpence, because Willie drives a hard bargain. In any case, the way the business has been going, his share wasn't worth more than fourpence. Grandma didn't leave anything. She only had an annuity which died with her. I can't imagine Tilly having money. Money comes with a cosseted look, whereas she has always looked slightly deprived. No, if you ask me, your father's robbed a bank.'

In the midst of all these changes, I also changed school, and joined Vesta at Helenslea, known as Hell for short. Stevie never referred to it as anything else because she had hated every minute of it. 'The girls were beastly and made fun of my name – they called me Whorelander. The food was awful, the rooms were cold, the beds were hard, and almost everything short of breathing was forbidden.' But father seemed determined to send us there and no place else, possibly in the belief that a school so detested by his sister could not be wholly devoid of merit.

I had by then become close friends with Callum's daughter, Grace, and I was hoping that she too would go on to Helenslea, but her mother had been to Cheltenham Ladies' College, so inevitably she went there as well.

Hell was not nearly as bad as Stevie had made it out to be. The main building was rather grim and forbidding and, as Vesta had said, it did remind one of the hospital in which mummy had spent her last illness. When we assembled for prayers in the main hall on cold, misty, autumn mornings, we felt we were there in expiation of some nameless sin. But the school was divided into six different houses, grouped round the edge of the playing fields, and the houses themselves were comfortable enough. I had imagined dormitories with an endless line of beds, like in the wards of an old work-house hospital, but there were only four or five of us to a room; and if the food wasn't exciting, my memories of grandma's cooking had inured me to plain fare at its plainest. The grounds were spacious and beautifully laid out, and the library was excellent. For the time being, however, I was more interested in events at home than in my new surroundings.

While I could imagine father as a farmer – albeit a gentleman farmer – I could not imagine Tilly as a farmer's wife; but in fact she took to farming as if she were descended from peasant stock, and was up before dawn to see to the milking. Even father was not afraid to get his hands dirty, mucking out the cow-shed, fetching fodder, digging ditches, laying hedges. We learned all this from Vida and Rocky, who were still at home. Tilly also looked after the chickens and kept the books, and both Vida and Rocky spoke of her as an ideal mother, which is to say, she left them largely to their own devices. Vida also spoke of having discovered 'a new father'.

'Not that there was anything wrong with the old one,' she added, 'but we hardly saw anything of him. Now when we come home from school, we all have tea together in the kitchen with him and Tilly – and he *talks*.'

'Aren't farmers supposed to be dour?' asked Vesta.

'Not gentleman farmers,' I said.

When we came home at Christmas, we could not wait to

see our new father and the new Tilly, but they had gone on a delayed honeymoon to the Canary Islands which rather peeved us, for we felt that at their age they might have reasonably waited for their honeymoon until we got back. Father was forty-five, Tilly could not have been much less, and the idea of a middle-aged pair going off on honeymoon at all sounded mildly obscene. Vesta and I were also unhappy about changes which had taken place in the house itself, though we should have been prepared for them, for the builders had settled in even before the wedding. The house was a Georgian structure and, although there had been Victorian additions, it was still substantially Georgian in character; but now some of the windows on the ground floor had been removed and replaced with what was called 'a picture window', a half-acre of glass which offered an uninterrupted view of the back garden and some of the fields beyond. Although there is something immensely attractive about the sight of ploughed fields under a glowering winter sky, the window just did not fit in with the character of the room, or the house. I was surprised, for although I by now had serious reservations about Tilly, I would never have accused her of lack of taste. The house had also been replastered and recaulked and seemed less open to the elements. In the olden days gale-force winds used to blow through the corridors, and we thought we could hear ghosts treading the creaking floor-boards. Now the whole place, for all its rambling size, felt too cosy and snug for our tastes.

We were invited to lunch to the Roscoes' on Boxing Day. The wine flowed pretty freely (though not at our end of the table – I felt that at thirteen I should at least have been offered a glass), and Callum asked me how I liked my new 'mum'.

'All right as mums go,' I said.

'Non-committal, aren't we? Good-looking woman. Don't know why he didn't make an honest woman of her years ago.' Sophie gave him a look which would have stopped a runaway express, but he continued on his merry way. 'Ever the Edwardian, your father. Kept her in a flat in Maida Vale. She's been married before, you know.'

Which was too much for Sophie. She rose from the table in silence and quickly left the room.

It was also a bit too much for me. I had suspected something of the sort. There was, of course, nothing reprehensible in the fact that Tilly had been married, as there had been nothing reprehensible in the fact that she was Jewish. What I found reprehensible was her determination to keep such facts from us, and father's readiness to aid and abet her. I felt that when he told us he was about to marry her, he might have told us more about her. I also felt, as did Vesta, that if we were to regard her as a mother, she would have to take us more into her confidence. Perhaps she did not wish to be so regarded, as was her right, but we resented the estrangement she was causing between father and us.

'I think we should say so when we see them,' said Vesta.

They had expected to be back before the end of the holidays, but were delayed by bad weather, and we returned to school without seeing them.

'I don't think we should write home,' I said, 'because I have no reason to believe that they're interested to hear from us.'

'Perhaps we're being too harsh,' said Vesta. 'They've only been married about six months and they're still wrapped up in each other.'

'They're not lovers in the first flush of youth,' I pointed out. 'They're ancient, and I, for one, don't intend to write.'

But a week or so later, Vida wrote to say that Tilly was 'big with child', which surprised us all, for we thought she was too old for that, and which thawed the chill even in my (already) ample breast. She added that Tilly had taken to her bed, and would have to stay there – 'flat on her back' – till the baby was due sometime in April. Then we heard that she had been moved to hospital.

'She'll lose it,' said Vesta, 'they always do at that age. Poor Papa.' When she was moved by ambulance to London, we took it as a bad sign and Vesta, who seemed extravagantly informed about such things, suggested that both Tilly and the baby must be in danger. We 'phoned Stevie to ask if this was the case. 'I'm afraid it is,' she said, 'but she's determined to have it.'

When we came home for Easter, Mrs Donelly tried her best to cheer us up, but the atmosphere in the house reminded us painfully of the atmosphere nine years earlier – almost to the day – when mummy lay dying. Father, who was at Tilly's bedside, would 'phone us daily in reassuring tones to say that everything was all right, but we by now knew him too well to take his reassurance at its face value. In any case, if all was well, what was he doing at her bedside?

'Do you think father will marry again?' asked Rocky.

Then early one morning, the 'phone went. We all dived from our beds, but I was the first to get there. It was father and his voice sounded odd, as if he had been crying. Tilly had been safely delivered of a boy. At this we all fell upon each other in tears. Only Mrs Donelly remained composed.

'I knew everything would be all right,' she said. 'I've been lighting candles to the Holy Virgin for the last two months.'

We were due to go back to school the next day, but were inclined to take it upon ourselves to extend our holiday till Tilly was home with the baby, but father warned us that that might take another week or two, and told us to go back. In the event she was in hospital for a further six weeks.

Stevie, who had been to see her, wrote to say that the baby was beautiful – 'the picture of your father' – but underweight and had to be kept in an incubator, and that Tilly was white and weak.

There was, for some reason, no half-term that year and we had to wait till the summer before we could see them. The baby had by then grown to enormous proportions, and it was difficult to believe that he had been underweight, but Tilly was still bedridden. There were grey streaks in her hair, dark rings round her eyes. She looked gaunt and far too old to be suckling an infant.

The house was full of people. A full-time nurse had been brought in, a prim, chilly thing with pale-blue eyes and a snub nose, who only thawed when Callum came over on a visit. Stevie was with us. Sophie was more in our house than in hers, and a small man in a velvet skull-cap, who turned out to be Tilly's father, appeared. He came for a week and stayed a month, during which time we largely subsisted on a vegetarian diet.

'You like your new brother?' he asked.

'I love him,' I said, 'he's beautiful.'

'My first grandson. The others are all girls,' and he grimaced with distaste. 'He's been circumcised, you know, a proper circumcision.' I had no doubts on the matter, though offhand I had no idea what an improper circumcision could be.

Sophie's father was in England and she brought him over to see 'the miracle child', as she called him, and introduced him to Tilly's father. The two old men scrutinized one another as dog scrutinizes dog, and both said almost simultaneously:

'Don't I know you?'

'My name's Abrahamson,' said Sophie's father.

'I'm Goshen.'

'Goshen? Goshen? Are you from Schwintzyan?'

'Yes, yes, I was born there. So you must be one of the Abrahamsons. Which one? Schwintzyan was full of Abrahamsons.'

'My father was known as Moshe *der reiter* [Moses the red one].'

'Ah, Moshe *der ganef* [Moses the thief].'

'Moshe *der reiter*, I said.'

'Moshe *der reiter ganef* [Moses the red thief].'

'He wasn't a *ganef*, but because he made a bit of money, people were jealous. They were jealous then, as they are now. Anyway, *mazeltov*.' And they shook hands and almost embraced. And they spent the rest of the day comparing memories and, I suspect, sons-in-law.

The Roscoes went up to their place in Scotland in the middle of August and, as we had no plans for a holiday that year, we were invited to join them. I was 'minded' (to use father's expression) to go, but all the others wanted to stay at home and ooh and aah over Tilly and the infant. I was by now getting a little tired of both, but I did not want to go off on my own (and I had a feeling that the Roscoes would not have welcomed me on my own), so I stayed at home with the rest. One evening, I was summoned to Tilly's bedside.

'Ducks,' she said, 'I have the feeling that you're unhappy about something.'

'Does one have to be happy about everything?'

'No, but one should be happy about something. You carry a general air of disgruntlement.'

'That's me I suppose.'

'Is it something I've done?'

'Well frankly –' and I hesitated.

'Go on.'

'You've kept your distance from us, which I suppose is natural and necessary for a governess, but it's a bit much now that you're married to father. If Callum hadn't told us, we wouldn't even have known you'd been married before.'

She gazed out of the windows for what seemed a long time and her eyes quivered with tears.

'I've nothing to hide, Ducks,' she said, her voice breaking, 'but there's a great deal I'd like to forget.'

I sat feeling very uncomfortable and saying nothing. I half-wanted to dive on her bed and embrace her. But she blew her nose, wiped her eyes and quickly recovered herself. 'But I'll tell you everything if you want,' she added.

'Not if it hurts,' I said.

'I'm afraid it may.'

At which I could restrain myself no longer, and dived upon her with tears streaming down my cheeks. I didn't know what was happening to me. That little infant seemed to be transforming us all.

When we went back to school the following month, I sent her long, intimate letters, and she wrote back with equal intimacy, without, however, delving into her past, as if it was something she had written off and was not to be mentioned. She also kept us posted on events on the farm. Father had brought in a new manager, a Mr Urquhart,

> alias, Urk, a long, lean, unsmiling figure, without hair, eyebrows, shoulders, without a wife, and almost without teeth. But the cows love him, which is just as well, poor things, for we have disposed of the bull, who was too fat and too lazy, and not really up to the demands made on him, and his good ladies are henceforth to be artificially inseminated. As we now have sixty head of cattle, including forty in milk, and as I have been rather slow in getting back on my feet, we also have a new cow-hand who has everything Urk hasn't and with whom Rocky has fallen unutterably in love.

I thought once she was back on her feet she would get a nanny to look after the 'miracle child', whom I was tempted to call Jesus, but whose actual name was Josh (or Joshua), but she wanted to look after him herself, which suggested that her farming days were over.

'You won't believe this,' Vida wrote, 'but Tilly's becoming a bore. It's Josh this, Josh that, nothing but Josh: his first smile, his first tooth, what he eats, what he doesn't, and what he brings up. I thought all young mothers of young children were bad, but they're not half as bad as the old mothers of young children. And father, if you can imagine it, is even worse.'

I had always regarded Vida as comparatively dull, having neither the beauty of Vesta, nor the sparkle and impishness of Rocky. She and Rocky had naturally become a pair, as Vesta and I had, and I hadn't had all that much to do with her, but she had changed greatly between her twelfth and thirteenth year and by the time she joined us at Helenslea she had – to my eyes at least – become an intelligent, lively and attractive young woman. I couldn't associate her with the giggly little girl I had known a year or two before, and she, Vesta and I became inseparable, a fact which occasioned the disapproval of our headmistress, a neat, white-haired figure, who reminded us rather of grandma.

'I sometimes feel', she said, 'that it is not a good idea to have too many members of the same family in the school at the same time, for they form a small, inbred clique and become indifferent to the school itself. It wasn't so bad when there were two of you here, but now that there are three it's become impossible. Other girls when they come to a school like this make friends who can see them in good stead through life. You three have become too self-sufficient both for your own good and for that of the school.'

'Are we falling behind in any way?' asked Vesta.

'Not in the least. I have no complaints on that score whatsoever, but you know one doesn't only go to school to pass exams. You three are privileged to be passing through one of the best schools in the country, but you are neither leaving a mark on it, nor is it leaving a mark on you. I'm afraid you people are rather like that.'

'What people could she have meant?' Vida asked later.

'What people do you think?' I said.

'I wonder why we didn't answer back,' said Vesta.

We slept on it, a restless night, and the next morning decided to ask for an appointment with the headmistress to clarify her remarks.

'I should have thought my meaning was obvious,' she said. 'Jewish girls bring obvious benefits to a school – scholastic generally – but they do tend to be cliquish. Usually where we have several members from the same family they tend to spread themselves through the school and become absorbed, whereas Jewish girls tend to form a solid, indigestible clique. And Jews are like that in general. It may not be a bad thing in other respects, and, of course, it explains why you people have maintained your identity, but it can be harmful to a school.'

When we were home at Easter we told father about the conversation.

'Frankly, I think she's an anti-Semite,' I said.

'Oh, for God's sake, don't be another Stevie,' he said. 'Of course Jews are cliquish – it's one of the first things you notice about them. In the Officers' Mess at GHQ there were several Jewish officers – doctors mainly – who always kept together and murmured about being ostracized, but they ostracized themselves.'

'How were you regarded?' I asked.

'That is not for me to say, but I wasn't one of them, that's for certain. Apart from anything else, their conversation was all of gonorrhoea and syphilis and blood groups.'

The following term brought many changes. Rocky joined us at school, and Vida turned Jewish. She later ascribed her conversion to our initial conversation with the headmistress. She began to study Jewish history and Jewish teaching. There was a Jewish girl in her class, called Hilda, who received private Hebrew tuition from a visiting tutor once a week, and Vida asked if she could join her; and then, when we returned to school for the new term, she asked to be excused chapel attendance. There was a precedent, for the Hindu girls – there were five or six of them at the school, large-eyed, studious, and quiet as mice – never went, and Hilda was similarly excused. But Vida was by now in her third year and had attended chapel the previous two, so her newly found Jewishness placed the rest of us in a slightly embarrassing position. The headmistress, for her part, was dumbfounded by it and she called us together in her study.

'I am perfectly prepared to excuse the genuine practitioners of another faith from chapel,' she said, 'but I have your application forms here and I have nothing to suggest that you three enter into that category.' She showed us the forms, and in each case the space after religion had been left blank. 'Is it only you, Vida, who wants to be excused, or all three of you?'

In common with most of the girls at the school, we found chapel attendance a bore, and I felt tempted to chirp in that I, too, had been restored to my ancestral faith, but Vida spoke up before I could open my mouth.

'My parents were never practising Jews and my sisters still aren't, but I've since become one.'

'Very well, I shall require a letter to that effect from your father.'

Vida did not anticipate any difficulties and 'phoned home that night. Father was away and Tilly said she was not prepared to write such a letter.

'But why not?'

'Because I feel that this is a matter which only your father should deal with.'

'You almost sound upset at the fact that I want to be Jewish.'

'I'm not upset, but I am unhappy at being placed in an awkward situation. You're only fifteen, too young to know the serious step you're taking, and I feel that if there is to be a letter to the school, it should come from your father.' And father eventually wrote it with much shaking of the head, and muttering: 'What's happening to the younger generation, what's happening to them?'

Vida's Jewishness did not stop with non-attendance at chapel. She turned kosher and took only vegetarian food, which she ate at a separate table with the Hindus and Hilda, and their food seemed so much less revolting than ours that I was half-tempted to turn kosher myself. Her habits persisted even when we were home, and she seemed to spend half her holidays preparing herself dinners of herbs.

Uncle Willie turned fifty about this time and Tilly gave him a party. He was almost our forgotten uncle. We used to see him frequently when we were smaller and of an age to be gratified by small pleasures, but as we grew older we rarely saw anything of him and might not have seen him at all, had he not taken the trouble to visit us at Christmas and for occasional weekends.

He had gone through a shaky stage in his early forties and father complained 'the poor man is falling apart', but new drugs had been developed to check his disorder. He no longer had his cyclical attacks of malaria, but if his health improved, his spirits deteriorated. He became silent and morose, his nose and ears turned mauve and his pockets rattled with pills. His hairless head seemed to have changed shape and was becoming pointed like a Gothic arch. Tall and thin, he walked with a solemn tread, and needed only a scythe on his shoulder to represent the picture of death. There was only a year between father and him, but they seemed to belong to different generations.

When I turned sixteen he took me out to lunch and was taken aback when I ordered wine.

'At your age?' he said. 'It'll go to your head,' but I suspect he was rather more worried that it would go to his pocket. Until father's situation had been so suddenly and so mysteriously transformed, we used to think of him as our rich uncle; now he thought of himself as the poor one, and grumbled incessantly that it was 'impossible for an honest man to make an honest living in England today'. He was still head of the family metal business which, as far as we were aware, was still solvent, though he was counting his pennies as if he was on the brink of bankruptcy, or even beyond.

He asked me what I planned to do when I left school and, when I said I hadn't decided, he suggested that I join the firm.

'You're the brightest of the girls', he said, 'and we need somebody from the family to keep it going.'

'But you keep telling me it's impossible to make an honest living in England.'

'It's impossible for someone of my generation with my old-world attitudes, but I have the feeling that you'd come with the right approach.'

'What is the right approach?'

'I'm not sure, I'm only sure I haven't got it.'

'Wouldn't you like to wait till Josh grows up, so that you could have another Courlander at the top?'

'How old is Josh now, two, three? I'd have to wait twenty years. I won't live that long, and I don't know if the company'll last that long even if I do. Besides, you're a Courlander yourself. I've never had any prejudice against women.'

Willie's birthday party was a family affair. Stevie had threatened to boycott it, arguing that birthdays beyond a certain age were a case for commiseration rather than celebration, but she eventually turned up in a new hat and with a large covered canvas under her arm as a present. When she unwrapped it, I had the sinking feeling that she had found yet another boyfriend, this time a painter, for I could not imagine even Stevie buying that particular canvas on its own merits. She also had a glow about her, which I presumed, did not derive entirely from her work with the BBC.

Tilly had prepared a fairly ornate lunch, and Willie noticed that the food Vida was eating differed from the fare the rest of us received and asked if she was on a diet.

'She's turned Jewish,' said father.

'Jewish?' said Willie. 'We've always been Jewish after a fashion.'

'Well she's turned Jewish kosher fashion. Didn't you know?'

'No, I didn't. Nobody in this family tells me anything.'

He seemed upset by the revelation and, after the meal, went over to talk to Vida to ask what had brought it on.

'You make it sound like a disease, Uncle Willie,' she said. 'I've been trying to find out what it means to be a Jew, and eating kosher is part of it.'

'Yes, yes, but these things are only tribal taboos. A few generations ago the family was full of rabbis and the like, but people move on, you know.'

'Yes, uncle, but not always in the right direction,' which for a fifteen year old struck me as a somewhat precocious remark. I had tended to regard Vida's 'return', as she called it, with a certain amount of indulgence, even amusement, but now I was beginning to find her insufferable.

'She's got time to grow out of it,' said Tilly, but there was a purposefulness about Vida's ample chin which made me doubt it.

5
The Candidate

We all had cause to remember the summer of 1958. Vesta won a scholarship to Somerville College, Oxford, I won the school history prize, and Rocky was sent down as a result of what she insisted was a miscarriage of justice.

'There was this grocer's delivery boy who had promised to get me back well before lights out, but his motor bike kept breaking down. It wasn't as if we *did* anything, and in the end I had to walk, four miles, through the darkness.'

The turn of events must have pleased the headmistress, for with Vesta removed for benign reasons and Rocky for malign ones, there was just Vida and me, and it takes more than two to form a clique. In any case, by my final year at Helenslea, there were no less than four kosher pupils in the school, and I did not see all that much of Vida for she now had a clique – indeed, something of a ghetto – of her own. Which didn't mean that I was left entirely friendless, for I had by then discovered the fellowship of books and I knew of very few people whose company could compare to a really good book or, for that matter, even a thoroughly bad one.

I also felt it important to enter university on a scholarship, for if Vesta, who had the looks, could win a scholarship, Ducks, who didn't, could hardly do less. If I look back on that year, I remember it as one of relentless toil, broken by one rather bizarre event – a coming-out ball.

The Season, as it was and, as I believe, still is known, dominated all conversation during the summer term at school and our headmistress would warn us of its pitfalls.

It disrupted the better part of a year, she complained, and a crucial year at that, in a girl's life. 'Of course, no girl who is scholarship material would have a mind for that sort of thing,' she added, 'but there is many a girl who might have done something with herself were it not for those wretched affairs. There was something to be said for them when they were marriage markets. The better-class English families tend to be scattered, not only over Britain, but all over the world, Singapore, Hong Kong, Kenya, the Argentine, so the Season did have its uses, but not any more. It's an occasion for licence and debauchery' – which immediately raised it in my esteem at least.

We used to read about the debutantes in the gossip columns and always had a good giggle about them. Then one day Grace Roscoe came to us with a long face to announce that she, too, was having a coming-out ball.

'Father says that all his sisters had one and he doesn't see why I should get away with it. Mummy says that all my friends were having them and were inviting us to them all, so she felt she had to reciprocate. I hate my parents, don't you?'

'There but for the grace of God go I,' said Vesta.

But God was not quite as gracious as she thought, for a few weeks later father asked her if she would like to have a coming-out party.

'You're not being serious?' she said.

'We would have it jointly with Grace.'

When she saw he was serious, words failed her; all she could do was shake her head in a mildly distraught way.

'Pity,' said father, 'I thought it might be fun.'

And that, thought Vesta, was the end of the matter till Tilly tackled her.

'I gather you don't want a coming-out ball.'

'Ball is it now? Father mentioned a party. No, I wouldn't want one or the other.'

'Can't say I blame you. They can be dreadful affairs, but this might have been rather nice – a joint ball with the Roscoes in their house. Sophie, as you know, does everything tastefully, and I know Grace would feel much happier if you went into it together. But still, if you don't want it, there's nothing more to be said for it.'

'Grace doesn't want it either.'

'Oh, I know, she told me. Callum bullied her into it. That, of course, isn't your father's style, though he was looking forward to it rather, and, of course, he's very proud of his daughters and would like to show them off.'

'I wouldn't have thought he was that infantile.'

'You don't know men, my dear. You may not know this, you've been away, but we've all been going through a difficult patch in one way or another: ill-health, setbacks on the farm, awkward suppliers. The ball would have been something to look forward to.'

'If father wants a party, have it for Midsummer's night or something – or his fiftieth birthday. He'll be fifty soon.'

'That's another reason why he would have liked to have a coming-out ball. It would help him forget.'

'Why? What's wrong with being fifty?'

'Nothing, if you've done something with yourself, but he feels he's achieved nothing.'

It doesn't take much to make Vesta feel guilty – it seems to me that people's capacity for guilt stands in exact ratio to their innocence – and in the end she and Grace had a joint ball.

There were bands and bars and buffets, and whole brigades of *bouffant*-haired girls and pink-faced young men. Grace had different groups of friends, 'Jews and blue-stockings,' as her father called them, and county, and the two did not mix.

Tilly looked quite regal, and it seemed to me that it was she who wanted the ball, rather than father, as an occasion to show off her glad rags. Sophie, though lacking her height, also looked magnificent, though I thought that she was overladen with precious stones. She had a natural glitter which tended to be a little dimmed by her diamonds.

Callum spent most of the evening dancing with Tilly, and I placed myself in a strategic position to be available when he was free, but almost every time I did so, a young man with glasses bore down upon me and asked me to dance. At first I found it difficult to refuse, but then I began to notice that he had taken upon himself the duty of dancing with every unattended or unattractive girl in the place. It was nearly midnight before I caught Callum on his own and asked him to dance with me. It was a tango and, for a man of his build, he was surprisingly light on his feet. I was particularly fascinated by the graceful movements of his empty sleeve every time we turned.

'You dance well,' he said.

'You sound suprised.'

'I am surprised. Didn't think blue-stockings were up to that sort of thing. Going up to Cambridge I hear.'

'Hope to.'

'To read economics?'

'Yes.'

'Going into politics?'

'Might.'

'Bolshie, I suppose.'

'Why Bolshie?'

'Well-to-do Jews have a bent for that sort of thing. Did I tell you I was standing for Parliament at the next election?'

'No. Tory, I suppose.'

'Why Tory?'

'Well-to-do Englishmen have a bent for that sort of thing.'

'Labour, as a matter of fact. Not that I'll get in. Macmillan's unbeatable.'

'Are you standing against Macmillan?'

'No, but people vote for the PM. It'll be Mac versus Gaitskell. Calibre of the local chap doesn't count. You could put up a horse and if it's a Tory horse, and there's a Tory trend, the horse'll get in.'

As I turned I saw father dancing with Vesta and felt an uncommon pang, almost a stab, of pride. Father was a trifle too fat, Vesta a trifle too thin, but they were a magnificent pair, with Vesta's long hair floating upwards from her neck every time they turned. She had the loveliest neck which, she always complained, was 'far too long – I feel like a giraffe'. She had just returned from a holiday in Greece and had a downy, tawny colour and wore a thin gold chain with a sapphire pendant which had belonged to mummy. I only wish she looked as if she was enjoying herself, but she never did, and there, as everywhere else, gave one the feeling that she was in this world against her better judgement. Father too was tanned, an even, glowing brown. They had been to Greece together.

Later in the evening, as I was talking to Sophie, I felt a pair of hands over my eyes.

'Guess who?'

'Aly Khan,' I said.

And he put his arms round my waist and kissed me on the ear. He must have been drinking, for I couldn't recall such a show of affection since I was small, and I found it almost embarrassing.

He seemed to have over-exerted himself and was sweaty and breathless, and we sat down for a drink.

'I was watching you across the room as I was dancing', he said, 'and thought you only needed one thing to look good.'

'A face-lift,' I suggested.

'Well, yes, almost, but an expression – lift I would call it. How old are you – nineteen?'

'Eighteen. You see, you don't even know my age.'

'I'm sorry, it's not only the fact that I have four daughters, but sixty head of cattle, and I have too many figures to keep in my head. You're eighteen. You've more or less come top of your school, with a scholarship to Cambridge. You've got every prospect of a brilliant future ahead. You're attractive, your family's fairly well off, you've got most of the things most people crave for. I know smugness isn't an attractive quality, even in people who have a great deal to be smug about, but I think I would prefer it to your constant air of displeasure. Vesta is even worse. Every time I see her I feel like taking her by the hand and murmuring words of reassurance in her ear. And even Vida, who used to be a straightforward, reasonable, if rather demanding child, has turned kosher and has been sulking all evening because the buffet table is dominated by a hog's head. I told her that I didn't order that hog's head, and that she doesn't have to eat it even if I did, and that there was plenty of salmon and other things which she could eat, but she'll hardly speak to me, as if I had expressly brought the wretched hog in as a premeditated assault upon her religious susceptibilities. Thank God for Rocky, she alone looks as if she may have an actual capacity for enjoying life. I'm proud of you all, as any reasonable parent would be, but will I ever be able to do anything to please you?'

'If we're being honest with ourselves,' I said, 'was this shindig put on to please us, or to please you?'

'I liked the idea – it came from Sophie, as you know – but if I had thought you weren't going to enjoy it, it wouldn't have occurred to me to do anything about it. The thing is, I suspect you are enjoying it, only you feel you shouldn't. I'm not sure if it's not a type of snobbery. You're bright, uncommonly bright, and you have acquired – goodness knows where from, perhaps it goes with brightness – a puritan streak which makes you feel that all this, the music, the dancing, the gaiety, the laughter, is, or at least should be, beneath you, and you are holding on to yourself in case you should lapse into the spirit of the occasion. It reminds me of something your headmistress told me. You were a highly intelligent girl, she said, and highly motivated and a credit to the school, but that you kept yourself apart and never entered fully into the spirit of the place. Even Vida, with all her religious quirks, is more part of the school. If you're going to continue like that through life, you're going to find the world a very lonely place.'

What he said about the school was perfectly true, but I had not *kept* myself apart, I had been kept apart. School society was not a loose association of individuals, but of little cliques. One joined the general society through one's membership of one or another of its sub-groups. I had at one time formed a sub-group of a sort with Vesta and Vida, but then Vida turned religious and Vesta left, until in my final year I was on my own. No one is more on her own than an individual in an association of groups, but it didn't worry me, for I had the library and books, and the scholarship to work for. I daresay if I had had a group to cling to, I probably wouldn't have got the scholarship, but there was no use explaining that to father, for I don't think he would have understood. And I didn't have the heart to tell him that the reason why I hadn't entered into the party spirit at the ball was that I wasn't aware of any such spirit.

No expense had been spared, but nothing like a party atmosphere had been engendered. Roscoe House had a vast mock-baronial hall which Sophie had been determined to fill, and fill it she did, but the crowds who assembled were not particularly familiar with each other, nor, it seemed, were they all that familiar with their hosts. I began to discern one of the factors which had drawn the families Roscoe and Courlander together. Both tended to keep their distance from the *petite bourgeoisie* about them, but neither had been fully accepted by the *haute bourgeoisie*. Both, moreover, had drifted from their origins, the one ex-Catholic, the other ex-Jewish. I daresay if they had remained Catholic or Jewish they would have counted for something, at least among Catholics or Jews, but their paganism had rendered them both somewhat *déclassé*.

The coming-out ball (or the COB as we called it), had, however, indicated to at least three of us – namely Grace, Vesta and me – that the class to which our parents aspired was not one in which any of us wanted a place.

But neither would we have been entirely happy to remain in the sort of social no man's land which they actually occupied. I was glad enough to come home on holidays, but that was because I liked to get back to my own room and my own treasures, and get a glimpse of Josh growing up and possibly see something of Callum and Grace, but glad as I was to come home, I was even gladder to leave. I could not explain my feeling of restlessness and discontent and I tended to ascribe it to overwork, except that I was at my most restless and discontented on holiday and hoped that it might change when I went to university.

One of the reasons why I had decided to try for a Cambridge rather than an Oxford scholarship was that Vesta was already in Oxford and I wanted to get away from the family altogether. Grace could spend whole nights unfolding the bill of grievances against her family. I had none, or none to speak of, but, through no fault of theirs, or, I believed, mine, I was tired of them all, so tired that I toyed for a time with the idea of studying abroad. If I had failed to get into Cambridge, I might have revived the idea, but I got the scholarship and went up to Newnham.

Stevie had been there before the war. It must have been long before, for when she visited me she could find only one don surviving from her day, who didn't even recognize or remember her.

'Shows you what an impact I made on Cambridge,' she said. 'In those days there were about twenty males to every female, and unless one was downright grotesque, one could have a ball all the year round. I know I did. And I felt entitled to it, after all those years in Hell. Time of my life. Nothing that's happened before or since can compare to it, except perhaps the war years.'

I must have been grotesque, or there may have been more women in Cambridge, for nothing like that happened to me. And in any case, I had hardly settled into the place before Parliament was dissolved and a general election was announced.

I remembered Callum telling me that he planned to stand for Parliament, but I didn't take him seriously until I saw his name among a list of prospective candidates. I immediately 'phoned to ask if I could be of help.

'Can you drive?' he asked.

'Yes.'

'Have you got a car?'

'I can get one.'

'You can be of help.'

Stevie was on holiday. I borrowed her Mini, commandeered her flat and used it as a sub-headquarters. Callum had a *pied-à-terre* on the Chelsea Embankment and offered me a room there, and, without thinking, I said no. I suppose I was familiar with Stevie's and felt safer there. I had never known myself to think in terms of safety first, but it was perhaps just as well that I had a place of my own to come back to last thing at night, for I had never worked so hard in my life and I needed a bed of my own to collapse into. At first I spent most of my time washing cups and making tea, then Callum took me over as his chauffeuse. He used to rehearse his speeches at me while I drove him, and I chipped in with so many suggestions that he finally said:

'Who's the fucking candidate, you or me?' He was not, however, completely unappreciative of my suggestions, and told me that I should think seriously about the possibility of standing for Parliament myself.

'You've got two handicaps. First, you're a woman, and secondly, you're bright. A man can just about get away with it, at least in the Labour Party, but not a woman.'

'There's a third handicap which you haven't mentioned,' I said. 'I'm not a particularly political animal. I wouldn't know which party to join.'

'That's a detail, though it helps to go for the party in which you look out of place. It fixes you in people's memory, otherwise one candidate looks much the same as another. You've seen all the publicity I've got, that's only because I'm Labour. I don't think I'd have got a line if I'd been a Tory. The Tory chap, a jumped-up lawyer, has been passing round photos of Grace's coming-out ball, in the mistaken belief that it would blacken me in the eyes of the electorate. He doesn't know the British working man. The working man has always liked people with the ready money to live it up. I've never been one of your hairshirt socialists. My opponent's even worse, a bloody hairshirt Tory.'

'He's a self-made man, Callum.'

'So the hell what? He's an upstart, son of a village butcher. Sad thing is, the Tories have lost faith in their own ruling class. The Liberals are finished. If you've got a bit of blue blood in your veins – not that I have all that much – Labour's your lot. The fact that I've picked up a few medals and lost an arm helps, but so does the fact that I've got a bit of money. They know I won't have to put my fingers in the till.'

We held a door-to-door canvass a few days before the election.

'Vote for Roscoe?' said one man. 'Why should I? He's a Yid.'

And another said: 'Didn't you know he's living on slave labour?'

This latter response was picked up by several canvassers, and it seemed that stories were circulating that his father-in-law had ten thousand blacks on his payroll, who were employed in the most atrocious conditions and on starvation wages. And to make matters worse – almost as if to confirm the charge – his work-force went on strike.

'I wouldn't call the old man a model employer,' said Callum, 'but he's no worse than most of the others, and a good bit better than some. Still, it's difficult to answer a charge which isn't publicly made, and I don't think it'll do me much harm. The British working man hates blacks.'

The canvass suggested that he might lose by about a thousand votes. His predecessor had lost by nearly two thousand four years previously in 1955, when there had then been a swing away from Labour. Now the swing was in the opposite direction and we had hopes that it might carry Callum into Parliament. Moreover, there had been changes in the constituency – a run-down inner-London suburb – and part of the area, which had been solid working class, was being refurbished and renovated; there had been a considerable influx of young, well-to-do middle-class families, a type which Callum dismissed contemptuously as upstarts, but many of whom, paradoxically enough, were inclined to vote Labour, so we thought that, in spite of the findings of the canvass, we might still win. One evening, towards the end of the campaign, Callum asked me home for a drink.

I was not particularly thirsty, but I was hoping his offer would not stop at drinks, and I gladly accepted. He poured himself a large brandy and I settled for some wine; as we clinked glasses, I said: 'To Colonel Callum Roscoe, MP.'

'I can't see it happening, can you? In a way I'm hoping it won't.'

'Then what made you stand?'

'Often asked myself the same question. Sophie, partly, partly ancestral pressures. The old man was in the House, so was his old man – a wop, you know. Never opened his mouth – don't even know if he spoke English. Mother's family's fairly ancient.' As he was talking he began to unbutton my blouse, almost absent-mindedly, but when he bent down to kiss the area exposed I thought my nipples would burst out of my breasts and ricochet round the room like bullets; as it was, my breasts burst out of their holders.

'My, you are a big girl,' he said admiringly, and bent down again, and then suddenly straightened.

'Are you a virgin by the way?'

'Why, what difference does it make?'

'My God, every difference. One doesn't deflower the daughters of one's best friend. If I had thought that your father had done anything like this to Grace, I'd kill him. Is she a virgin, by the way – Grace?' He looked at me almost imploringly.

'I wouldn't know,' I said, placing my breasts in their receptacle. 'We don't talk about such things.'

'Don't you, by Jove? When I was your age we never spoke about anything else.'

I re-buttoned my blouse, put on my coat and, as I turned for the door, I said: 'When I'm deflowered, I'll send you a postcard to come and get me.'

When I got back to the car, I had to sit at the wheel for some minutes before I felt calm enough to drive back to the flat.

Sophie came down with Grace for the eve of election meeting, but to my surprise did not stay for the election itself, or the count.

'She's convinced father will lose', Grace said, 'and doesn't want to be around to share his humiliation.'

'But didn't she put him up to it in the first place?'

'What makes you say so?'

'Your father told me.'

'In which case he's preparing to blame her for his débâcle. More drink, more rages. Oh, how I hate it all.'

'He's got more than a sporting chance, you know,' I said.

'I wouldn't vote for him,' she said, 'not even if I was in the Labour Party.'

I was surprised by her attitude.

'He's campaigned very hard, you know, the people like him. He'd make a very good and very conscientious MP.'

'For the first year or two, maybe, but he'd tire of it as he tires of everything. You've heard him, haven't you? "Oh, I say, wouldn't that be fun, let's try it." Everything's fun and games to him. His whole life's been one long escapade.'

'I can't think your mother would let him get away with it.'

'They've been married nineteen years, you know. She tried, and she's given up. I only hope Robin won't go the same way.'

'I'm beginning to understand why most fathers would rather have sons. We're harsh judges, you and I.'

'Harsh? Have you ever lived with him? Oh, he's attractive enough when he breezes in for a minute and then breezes out again, but you can't imagine what it's like having him around all the time, usually half-drunk, and not infrequently in a complete stupor. Mother tries to be understanding and explained that he was so near death that he has come to regard what's left of his life as a bonus to be squandered, the way people might squander an unexpected windfall. But it's her fault really, she's *too* understanding and has made too many allowances for him. If she had taken him in hand when they first married, she might have done something with him, but it's too late now, of course.'

'This could be a new start for him. It would give him new responsibilities.'

'*New* responsibilities? Isn't a family a responsibility enough? No, I have sufficient confidence in the good sense of the British voter to feel sure that he will be rejected by a very sizeable majority.'

That night I dreamt I was at the count and that Callum was walking up and down outside the counting hall like an expectant father awaiting his first child. There was first one count, then another. Finally after a third it was announced that he had lost by three hundred and forty-seven votes, at which point I woke with a start. It was still dawn, but I got out of bed, had a shower, gulped down a mouthful of black coffee and rushed out. It was election day and I spent most of the next twelve hours bundling voters into my car and driving them to and from the polling booths. I forgot to have lunch and when I sat down for my first meal of the day shortly after polling closed, I was too tired to eat. But I came to life when the count began. Callum's election agent was for some reason hopeful, and father had arrived to see Callum 'in his hour of triumph' as he put it.

'What makes you think he'll triumph?' I asked.

'One gets a feel for these things, dear child.'

There were six candidates, three from the main parties, one Communist and two cranks standing as Independents. They were all there with large rosettes on their lapels like prize cattle, and their wives, and their hangers-on, all trying to exude confidence.

'Don't get too hopeful,' Callum cautioned me, though I felt and must have looked anything but hopeful. 'I'm a born loser. That's what drew me to your father in the first place. We were always among the laggards in the cross-country runs, and developed the habit of dropping out altogether and going for a smoke. In any case the first returns are in and the Tories seem to be doing well.'

The hall was full. Sweaty, purposeful young men, with microphones in their hands, were pushing their way here, there and everywhere. There were two television cameras on the platform and a further two in the body of the hall, and one couldn't move without stumbling over cables. I too wore a large rosette and, statements having been obtained from anybody who was anybody, someone thrust a microphone in my face to see what prognostications I had to offer. I had nothing to say, nor the breath to say it, but I was caught up in the excitement of it all and I could see what made Callum run. This was a game worth playing almost for its own sake.

It was hot and stuffy and he was drenched with sweat. I took out a handkerchief and wiped his cheeks and forehead with a quivering hand.

'It's all right,' he said, 'don't get excited. They don't hang you if you lose, though perhaps they should.'

By one in the morning the first count was over, and the Returning Officer, his face impassive, ordered a recount. It must have been a close thing.

Father saw it as a hopeful omen. 'You've won,' he whispered.

Callum's election agent sounded equally hopeful. 'A recount's always a bad sign for the sitting candidate. You're as good as in.'

'D'you really think so?' said Callum. He seemed mildly perturbed at the prospect.

I looked over towards the Tory candidate – a tall, lean figure in broad-brimmed glasses, whose eternal smile did not quite hide the air of despondency which seemed to have descended over him and his co-workers – and for the first time I began to take heart. The excitement, or perhaps my hunger, began to affect my bowels. I left the room. When I returned a few minutes later, I found that the Returning Officer had ordered a further recount. At this I was gripped by something like despair and I was afraid to look in Callum's direction.

'It was only a dream,' I kept telling myself, 'there's no reason why it should be fulfilled in every detail.'

The tension was by now unbearable and I went outside for a breath of fresh air.

When I returned all the candidates were lined up beside the Returning Officer. All were smiling broadly, some desperately. Callum gave me a broad wink. The result was about to be declared. He lost by four hundred and seventy-three votes. I rushed over and threw my arms round him and broke down.

'What's that for, dammit?' he protested. 'If I'd won that would have been something to cry about.'

For a long time after that I was afraid to fall asleep because I was afraid to dream, and I was afraid to dream in case my dreams came true.

6
Otto

When I began my first year in Cambridge, Vesta was already in her second at Oxford. There had been a spate of suicides and a number of students, including Vesta, had formed themselves into an organization calling itself sos and put up posters round the various colleges inviting anyone in distress to 'phone them. I asked the secretary of the organization if there was not already in being a body called the Samaritans to cope with such things, and she replied that there were people 'who wouldn't be seen dead talking to the Samaritans'. sos, in other words, was a sort of Top People's Samaritans. Frankly, if I was on the point of suicide and found myself in conversation with someone like Vesta, it would more or less confirm me in my intentions. One night when she was on call I 'phoned and said: 'Good evening, you don't know me, but I wish to hang myself', to which she retorted 'please do', and put the 'phone down. She later reproved me for my little joke, suggesting that it was in poor taste, and warned me that my sense of humour would be the death of me. She added, 'It wouldn't be a bad thing if it was.' Such asperity was uncommon in my sister. Oxford was obviously doing something for her, or, at least, to her. A month or so later I came to spend a weekend with her, and by chance (or perhaps not) she happened to be on call while I was there. It was near midnight and I was getting ready for bed when the 'phone rang. Vesta was out of the room and I picked up the receiver:

'Hello,' an American voice asked, 'is that sos?'

Before I could answer, Vesta dashed in and snatched

the receiver from me.

'Hello,' she said, 'yes, yes it is. Can I help you? Could I have your telephone number? No, no, you don't have to give me your number, but it would be useful to have in case we're cut off. And your name? No, no, you don't have to give it. It is anonymous . . . Is British domestic gas what? Lethal? I should imagine it is . . . You've done what? Could you speak up please, it's a bad line. I think you misunderstand our purpose. We don't exist to advise people on how to commit suicide, we're here to talk them out of it. Are you sure you wouldn't like to give me your name – only the first one – if only to facilitate conversation. Bob? Your accent sounds vaguely American? It is? I see. What brings you to Oxford? Oh I am sorry to hear that . . . How dreadful . . . Good God . . . Gracious . . . She sounds like a monster. But what would killing yourself do? Think of your loved ones, your parents . . . Oh, you hate your parents? Did she? . . . Good grief . . . It hadn't occured to me sane people could behave like that . . . Oh, she's not sane . . .'

This went on for about an hour and, by the time she was finished, she was nearly suicidal herself; I daren't think what she might have done if I hadn't been there.

He 'phoned her again the following morning to tell her she had saved his life, which bucked her no end, and she invited him round for coffee. He was a graduate history student from Yale, a lean figure with an emaciated face, thin, sandy hair, a freckled complexion and blue, lustreless eyes behind large glasses. He had a drooping stance, with his head slightly to the side, and he spoke in a flat woebegone voice, as if he was imparting sad news. His name was Reed and, in keeping with the family tradition of not calling anyone by their actual names, I immediately christened him Weed, or Weedy.

She brought him home for a weekend once, and he seemed frightened of the cows.

'They're not bulls, you know,' I said.

'But they're so large and menacing,' said Weedy, 'in fact un-English. I like the scale of England – everything is small and in proportion to mankind, but the cows are too large.'

'I don't care for your young man,' father said to Vesta.

'He's not *my* young man,' said Vesta, 'and besides he's not all that young.' But he was back again at Easter and I said to her:

'You know he's becoming too dependent on you. What'll happen when you leave Oxford, or get married?'

'He's leaving in the summer,' she said.

When I came home in the summer, however, I found him sitting cross-legged on the patio, reading poems to Vesta and stroking her calf.

Stevie, who was staying with us, thought Weedy was 'rather nice'.

'You don't mean it,' I said.

'He's gentle.'

'He's more than gentle, he's inert. He began as her good deed for the day. He's become her good deed for the year. If she's not careful, he'll be her good deed for life.'

One evening I said to Vesta: 'I thought you told me he was going back in the summer?'

'The summer isn't over yet.'

'Did he have to come here?'

'He didn't have to, I asked him to. I rather like his company.'

'Now you know that's not true,' I said. 'You haven't the courage to tell him to leave because you're afraid he'll hang himself. Now you're trying to convince yourself that you like his company.'

At which she sighed.

'Ducks, you know, you may be very bright in other ways, but you don't understand people – or at least you don't understand me.'

Vesta must have told him about our conversation. Father and Tilly were away, we had little domestic help and we took it in turns to wash up after meals, and the next evening, when it was my turn, he offered to join me at the kitchen sink. He rolled up his sleeves, put on an apron and rubber gloves, and went about it in a surprisingly workmanlike manner.

'Somebody's trained you well,' I said.

'My wife,' he said.

And I stopped with my hands in the sink.

'Your what?'

'My wife.'

'You've been married before?'

'I'm married still.'

'Nobody told me.'

'I shouldn't imagine anyone knows.'

'Does Vesta know?'

'Vesta knows.'

'She didn't tell me.'

'I don't suppose she thought it important.'

On the one hand I received the news with surprise and relief, on the other with consternation. Could Vesta, of all people, be having an affair with a married man, and a married man, moreover, with suicidal tendencies?

It was nearly midnight before I could get Vesta on her own, and I asked why she hadn't told me that Weedy was married.

'There's lots of things about him I haven't told you,' she retorted. 'But why do you want to know? Do you insist on a curriculum vitae on everyone who sets foot in this house?'

At which I lost my temper.

'Don't be so bloody coy. You know yourself he's more than just another visitor.'

Now I finally understood what I really resented about Weedy. He had come between Vesta and me. Our headmistress had been right: we were so close as a family that we hardly had any friends outside it, but more than that, we actually resented the intrusion of outsiders. Grace had been admitted to our charmed circle, but then she was almost a member of the family herself and I had initially resented even her. I had been particularly close to Vesta, and Weedy was the nearest thing to a man to have come between us. She knew how I felt about Callum, but she dismissed it as a schoolgirl crush. 'Schoolgirl crushes don't last for five years,' I said to her. 'They can last for ever if you nurse them,' she replied.

Weedy left the next day. He regarded me with an amused, hesitant look as he said goodbye and then, on an impulse, he leant forward with a jerky movement, like a heron pouncing on a fish, and kissed me on the cheek.

'Going back to Oxford?' I said.

'No, my love,' he said, 'going back to the States,' but I had an unhappy feeling that I wasn't seeing the last of him.

When Grace returned from holiday, she was sorry to have missed him.

'He's rather good looking in an insipid sort of way,' she said, 'and makes a powerful appeal to one's maternal instincts. That's why Vesta was so fond of him, I'm sure.'

'Vesta's not that maternal,' I said, 'she's no Yiddisher mamma.'

Towards the end of that summer, Stevie announced that she was experiencing what she called 'a second spring' (or was it a third one?), which I took to mean that she was resuming her love life. I anticipated a further succession of callow youngsters, medical students with stethoscopes still raw in their ears, out-of-work actors, budding composers, would-be writers, aspiring painters, unemployed social workers, and maybe even schoolboys, all of which left me unprepared for what actually followed.

One day, shortly after I had returned to Cambridge, she 'phoned to ask if she could come for a weekend, and I offered to put her up in my rooms.

'No, no,' she said, 'I'm coming with a friend. Could you get me rooms at the Blue Boar?'

'A room,' I said, 'or rooms?'

'For God's sake, Ducks, what do you think I am? I said *rooms*.'

The chaste tone of reproof sounded strange coming from her, and I couldn't wait to see what she'd come up with.

She asked me to join them for dinner at their hotel on the Friday night, and when they came downstairs, arm in arm, they looked like a middle-aged married couple.

Middle aged they were. Stevie was forty-six, her friend, whose name was Arnold, looked some ten years older. He was of medium height, with thin, jet-black hair (which I took to be dyed), thick glasses and a kindly but hesitant smile. His conversation at table was largely confined to the failing health of his mother, the failing fortunes of the country, and his Persian cat, or maybe his mother was Persian and his cat was in failing health, for I did not follow his conversation with much enthusiasm, and neither, for that matter, did Stevie. She kept glancing in my direction for my reactions and I did my best to appear interested, even concerned, but I must have looked glazed, or perhaps even dazed, for he paused after a while to ask if I was all right. He was a solicitor and, to judge from the expensive wines he ordered, presumably solvent. He sounded a thoughtful, considerate man, though I wondered how much room he would have in his affections for Stevie, when he was so devoted to his mother and his cat. They did not, in fact, make an improbable pair, but I should have liked to see our adored aunt in the hands of someone more adorable.

In a way I was disappointed with her. She had spent the best years of her life, and not a little of her money, chasing after cads, happily without success, but the cads, at least, had been upper class or at least *déclassé*. If she had finally come to her senses and settled upon someone probable, could she not have found someone more polished, with wider interests, who had travelled and lived a little? Vesta, who met Arnold briefly, said that he looked as if he had his life behind him, but that suggested that he had at least lived, whereas the impression he left on me was that life had passed him by completely. Everything about him suggested constriction, a cramped life, cramped imagination, cramped ambitions and, probably, cramped prospects. His accent was lower middle-class cockney, and as soon as he opened his mouth, I could sense his whole history. His parents were probably penniless immigrants living in the East End, and he had managed, by dint of hard work and constant application, to get to university and into the professions. He had had a commission during the war, but that was in the Army Pay Corps, and was an authority on war widows' benefits, on which he could speak endlessly and sometimes did. He was a worthy individual in every way, but Stevie, to my eyes at least, was still attractive, with a bit of money and something of a career, and I felt that if she had at last reconciled herself to reality and was prepared to accept the companionship of middle-aged or even elderly men, she could have done better. I did not care to think of Arnold as an uncle.

When I came home at Christmas, the matter was the subject of constant debate, and even acrimony. Uncle Willie was scathing.

'Dammit, the woman's nearly fifty, what does she need it for?'

Father was hardly more enthusiastic, and Tilly said to him:

'It may be her last chance.'

'What do you mean, her last chance?'

'If she doesn't marry him, she may never marry.'

'Who says she must marry? The country's full of spinsters who seem to lead perfectly normal, even happy lives.'

'They're English spinsters,' said Tilly, 'and upper-class English spinsters know how to accommodate themselves to being single. Stevie isn't that English.'

'How English does one have to be to be reasonable?'

For my part, I would have been less unhappy with Arnold if Stevie had been more happy with him, but she did not regard him with the sort of adoring glances she used to cast at Nick and, in fact, seemed to avoid looking at him altogether. But she did have the relaxed attitude of someone who had taken the measure of her situation and was content to live with it.

Shortly after the New Year Stevie was having dinner with Uncle Willie. She did not say what the subject of their conversation was, but I suspect that it may have had something to do with Arnold, for Willie had a stroke and had to be rushed to hospital. Stevie came with him in the ambulance and sat by his bedside. A top neurologist was called in, but she was too engrossed in her own thoughts to notice who he was, till he came over to her and said:

'Have I changed that much?' Stevie looked up and thought she was having hallucinations:

'Nick?' she said. 'It isn't Nick, is it?' And that ended the Arnold affair, although I'm not sure to this day whether it was Willie's stroke which caused her to change her mind, or the sight of Nick. Uncle Willie (who made an almost complete recovery) was convinced it was his stroke. 'It's an ill wind that blows no one any good,' he muttered.

Although I had not taken to Arnold, once I was reconciled to the thought of him as a member of the family, I viewed the situation with a certain amount of relief. For, as Tilly had so truly observed, Stevie was not the sort of person who could accommodate herself readily to spinsterhood, and the longer she remained single the more she would become a problem to herself and her friends.

'She'll have to grow up,' said Tilly. 'She's frivolous, frivolous in the way she entered into the relationship and frivolous in the way she finished it.'

'Perhaps there's something to be said for frivolity,' said father.

The post mortem over the Arnold affair took place when we were all home over Easter, and Vesta said to me: 'You know, Ducks, you're taking all this too much to heart.'

But if I did, it was possibly because I sometimes looked at Stevie and saw myself. I too found it difficult to form stable relationships, and my emotional life was bleak and empty.

On cold winter nights my fancy lightly turned to thoughts of Callum, but apart from that one time when he tinkered absent-mindedly with my blouse, he seemed barely aware of my existence, though I sent him birthday cards and even Christmas cards with crude, *double entendre* inscriptions which he never acknowledged.

Grace once mentioned, almost in passing, that he went for 'anything on two legs', but I had my doubts about the libidinousness of a man who was afraid of virgins.

Vesta, Vida, even little Rocky had their throng of admirers, I had none. Little, or not so little, Rocky went to America with father as a fifteenth-birthday treat, and received more of a treat than father, I'm sure, had bargained for: for when she came back her eyes had the glitter of someone who had seen the glory, and she brought all her sisters (with the exception of Vesta) together to announce that she had lost her virginity. Vida and I exchanged envious glances.

'How was it?' I asked.

'Delicious. Much nicer even than American ice-cream.'

'How did it happen?'

'Oh, by accident. Father had ordered some drinks to be sent up to his room and the waiter came into my room instead. I was in my underclothes, changing. He looked at me and I looked at him, and he put the drinks down and the rest followed.'

'With the waiter?'

'Why? What's wrong with waiters?'

'Aren't you romantic at all? Seeing this was your first experience, wouldn't you have preferred it with someone you loved?'

'Oh, but I loved him. I still do. He promised to write to me and to try to come over at Christmas. You should have seen him, he was so big and strong, and it all happened so quickly.'

'Didn't it hurt?'

'A bit, but it was worth it.'

'Didn't you bleed?'

'Why? Was I meant to?'

'They say virgins do.'

'I didn't really look, it all happened so quickly. The thing is once you've had it, you keep wanting to have more and more of it. I'm dying for it now.'

A few weeks after that I was pedalling furiously down King's Parade, when my scarf got caught up in the rear wheel of my bicycle and I went flying over the side and landed in the arms of a fresh-faced, young man with a short, fisherman's beard.

'Good job you weren't driving a Bugatti,' he said, 'or you'd have done an Isadora Duncan.' He was slightly shorter than me, with the pugnacious chin of a boxer, black curly hair and dark, amused eyes behind rimless glasses.

'Thank you,' I said and tried to get back on my bike.

'You won't get far with that,' he said, 'your wheel's buckled. Still, better a buckled wheel than a buckled neck.'

'I'll be late for my lecture,' I said.

'What are you reading?'

'Economics.'

'You can't be too late for that. Let's have a coffee.'

His name was Otto Schoenberg. He was a final year physics student and spoke with a Yorkshire accent.

We went to the pictures that evening to see *Pal Joey* with Frank Sinatra, and we were hardly in our seats, with our overcoats over our laps, when I felt a horny hand working its passage under my skirt.

'Don't do that,' I said, in what I thought was a whisper, but which caused people five rows away to turn their heads.

'I'm not a prude,' I said when we emerged, 'but when I go to the pictures I want to see the picture. When I go to fornicate I fornicate.'

'All right then, let's fornicate.'

I looked at him for a moment. The idea was attractive, but he wasn't, or not attractive enough for such an occasion.

'I've got an essay to prepare,' I said.

'We'll prepare it together.'

'What? While fornicating?'

'You'd be surprised the things you can do while fornicating.'

'I need a clear head.'

'Your head won't come into it, love.'

He had a way with him, but he didn't have his way, and I

spent a restless night wondering why I had refused him and wishing I hadn't.

I suppose one of the reasons was my shyness at being a virgin at all. I had, or thought I had, the air of a woman of the world, and my manner did not go with my condition. Moreover, unlike Rocky, I was fond of ceremony. In those days, undergraduates in most colleges were not allowed to entertain friends of the opposite sex in their rooms after ten at night (in some they could not entertain them at all). I felt that, if I was to be deflorated, a minimum degree of delicacy should attend the occasion, and a quick cut and thrust against a garage door in a back lane on a damp night was not my idea of a beautiful experience.

'The next time,' I told myself, 'the next time.' But it looked as if there would never be a next time. We had had a pleasant evening out and had parted on amiable terms, and I thought he might call me the next day, or sometime in the course of that week. I kept racing back to college between every lecture and after every tutorial to see if there were any messages for me, but there were none. When a second week passed and he still hadn't called, I presumed that he had picked me up in the hope of 'a quick bit of the other', as they used to call it, and when he found that it wasn't coming so quick, and mightn't come at all, he had called it a day. On the one hand I felt pleased to be thought of in such terms, on the other I was pained that he had thought of me *only* in such terms: I liked to think I had more to offer than that. On balance, therefore, I was hurt. I was also lonely. In my first year at Cambridge, there was the novelty of the place to sustain me, the different tutors and lecturers, the very buildings. I made few friends, partly because I did not feel any particular need of them. The course was demanding. I generally had time to spare only at weekends, and these I often spent with Vesta or Grace in Oxford, or they came down to stay with me; but Vesta was now in her final year with her final exams before her and Grace had a demanding love life, so that they had no time for visits or visitors, and there were frequent occasions when I found myself alone, sitting in my room, longing for a knock on the door, while the sounds of distant bands and revels and revellers came wafting in on the moist night air, and I began to ask myself if Otto did not want to call me, what was to stop me calling him? He was in Trinity, in a room overlooking Trinity Lane, and I often saw his lights burning late into the night. I could have quite easily tapped on his window with a stick and asked him out for a walk or a drink, or even 'a bit of the other'. I was not so hidebound as to find such thoughts unthinkable, but decided not to, not out of pride, but out of the conviction that if I did, he'd say no.

But perhaps he was afraid to ask me out a second time, because I had said no so often during the first (well, not all that often, but the no I did utter was a crucial one). Perhaps I had hurt his pride?

The matter finally resolved itself a month or so later when my bicycle chain slipped; when I stopped to adjust it, who should I find standing over me, but Otto. I began to think of him as the genie of the bike.

I was on my way to the library, and so was he (or said he was), and he walked me there. We went out to the pictures again that Saturday night (the cinema was his favourite form of entertainment, and mine), but this time, to my regret, he didn't try to push his hands under my skirt. We had coffee after. I was curious to know how somebody with a name like Otto Shoenberg could have a Yorkshire accent.

'I came with a children's transport with my older sister from Dusseldorf shortly before the war and we were adopted by a Leeds family.'

'A children's transport?'

'Aren't you Jewish?' he asked.

'Sort of.'

'I had no idea we were Jewish at all till my mother woke me and my sister early one morning and told us we were going on a long journey. She in fact accompanied us only to the station. The train was full of other youngsters. I was only six at the time, but in the course of the journey, my sister, who was about three years older than me, tried to explain what it was all about. Hitler wanted to get rid of the Jews and nobody wanted to have them. But special arrangements were made to allow Jewish children into Britain and my sister and I were among them. What I couldn't take in was the fact that I too was a Jew, and I was in Leeds for some months before. I could understand that I had been on that train because I, little Otto, was not a German like all the other Germans I'd known.'

There was no talk of fornication either that evening or the next time we met, which, paradoxically enough, made me think that he really was fond of me. I was certainly becoming fond of him. He too was working for his finals, so that we could not meet often, but we went out on long walks on most Sunday mornings. The weather was almost invariably atrocious and we usually got soaked, but we found an old pub called The Coal Scuttle, well away from the usual student routes, which had an open fire and we would sit beside it, our clothes steaming, with large mugs of beer in our hand. Then towards the end of the term he asked if I would like to come up to Leeds with him.

I had thought of asking him over to stay with us, but I was mildly apprehensive about exposing him to the scrutiny of my family, or exposing our establishment to his scrutiny. I had not thought of ourselves as particularly prosperous because most people we knew were as well off, if not better off than us. In Cambridge, especially after I moved from college quarters into lodgings in the city, I discovered for the first time, that even successful people, distinguished professors whose names were a household word, lived in comparatively humble circumstances, in small, servantless homes, and drove small rickety cars, and I realized that in the eyes of most people we were now meeting, we would probably be thought of as millionaires. And I was a little afraid how Otto would react to our house with its many rooms and its antique furniture (the accumulation of which had been Tilly's principal interest once she had been safely delivered of her miracle child), and the ornate gardens and tennis court, to say nothing of the farm. On the other hand, the idea of spending a week in a place like Leeds, even in his company, did not sound particularly inviting.

'It's got some civilized people,' he assured me, 'not many, but enough to make a short stay passable, and there are lovely walks within easy reach, the Dales, the Bronte country. And you'll like the family, though I should warn you, they're kosher. Do you know what that means?'

'Yes. I've unfortunately got a mad sister who's come down with the complaint.'

'But they're strictly kosher. We'd be there over *Pesach* – Passover – no leavened bread or anything like that, and rituals which may strike you as bizarre if you're not used to them.'

'Are you trying to talk me out of coming?'

'No, not at all, but I feel obliged to warn you of some of the hazards you'll face.'

We went up by train and were met by his foster father, a large, plump man with a red face, thick glasses and a genial smile, who had the somewhat improbable name of Cavendish. He embraced Otto and, before I could retreat, he was upon me and I was suffocated both by the force of his embrace and the smell of stale cigars and a particularly pungent after-shave lotion.

'So this is your young lady,' he said.

'She's no lady,' said Otto, 'she's an undergraduate.'

Mr Cavendish lived on the outskirts of the city in a sizeable house, with numerous low-ceilinged rooms, though the ceilings may have seemed low because the carpets were so high. There were carpets everywhere (in some instances with rugs on top of them), brand new, with a strong smell of rubber underlay. Every room had fitted carpets. There were carpets in the bathroom, the kitchen, the laundry-room, the attic, so that one half-expected to find carpets in the garage. Mr Cavendish, I was not surprised to learn, was in the carpet trade. His wife was a pleasant-faced woman with smiling eyes and neatly coiffured hair, bleached a platinum blonde, and an ample figure kept under severe restraint by an undergarment whose outlines showed through her woollen frock. From the back she looked about thirty, from the front about fifty, but back or front, restrained or loose, there was a generosity to her build which somehow went with her temperament.

She fell upon me the moment I entered and showered me with kisses. She had been at the kitchen stove and the smell of onion mingled with that of Chanel No. 5. The ardour of their greeting made me wonder in what terms Otto had defined our relationship. I could not have been more warmly received if I had been a prospective daughter-in-law, but it soon became clear that I was benefiting from the adoration they had for Otto. They could not have been more proud of him if he had been their actual son.

'He was only a lad when he came here, this high,' she said, 'and I was wondering how we'd manage, because he didn't speak English, and I didn't speak German – but in a matter of weeks his English was better than mine, and soon he was winning scholarships right and left. Eddy, that's my husband, wouldn't have minded putting his hand in his pocket and paying, but he didn't have to – not a penny. Scholarships and prizes all the way, you see. You're at Cambridge yourself, aren't you?'

'Yes.'

'Oh, what wouldn't I have done to be clever, but I'd never have gone to university even if I was. Girls didn't, not in those days, not in Leeds, though I could have done with a bit of education, but our daughter, Selina, went to finishing-school in Switzerland.' And she trotted over to a drawer and pulled out an album, with numerous glossy plates of a rather glossy, attractive, but empty-faced young woman.

'She speaks five languages, six if you count Yiddish, but she doesn't like to give on that she knows it, you know how it is.' I didn't know how it was, but I didn't interrupt her. 'She married at nineteen, can you imagine it? It was a lovely wedding, in the Queen's Hotel. Six hundred guests, including the Mayor. There were people up from London in grey toppers, grey ones, mind you, not black.

Oh, it was a lovely wedding. We don't see all that much of her now. She married a Londoner, you see. No family yet, unfortunately. Young people like to bide their time these days, but if they're slow about starting a family, I don't see why they're in such a hurry to get married.' She paused. 'You've got four sisters I hear.'

'Three.'

'But four of you altogether – that's no joke for your poor father, is it?'

'He'd agree with you.'

'He's a farmer, I hear. A Jewish farmer, imagine. Are you and Otto – well it's none of my business, but this is the first time he's brought a girl home. Very serious type. Well, he's German, you see, not like us. Takes everything very seriously. Lovely boy. He's like a son to us, and his sister was like a daughter. She's in Canada now. Lovely girl, but very serious. She married in Canada. Small wedding. Eddy, that's my husband, was ready to put his hand in his pocket for something bigger, but she wouldn't hear of it. "There's hardly anyone I want to invite," she said. To a *wedding*! Can you imagine it?'

They threatened to make a party for us, but Otto managed to talk them out of it, and they took us out to the theatre one evening, and to a fish restaurant the next. On the third, after many apologies, they went out to some sort of business reception.

'We won't be back till after midnight,' said Eddy, and gave me – not Otto – a wink, as if to say, 'now's your chance'. What made him think that the initiative rested with me? Perhaps he knew Otto better than I did.

The Leeds Otto was a different person from the Cambridge Otto, as if the presence of his foster parents, or perhaps the smell of the carpets, or perhaps both, cramped his style. It is true that we were hardly left alone even for a minute, but when one is disposed towards a certain course of action one can always find, or if necessary make, opportunities for it. He could have easily come into my room last thing at night when his foster parents were asleep, and I always sat up hopefully, in a particularly tarty nightie, in case he might, but he never did. Even now, when we were alone together in an empty house, he showed no inclination to lay a finger on me, but sat bolt upright watching the television news. After a time I leaned over and, very gently and tentatively, put my head on his shoulder. He put his arm round me, but still remained upright (come to think of it, he must have had long arms), and I put my hand on his knee and allowed it – allowed it – I propelled it – gradually upwards. That did it. He pushed me over on the sofa, tore off my underclothes, and before I knew what was happening he was pounding away inside me. It was like being set upon by a pile-driver. It was all over in a minute, and in that minute he lost his glasses (which were crushed under me) and I lost one pair of knickers, one pair of stockings, and my virginity. We also stained the fawn-coloured sofa. I tried to clear it up with detergent but only made it worse, and finally tried to hid the evidence under a cushion. As an experience it was nasty, brutal and short.

'Was that the first time?' he asked.

'Yes, and if that's what it's really like, it's going to be the last time. I can't for the life of me understand what all the fuss is about. Give me ice-cream every time.'

'Ice-cream?'

'Family joke.'

We slept together the following night and that was a far more delicate and tender experience. It was also more dignified. Everything happened gradually. I fell asleep in his arms with a feeling of contentment bordering upon ecstasy. When I woke the next morning and reflected almost disbelievingly on the events of the night before, there he was, asleep beside me, his prickly little beard standing on end. I stretched down my hand to his nether beard, which was far more luxuriant, and grabbed his penis. It seemed to have a life and will of its own and awoke while the rest of him seemed to sleep. I pulled the blankets back and lowered myself on top of him. His eyes remained shut, but a broad smile spread across his face. 'Be gentle with me,' he murmured.

The following week was Passover and Mrs Cavendish, or Amy, as I had learned to call her, who had been on the go since the moment I arrived, accelerated to a frantic pace. An elderly cleaning woman came in most mornings, but it was a large house and apparently the traditions of the festival demanded that every corner had to be spring-cleaned and purged and turned inside out before the festival began. There were also cakes to be baked and special meals to be made, but no matter how busy she was, her tongue never stopped.

'We like to have a few guests for the first night – the *seder*, you know, it's very special, and it wouldn't be a *seder* without guests.'

I helped in whatever way I could (and not without loud insistence from her that I mustn't, for she had a habit of treating me like a frail mother in the final stages of a difficult pregnancy).

They had two large communicating rooms with a long, glass-topped table in one, which could have sat about a dozen guests, but she expected more like two dozen and I helped to bring in a table from the breakfast-room and spread damask cloths over both.

'The tablecloths belonged to my late mother, her proudest possession, brought them from Russia. Used once a year, laundered and starched once a year, packed away till the next year and still good as new. I wanted to give them to my daughter, Selina, but she wouldn't have them – can you imagine? Please God, when you marry, you can have them.' I felt touched and embarrassed.

She had a special set of crockery and cutlery, which she kept in the attic and which I helped to wash and polish. The crockery had the willow pattern design and evoked vague memories of meals in grandma's house while grandma was was still alive.

'Your people don't keep Passover?' asked Amy.

'No, I'm afraid not.'

'Like my Selina. Her husband's Jewish, though you wouldn't think it, or at least he doesn't like to think he is. He wanted to marry in a registry office – can you imagine?

I said "over my dead body".'

I arranged the place-settings, the gleaming glasses, the spotless, white napkins, the silver goblets for the wine, the special plate for the matzot, the flowers, while Amy busied herself in the kitchen, and we continued our conversation at the tops of our voices.

'It must be an expensive festival, Passover,' I said.

'Expensive isn't the word. I'm afraid to show Eddy the bills, and we're quite comfortable. But I'll tell you something. My poor father was a cabinet-maker, more out of work than in. We couldn't afford to keep warm and in winter me and my sisters were covered with chilblains. Passover couldn't have been all that cheap even then, but when it came to the *seder* we always managed. Do you know Yiddish?'

'No.'

'There's an old saying. It's all right being a *schnorrer* for a year if you can be king for a night, and on *Pesach* every Jew is king.'

A delicious aroma compounded of boiling soup and roasting fowl came from the kitchen and hovered over the house like a friendly, divine presence.

As the day darkened, Eddy and Otto, the latter in an ill-fitting blue serge suit, went off to synagogue, while Amy went upstairs to have a bath and change.

I had a shower but, when I began dressing, I was not quite sure what sort of outfit was appropriate to the occasion. I had never given much thought to clothes, but at Otto's behest I had bought a mini skirt in Leeds. I decided to wear it, till Amy came down in a scarlet evening gown with a gold belt and a gold choker. In her crude way she looked quite regal. I almost pulled off my mini skirt there and then, and hurried back upstairs to put on the evening dress which had been made for Vesta's coming-out party three years earlier.

'You've got a beautiful figure,' said Amy, by which I took her to mean that I had big tits.

I was sorry I had put on that dress. The world I was visiting was very different from the one I had known, but I thought I had adapted myself to it with aplomb and was beginning to enjoy it, till I pulled that dress over my head, and echoes came wafting in of the unreal world in which I had matured – of large houses, servants, broad acres, panelled halls, horses, hunts and debutantes. Had we been native to that world – or integrated in it – it might have seemed less unreal, but we were really on the periphery of it and, but for our friendship with the Roscoes, strangers to it. We had been living in a never-never land, created by my father's fancy.

While I was thus lost in thought, people began to return from synagogue and within minutes the house filled up. Men, women, children, sisters, brothers-in-law, uncles, cousins, all looking vaguely alike and sounding alike, but among them all I noticed one dapper figure I had seen before and wondered if he had been evoked by my imagination. It was Tilly's father, or, if not, someone who bore a striking resemblance to him. He was also looking at me as if he had seen me before somewhere, but hesitated to approach me in case he hadn't. I went over to him and held out a hand.

'Good *Yom Tov*,' he said, a little hesitatingly.

'Aren't you Tilly's father?'

'Yes,' he said, his eyes lighting up. 'I thought it must be you, then I think it can't be. I mean, what would you be doing here in Leeds? You married yet?'

'No, not yet.'

'Please God, you soon will. You're a lovely girl, they're all lovely girls.'

He was, he said, staying with one of his sons, a few streets away.

'His wife, bless her, is kosher, but not very kosher. On the *seder*, you see, you've got to be very particular. Particular she's not, and very particular she certainly isn't, so I come here to Amy's. Amy's a *tzidkonis*, a saint, bless her. I knew her father. Didn't have two pennies to clink together. Look at her now, bless her, a queen.'

But he too, possibly because of the surprise at seeing him, added to my unease. We all took our place at table, opened small books which I took to be the order of service for the occasion, filled our goblets and stood up while Eddy began with a blessing over the wine. Otto was next to me, and all eyes were trained on us, or rather on me, while people tried to work out the exact nature of our relationship. Amy had treated me as a member of the family from the moment I arrived, and presumably to be present at a family gathering of this sort was tantamount to a publication of banns. The glances cast in my direction were not unfriendly, but they did seem uneasy, as if I was a spectre at their feast, or perhaps they seemed uneasy only because I felt ill at ease, out of place. I admired it all, regretted the fact that there was nothing like this to our life, but felt apart from it all. Otto must have sensed my unease and he gripped my hand, and Tilly's father beamed at me across the table from over the top of his glasses, yet I still couldn't relax. But as we continued through the service which preceded the meal to the meal itself, and downed cup after cup of the rich, sweet wine, I began to feel the tensions seep out of me.

A cousin of Amy's, a perky little woman, with long, false eyelashes which almost brushed my bosom, said to me:

'So you're Otto's little secret? We call him the little genius. It's always been books, books, books, for as long as I've known him, and I said to him only last year, you know Otto, there's more to life than books.' And she gave me a nudge. 'I'm glad to see he's taken my advice. It's no good being on your own, even if you are a genius.'

The meal was followed by traditional Hebrew songs, in which everyone joined, except Tilly's father, who was asleep, and me, though, as they went on for some time and had endless refrains, I was able to chip in before they were finished. The dominant voice, to my surprise, was Otto's.

'The songs are my favourite part of the *seder*,' he said. 'They remind me of the German folk-songs my mother used to sing.'

We had eaten stuffed carp in jelly with horseradish sauce, chicken soup, roast duck and stuffing and roast potatoes and pickled cucumbers, and fruit salad. The evening finally closed with lemon tea, and I said to Otto:

'From what you, or someone told me, I was under the impression that Passover was meant to recall some black period in Jewish history.'

'It does. Don't they teach you the Bible at all in girls' public schools? It's all in the first chapters of Exodus, how the Jews were slaves –'

'And is all this meant to remind us of slavery?'

'It's nice to recall hard times when times aren't hard, isn't it? Nicer than Christmas, don't you think?'

'What happens now? Do I hang up my stocking when I get to bed?'

'Do, by all means,' he whispered, 'and you'll get something from Santa you've never had before.'

'What, never?'

'Well, hardly ever.'

It was well past midnight before the company began to disperse. Amy thought it was too late for Tilly's father to walk home, and offered him a bed.

'No, no,' he said, 'My daughter-in-law will worry about me. And in any case I like a walk. It's good for the digestion.' And Eddy put on his coat and walked him home.

'Ironic that,' said Amy as we were clearing up, 'his daughter-in-law doesn't give a damn about him. He set up both his sons in business and they treat him like a lodger who's late with his rent, poor *nebbish*. He hasn't had much *mazel* with his children. Even his daughter, beautiful girl – girl? She must be nearly my age, but very good-looking and very clever, wasted her life.'

'How many daughters has he got?'

'Only one, Tilly – a wasted life.'

'Did you know her?'

'Know her? We grew up together – well not quite, she was more my sister's age than mine. A tomboy. She used to come and make wooden toys in my father's shop. She still probably has a mark on her hand where she cut herself with a chisel – but why do you ask?'

'She's my step-mother.'

At which she sat down open-mouthed, with a bump. It took her some time to recover her voice.

'I'm sorry, I shouldn't have said anything. Well, I didn't say anything, did I? All I said was she was beautiful, which she was. I haven't seen her in twenty years and don't really know what's happened to her. Tilly your step-mother?' She seemed on the point of tears.

— 7 —
Vesta

When I 'phoned from the station for a lift, Tilly came to meet me, but she seemed anything but welcoming, and her first words were:

'You didn't tell me you were going to Leeds.'

I was rather taken aback both by her manner and her question, as if I had to report every movement I made. She had reverted to Tilly the Governess.

'What do you mean? Why do I have to tell you anything?'

'There's no *have* about it, but we do happen to be a family. Would I vanish for the better part of a week and not say where I was going?'

'You weren't around, and I only decided at the last minute.'

'You didn't tell Vesta either, you didn't tell anyone. The 'phone was ringing, people were asking for you. I know I'm only your step-mother, but I felt damned silly not knowing where you were, how long you'd be away for, or if you were coming back at all. You could have left a note, 'phoned, something. And Leeds of all places.'

'How did you know I was in Leeds?'

'How do you think I knew? Father 'phoned me. "And she was with soch a nice yong man", she added in her father's heavily accented English, "they should be very happy together," which, of course, was all news to me.'

Her hands were shaking and we were driving at such speed along a narrow, winding, country road, that I was afraid she would go into a hedge. A cigarette was smouldering in her mouth, and her complexion had coarsened, which it always did when she was angry or strained.

'I thought your father might have known something about it, or Vesta, but it was news to them all. Why are you so secretive?'

Which was too much, even for me, and I exploded.

'Why am *I* so secretive? What about you? What about father? I've been surrounded by secrets all my life. If we should ever acquire a family crest with a family motto, it'll be: "Don't ask!" As children we had to move around the house like shadows because mummy was ill, but we were never told the nature of her illness, and to this day I don't know how she died or what she died from, though it seems reasonably clear that she kept lapsing into insanity and probably killed herself. Then there was the great unmentionable, money. One moment we were sliding towards destitution, the next we were awash with wealth, but again, never a word of explanation. And on top of that you suddenly reappear, ready-made like Aphrodite rising from the sea. And you accuse *me* of being secretive? And you're even worse than father. Father is secretive about money, you're secretive about everything. Perhaps as a governess you had a right to be, but you're supposed to be our mother, and we still hardly know a thing about you.'

'Is that why you went to Leeds, to find out?'

Her driving was getting dangerously erratic and I suggested that we continue the conversation when we got home, but she pulled up by the village green and switched off the engine.

'No,' she insisted, 'I asked you a reasonable question and I want a reasonable answer.'

'I don't think your question was reasonable.'

'All right, let me rephrase it. Leeds is a small place, at least Jewish Leeds is. My family was quite well known. I know you met my father, but did no one else mention me?'

Her attitude was a revelation. This was a Tilly I had not known before.

There was a strange note of urgency, even of alarm in her voice. Was her past so unsavoury that she was actually afraid of what I might have discovered? For a moment I felt tempted to play on her fears, but thought better of it.

'The woman I stayed with claimed to know you,' I said.

'I was wondering when you'd be coming out with that. She more than knew me. She's my former sister-in-law.'

'Amy –'

'I was married for a time to her younger brother.'

'She didn't say a thing about it.'

'What *did* she say?'

'She spoke fairly scathingly about your brothers and their wives.'

'And said nothing about me? I don't believe it, she's the biggest gossip in town.'

'She said you were a tomboy and that you had wasted your life. She might have told me more, but when I mentioned you were my step-mother she more or less broke down.'

She lit another cigarette and gazed through the windscreen in silence. It began to rain. The window misted up, and the raindrops rapped on the roof like a prolonged burst of machine-gun fire.

'Perhaps I should tell you everything. You certainly have a right to know, but I don't know if I can take you into my confidence if you don't take me into yours. I know I'm only your step-mother, but there were times when you led me to believe that there was more to our relationship than that, but as a matter of fact you keep even your father at a distance and in the dark.'

'I've never been able to talk to father, because he hardly ever talks to us. Oh, he may amuse us with occasional pleasantries, or some facetious remark, but even when he has something important to say – as when he remarried – he doesn't really speak to us but calls us together to make a public announcement.'

'You don't even do that. I didn't know you had a boyfriend. All right, that's not important, not these days, but if your relationship with him has reached the point where he takes you to see his family, it does become important. Why didn't you bring him here? Are you ashamed of us?'

'In a way I am, yes. Amy and Eddy are only his foster parents, but there was greater warmth and affection in his family than in mine. Amy may be a mindless gossip, but she's a real, throbbing, living individual, but, our family – apart from occasional tantrums and bursts of temper – we seem to be devoid of emotions.'

'Ducks, I thought you were more perceptive than that. The Amys may be all right for a week, or even a fortnight, but if you had spent the first twenty years of your life among them – as I did – you would run screaming from them with your hands to your ears.'

'I'm not sure. To be honest, I didn't care for the smell of their house, but I found my stay refreshing. I rather liked Leeds. I'm sorry you never told us more about it.'

'You make it sound like some never-never land.'

'But don't you understand? This is a never-never land. Leeds was my first excursion into the real world.'

'Didn't the fact that you were staying with your boyfriend have something to do with it? This was the first time, wasn't it?'

I wasn't sure what she was getting at, and she also thought she might have been misunderstood, for she quickly added:

'You haven't been away with a boyfriend before, have you?'

'I haven't, but I'm not sure if I can call him my boyfriend.'

'And you went to stay with his family? You don't know what that means in Leeds.'

'I do now. It was premature, I suppose, and probably rather silly, but he asked me, so I went.'

'Aren't we going to see something of him here?'

'I suppose you will, eventually.'

'It all sounds very tentative.'

'It all is very tentative.'

I wasn't really sure how far my visit to Leeds had advanced my relationship with Otto, but I had the feeling that it had impaired my relationship with Tilly, for once it became clear that Otto and I were in fact no more than 'friends' (as they say in the gossip columns), she became convinced that I had gone up to Leeds for the express purpose of unearthing her unsavoury past and that I had in fact discovered a good deal more than I was ready to admit, and she became obviously uncomfortable in my presence. What was rather more surprising was that I became uncomfortable in hers, as if her convictions were well founded.

Vesta told me that she had happened to be around when Tilly's father 'phoned from Leeds. 'She kept repeating, "Are you sure it was her?" as if the idea of your being in Leeds was unimaginable, as indeed it was, for I certainly couldn't imagine what you could be doing there. And when she added, for good measure, that you were there with your boyfriend, I was sure he was mistaken.'

I didn't like the way she put that, as if the very idea of her sister, the Ugly Duckling, having a boyfriend was unimaginable. I told her about Otto, but I spared her some of the grosser details, for I wasn't sure how she would react to them, and I couldn't fully unburden myself till Grace turned up. And with Grace I didn't even have to say anything. She looked at me, turning her head now to this side, now to that, as if trying to get me in focus, and said she thought there was a mellowness to my face she had not seen before, and added, in her abrupt, deep, rapid, public-school voice: 'Have you been screwed?' I nodded. 'About bloody time,' she said. She had been through it herself, she said, when she was fourteen.

'A picture restorer did it for me. A large, middle-aged man, with a paunch and a small beard. He didn't do much for our pictures – almost restored them out of existence – but I shall be eternally grateful for what he did for me. Every part of him smelled of paint, varnish and chemicals, and I mean every part – it made me wonder what he restored the paintings with – but he was marvellous. The only thing is I can hardly get an orgasm these days without the attendant smell of varnish.'

She questioned me in detail about events in Leeds in

terms which made me blush.

'What you need now is a Dutch cap,' she said. 'Try our doctor. He's young and good-looking, and he has a unique way of measuring you for size.'

We saw a lot of the Roscoes during those weeks, including Callum himself. I wondered if I should pull him aside to let him know that I was no longer a virgin, but he somehow no longer carried the same allure, as if his particular type of dash and virility appealed mainly to maidens, or rather that his attractions were merely skin deep and that I, as a woman of the world, was now able to see through them.

In the meantime, Rocky appeared to have struck up what was, for her, a fairly lasting relationship with his son, Robin. When I first heard about it I thought it rather unlikely, for he was very tall, very thin and rather callow, with a pink baby face, carefully parted black hair, carefully spoken and rather priggish, but he was now in his second year at Sandhurst and had changed. He was still carefully spoken and rather priggish, but he had filled out slightly, and was red rather than pink, yet I still couldn't see quite what he had in common with Rocky. It wasn't sex for a start, for he seemed above it, or beneath it, but certainly impervious to it, whereas she was impervious to almost everything else. His main interest, as far as I could recall, was his collection of toy soldiers, mounted and on foot; while he was still a schoolboy he would fascinate us (though not Rocky) with his reconstruction of the Battle of Waterloo, but he was also interested in horses and this may have brought them together. Rocky was not a great horsewoman, but she looked great in jodhpurs, and was rarely out of them. She was, in fact, the only one among us who had turned native, for she had the upper-class habit of talking through her nose, and her talk was all of horses and jumps, and scents and trails. One or another of us might go out riding for an hour or so during the weekend, but Rocky had her own horse and her own horse-box and was a member of the local hunt.

Vida, who was in her final year at Helenslea, also had a

boyfriend, a second-year medical student with pearly teeth and smiling eyes, the brother of a member of her little kosher set.

I had thought of asking Otto up to 'West Wynds' for a weekend, but apart from my hesitation about bringing anyone to the house, I wasn't too sure if he would come. He was within weeks of his final exams. He hoped to get an academic appointment and there was no prospect of doing so with anything less than a first-class degree, and he had warned me that he would not have much time to see me till the exams were over. In the event I hardly saw him at all, and I began to wonder, as I am told most ex-virgins do, if having 'got what he wanted' in Leeds, he had no further interest in me.

I passed through a desolate month. Before I met Otto I would often travel through to Oxford and spend the weekend with Vesta or Grace, but they too were now working for their finals, and Vesta in particular was unapproachable.

'It's not the end of the world if you don't get a first, you know,' I told her. 'I know of dozens of people who have taken a second or even a third, but who manage to go through life with reasonable equanimity.'

'I won't even get a third. I've lost all capacity for absorption. I read, take notes, take notes and read, and the moment I close the book, I forget everything I've noted.' She wore a thick white jumper and slacks, looked painfully thin and distraught, and her complexion seemed yellowish. She used to have a slight but finely shaped bust, which seemed to have caved in and now she was as flat as a tombstone. When she came down for meals, she would pick erratically at a bit of fish, or potato, and lived mainly on black coffee.

One evening, about halfway through the summer term, I returned late to my room and found a message: ' 'Phone home at once. Urgent. Tilly.'

I 'phoned and father answered. There was, I thought, a slight tremor to his voice: 'It's Vesta,' he said, 'she's been taken rather ill. I think it would help if you came down.'

'What sort of illness?'

'I wish I knew. We've had doctors coming and going for the better part of a week.'

'But what's the matter?'

'She hardly takes food, and if she does she can't hold it. She's been on a glucose drip for the past day or two. Tilly thought it might help if you saw her.'

I borrowed a car and left right away. It was nearly one by the time I got home and lights seemed to be blazing in every room.

Vesta was sitting up in bed with a sunken face and eyes which seemed to be glowing either with amusement or fever. She had recently taken food – a thin soup – and Stevie, who had persuaded her to take it, was particularly pleased with herself. 'The thing now', she said to me, 'is to see if she can keep it down.'

'They're treating me like an invalid,' said Vesta.

'Well, you're hardly a picture of health,' I said.

'It's some sort of bug in my intestines.'

'Is that what the doctors told you?'

'It's what I told them – and one of them did say it could be a virus.'

'Virus is medicalese for we haven't a clue.'

Father was walking round the house like a shadow.

'He looks at her and keeps seeing her mother,' said Tilly. 'They were never able to establish a physical cause for her illness, and it's the same with Vesta. Someone suggested bringing in a psychiatrist and, for the first time in the many years I've known your father, he almost lost control of himself. "Psychiatrist!" he shouted. "Those charlatans, not in this house, not for my daughter." '

'It's fifteen years since mummy died,' I said, 'and psychiatry's made great strides since then.'

'Frankly I'm not sure if it has. It seems to be going round in circles and the orthodoxies of one generation are the heresies of the next. But the fact is physical medicine hasn't been of much help either, and if she continues like this she'll waste away.'

'She's taken some soup.'

'I know, and she's trying to hold it down, but as soon as your back is turned, she brings it up. I think it's all due to overwork, but your father is obviously afraid it may be something she inherited from your mother.'

I had the very same fear. I liked to have a walk last thing at night before going to bed, and that night I asked father to accompany me. He was at first reluctant and complained that it was late, that he had many things to see to and that, in any case, farmers didn't need walks because much of their working day was spent on their feet. I almost had to pull him out forcibly. It was a balmy Mediterranean evening, with only the hint of a breeze rustling through the trees.

I put my arm through his and said:

'Do you know what you are? A coward.'

'Oh, that's well established, but what particular form of cowardice have you in mind?'

'The worst sort, moral cowardice. You're afraid to be alone with me, and I can only imagine you're afraid because you may find yourself talking, and you're afraid to talk because – well, that's the mystery. Why *are* you afraid to talk?'

'Has it ever occurred to you that I may have nothing to say?'

'Haven't you got problems?'

'Without end, but presumably you haven't dragged me out here to hear my problems.'

'Yes, I have. Tilly keeps saying "I know I may only be your step-mother, but –" Well I'm not your step-daughter, but I'm often made to feel like one. Oh, I know you may be generous with your money and things like that, but you're mean with your attention.'

'Are you trying to tell me that I'm unconcerned about the welfare of my children?'

'Oh, you're very concerned, perhaps too concerned, but you don't share your concerns, at least not with me. I know you're very worried about Vesta, as we all are, and you brought me down specially, but I've been here two days and you've hardly said a word about it to me.'

'I explained the situation on the 'phone. There's nothing to add.'

'Was mummy like this?'

He sighed.

'For a time, but then your mother had cause for her breakdown.'

'In what way?'

'She was from an old Rhenish clan and her father owned a small banking house in Cologne. She was an only child and they were an extremely devoted family. Then, when she was only twelve, her mother died, and worse was to come. Her father was of Jewish origin, but he had never thought of himself as a Jew. When Hitler came to power, he regarded him as a passing phenomenon and, in any case, he didn't believe that he would be affected by his policies. But he was. His bank was seized and he himself was arrested by the Gestapo. All this happened shortly after our engagement. Against all advice, she went back to Germany to see if she could be of help, but she came too late. Her father had either hanged himself, or been hanged while he was in jail. She wasn't the same person after that, but who would have been after such an experience? You wouldn't believe this, but she was like Rocky when I first knew her – lively, vivacious, pert – but a disciplined Rocky, for she was hard-working as well and very studious. But when she returned from Cologne, all life had gone out of her and she never fully recovered.'

'In which case you've no reason to believe that Vesta may be suffering from some sort of inherited illness.'

'None. And yet – well, most fears are irrational, aren't they?'

Later, as I was preparing for bed. Mrs Donelly knocked on my door.

'There's something I've been wanting to tell you. I'm going to Lourdes next week and I'll put in a word with the Holy Mother. She'll be all right.'

Sophie came the next day, spent some time with Vesta, and suggested that she see a cousin of hers who was a Harley Street consultant.

'He's not a psychiatrist?' asked father.

'To be honest, I'm not sure what he is. I would call him an all-rounder.'

He arrived that evening, a stocky man with white hair and a red face, spent an hour with Vesta, and suggested that she enter a clinic with which he was associated near Epsom.

'What sort of clinic,' asked father, 'and how long will she need to be there?'

'A clinic much like others,' said the doctor, 'but the standard of medical and nursing attention is high. I've handled cases of this sort before and they've generally been able to leave after about a fortnight, sometimes after a week.'

'Will she need an ambulance?'

'No, no,' he said, 'she's quite capable of a car journey. She may look frail, but she's wiry.'

I drove her there the next day. She slept all the way with her head thrown back and her mouth open, and I stopped a number of times to satisfy myself that she had not passed out.

The clinic was a modern building on high grounds, with numerous chalets in a woodland setting. It did not have the look or smell of a hospital, and I presumed it was some sort of psychiatric institution.

She woke up as soon as I pulled up, and looked around with bewilderment.

'Where am I?' she asked. 'What am I doing here?'

'It's a clinic run by Sophie's cousin, don't you remember? The man who came to see you yesterday.'

'The red-faced man with white hair?'

'That's right.'

'Was that yesterday? It all seems so long ago. Everything seems long ago.'

She looked so thin, so white and strained that I could have cried, and when I saw her being pushed away in a wheelchair with her head drooping between her shoulders, I did cry.

I went back to Cambridge the next day, but was too

distressed to attend lectures or do any work. I half thought of 'phoning Otto, but hesitated partly because I knew he was working furiously for his exams, and partly because I didn't feel I really wanted to talk to him about Vesta and my worries. My hesitation, I felt, told me something about the true nature of our relationship. The only person I would really have cared to talk to at that moment was Grace.

An assistant at the clinic, a young doctor, suggested that we waited at least a week, or preferably a fortnight, before coming to visit her.

'The patients often get worse before they get better,' he explained, 'and it could be distressing both for them and their families to have visitors.'

I couldn't imagine her looking much worse, for she seemed barely alive as it was. Father complied with the advice, but I didn't and went to see her after about a week. I could see what he meant. She didn't look any worse physically, except for her lips which seemed crusted and chapped, but she looked at me without the slightest flicker of recognition in her eyes. I took her hand, but she jerked it back, as if afraid I might take it away, and I had the feeling she was slightly alarmed by my presence.

'What have you done,' I asked the doctor, 'erased her memory?'

'It's a new drug we've been trying,' he said, 'and amnesia is one of its side-effects, but in our experience it wears off after a week or two.'

I liked the description of amnesia as one of the 'side-effects'. I could imagine being told, 'She's dead, but that's one of the side-effects.'

I returned the following week with father. She wasn't quite as inert as she had been, but she was lifeless enough to give him a shock. She didn't say anything when we spoke to her, but she didn't seem oblivious to what we were saying. When I took her hand, she was prepared to let me hold it.

'She is a little better,' I said, trying to reassure myself, as much as father, but he would have none of it. From what he could see, she had plainly deteriorated.

'She was ill when she left,' he said, 'but she wasn't a vegetable.' He demanded to see the head of the clinic, but was told he wouldn't be available before the following week.

'That isn't good enough,' he retorted. 'I am extremely concerned by my daughter's condition and I want to see him right away.' I had rarely known him to be so assertive, but it didn't help, for the doctor was out of the country and would not be returning till the weekend.

We returned the next day. Father spoke of the place as 'a rich man's nut-house', and was in half a mind to take Vesta back with him in his car there and then, but I was certain that as we came into her room something like a smile had flickered across her eyes.

'You're imagining it,' said father. I possibly was, but I pleaded with him to leave it till the weekend, and he turned upon me:

'Why? What for? Can't you see these people are quacks? They've drained the life out of the poor child.'

'She's been here two weeks. Leave it another three days.'

'Have you seen what she's like? Not another minute.'

'She's making progress.'

'I can't see it.'

'I can feel it. Another day, that's all. You can't take her away now.'

When we got home, I 'phoned Sophie to tell her about father's intentions. She came over right away and pleaded with him for the better part of the evening, but without effect, and he told her he couldn't forgive himself for having listened to the specialist in the first place. Tilly entered the argument and said he was being irrational.

'The girl's been very ill. You can't expect miracles overnight.'

'*Overnight!* She's been there more than a fortnight, which wouldn't have bothered me if I had seen any signs of progress, but she's getting worse every time I see her.'

He had spoken to the family doctor and had arranged to travel with him to the clinic the next day. I went with him and, as soon as I saw her, I realized that my belief that she had been making progress was, indeed, illusory. What I had thought was a smile in her eyes was a fever. She was obviously very ill, and too ill to be moved.

That afternoon Sophie 'phoned the head of the clinic, who was attending a medical congress in Vienna, and he flew back on the first plane. Father in the meantime stayed on at the clinic and he 'phoned us in the evening to say that she had pneumonia.

I couldn't imagine that she would pull through, not in the state in which we saw her. She had seemed lifeless enough as it was.

I was distraught, but not as deeply distraught as I felt I should have been. Vesta was everything to me and the thought of her dying should have meant the end of life, but it didn't, as if I had long ago reconciled myself to the thought that someone so good and so beautiful could only be ephemeral and could not expect the sort of life-span accorded to mortals. For the moment I was rather more concerned about father, and felt that he shouldn't be left sitting by her death-bed on his own. I asked Tilly if I could borrow her car to drive to the clinic. She was reluctant to lend it.

'You look rather shaky yourself, you know. You've got to cross London to get there. It's a three-hour drive. I'll drive you to the station. You'll be safer and quicker by train.' And for the first time a stab of hatred ran through me. I was sure that she was more concerned about her car than about me, father or even Vesta, but she was proved right by events.

When we got to the station we found that the last train to London was no longer running, and I had to use her car after all. I can't remember how far I'd driven, or where I was at the time, for I was deep inside myself and paid only cursory attention to the traffic around me or to anything else. I do remember skidding, a loud bang and the sound of breaking glass; when I opened my eyes I was in hospital, not beside Vesta, but in a dimly-lit room on my own.

It was a moot point who was nearer death that night, Vesta or me, for in the course of the crash I had broken a rib which impinged upon my heart and nearly went through it. It must have been quite a night for poor father. According to Tilly he nearly died himself when he got the news, but we all pulled through and as soon as I was on my feet – which took the better part of a month – I went to see Vesta. The sight of her completed my cure. She was a new person.

I found her in a deck-chair, wearing dark glasses and reading a book, still rather thin and pale, but happy, or at least smiling. The doctor was, indeed, a miracle worker.

'How did it happen?' I asked. 'What sort of treatment have you been getting?'

'I was on drugs for the first couple of weeks, a sort of psycho-enema, the doctor called them. They clear your mind of almost everything in it. In my case the process was complicated a bit by pneumonia, but in the main they leave everything to time. I've spent most of my stay on long walks, sometimes with a doctor or nurse, sometimes with father.'

'But your mind,' I said, 'it's no longer a blank, I take it?'

'No, not now. Things come filtering back, but the doctor hasn't allowed me to touch anything resembling a text-book and I've no chance of taking my finals.'

'So?'

'That's the odd thing. I don't really care if I do or don't.'

'You can take the exam in the winter, or next year if necessary.'

'But you don't understand. I don't even know if I want to go back to Oxford at all.'

'You'll probably change your mind when you're a little better. I mean what would you like to do?'

'That's just it. I think the effect of my stay here was to clear the mind of all long-term ambitions. You revert to a sort of childhood I suppose, and to be honest the only plans I have for the immediate future are to sit in the sun and read. I've got such a bad memory that I can return to all the books I used to enjoy at school, like *Emma* and

Pride and Prejudice, as if I'm reading them for the first time.'

When she returned home the following week, she decided to remain there and gave up further thought of Oxford, for the time being at least. Instead, she made herself useful round the house and in the dairy.

So that was it. Vesta, whom all of us had regarded in one way or another as the queen of the family – though she was always diffident and had never tried to assert her status – who had emerged as top scholar of her year at school and had entered Oxford on a Scholarship and who, according to her tutor, was well within sight of a 'first' and was destined for a brilliant academic career, was reduced to being a farm-hand. But she was apparently happy with her new situation, and a good deal happier than she had been at Oxford.

Father, however, was rather less happy.

'She seems to be enjoying herself,' he said, 'and I suppose it's doing her some good, but I want her to be back at Oxford as soon as possible. Her tutor was here the other day and said it would be a crime if she didn't complete her course.'

'It would be an ever bigger crime if she was forced to complete it if she wasn't up to it.'

'I wouldn't dream of forcing her, but I know she sets great store by your opinions.'

'I don't know if my opinions would count for much, but if I made her feel guilty about staying on here, she might drop everything and go back to Oxford, but I don't know if she's got the necessary stamina –'

'I don't mean now – next term.'

'If she had had the necessary stamina, she wouldn't have collapsed in the first place. She's got a quick and perceptive mind, but I don't know if it can stand up to all the pounding that a degree course entails – especially if she is anxious to have a first.'

At which he put his hands in his pockets and sighed a deep sigh. He had been having trouble with his cows. One of them had turned barren, another had developed mastitis, and one or two others were showing incipient signs of the same disorder. I had the feeling that when he was troubled by his cows he sought consolation in contemplating his daughters, but now he was having trouble with all his livestock.

He had hoped that Vida, who was not particularly brilliant at school and was in some ways the most domesticated among us, would take a course in farm management or dairying, or perhaps a university degree in agriculture, but she decided to take up teaching and had been offered a place in a teachers' training college on the outskirts of London.

And Rocky was, of course, Rocky.

As a result I became increasingly conscious of the weight of the hopes which he was vesting in me, but there were signs that I too might become a disappointment. At school, though we may have been awkward customers in other respects, 'the Courlander girls' were generally reckoned to be bright – and there is nothing like a general belief in one's ability to make one able – but we seemed to have been born with an impetus which had since petered out. I had not done too badly at Cambridge in my first year or two, but when I began my final year, my tutor complained that my essays were beginning to show signs of deterioration rather than improvement.

Events at home and my accident were not entirely to blame. Otto had taken a brilliant first in physics and, after weighing up various alternative offers, he had accepted a research post at the Weizmann Institute in Israel. I was surprised, because the whole world was open to him and he had not expressed any interest in Zionism or the Jewish state before, but he said: 'It has nothing to do with Zionism or Jewishness. The work they happen to be doing is right up my street.'

We spent his last night in England together at an hotel near London airport and he promised to write to me regularly, but his idea of regularity was not mine. He wrote every five or six weeks, interesting letters with perceptive observations on life in Israel and the Institute, but with hardly ever an intimate aside or an expression of affection, and it was clear that I had misconstrued the nature of our relationship. I had mentioned the possibility of my visiting him in Israel over Christmas, but he never broached the matter, and after about four or five months of this I stopped writing, in the near conviction that if I didn't, he would.

One tends to arrive at a university as a stranger among strangers and gradually make friends among one's contemporaries, but in my first year I spent much of my free time with Grace and Vesta in Oxford. In the second year there was Otto. Now all my contemporaries had their own little groups. Otto was gone, Vesta was down, and Grace had taken an upper second and was working in a publishing house in New York. I was aware when I began term of the isolation ahead, but I had thought of myself as self-sufficient and looked forward to eight months of hard slog till I had finished my course and would be a free woman. But my studies did not offer the satisfaction in the final year that they had given me in the first two, and often I would look up from my work and hear – or think I heard – the sound of music and laughter and merry-making and found it difficult to continue. Stevie would sometimes come and visit me, but she was nearly fifty and was not taking the onset of age cheerfully. She was, she said, having problems with her health. She would not define them, though I felt that there was little wrong with her which a decent man couldn't cure, but I was afraid it was a little bit late for that. She had begun to neglect her appearance and clothes and was beginning to look drab and dishevelled. She came to see me because she was feeling low, but I think we rather depressed each other, and then as the year progressed even her visits stopped.

The winter was long and severe. Cambridge in the snow looked like a Christmas card, and I took some pleasure in walking round the silent quads at the dead of night, with the crunch of my footfalls, but the snow turned to slush and the slush to a quagmire. It was nearly Easter before the roads cleared and I could take my bike out for a run in the country.

Then, one evening, as I was poring over a volume of statistical abstracts – an exercise which left me on the brink of despair at the best of times – there was a loud knock on the door. I sat up for a moment, wondering who might want to see me at that time of the night, or for that matter who I might want to see, and rushed expectantly to open it. It was Callum. For a moment I was afraid that he had been conjured up by my imagination, but when it became clear it was him, I threw my arms round his neck and for a moment was unaware that the cigarette in the corner of his mouth was burning a hole in my armpit.

'What are you doing in Cambridge?'

'Piece of new machinery – electronic. We'll have the most up-to-date milking parlour in the country. And disposable tit-grips. No more rinsing, boiling, sterilizing. And talking of tits, what happens if they find you with a man in your rooms at this time of the night? I suppose with somebody of my age you're safe.'

'If my previous experience is anything to go by, I would say yes – you do know I'm not a virgin anymore, by the way, don't you?'

'No, it's not the sort of thing they shout across the meadows in my part of the world. I rather imagined you weren't though.' He put his arm round me and squeezed me against his chest. 'Cambridge has done something for you in that respect at least.' He smelt of stale tobacco, stale wine and stale breath. My joy at his unexpected arrival ebbed slightly.

'Would you like a coffee?' I asked.

'No, no, there's only one thing I'd really like,' he said and put his hand on my breast and began to turn it in an anti-clockwise direction.

'Are you trying to screw it off?'

'I wouldn't mind having one as a souvenir. They're a lovely pair.'

He still had his coat on, and the cigarette, which had singed my armpit, was still smouldering in the corner of his mouth. Possibly because of his graceless manner, I felt none of the sensation which even the thought of him could sometimes arouse. Perhaps I was too weary or dejected for such arousal or perhaps he was too dejected and weary to arouse.

Callum was the first man I had become aware of as a man, but apart from his looks, the fact that he was a soldier and a hero added to his attraction, and the thing I liked best about him was his breezy self-assurance. I was also aware of his fecklessness, but he carried his defects lightly and, in a way, they added to his attractions for he had an air about him of the eternal truant schoolboy, so that even when I was twenty and he fifty, he tended to arouse my maternal instincts. But the breeziness seemed to have gone out of him. Possibly it had always been contrived, but if so he now lacked the energy to contrive it, and I saw before me a middle-aged man with floppy jaws and the debauched remnant of good looks, who was hoping to comfort himself with a quick screw. Or was it simply that I was beginning to see him through Grace's eyes rather than my own?

'Let's have a coffee,' I said, moving out of reach.

He clearly had not expected the rebuff.

'Don't you –'

'Not at this moment.'

He sighed, sat down on my bed and reached for another cigarette.

'I've fallen from favour, have I?'

'No, no,' I said – quite untruthfully – 'it's not that at all. I don't know how men work, but women don't always feel like it.'

'Neither do men, but you gave me the impression that you were one of those women who always did.'

'Callum, my love, you're a married man, and your wife is a close friend of the family.'

'I shouldn't think my wife would mind, if you didn't. And besides, it's all over – didn't you know?'

I was filling up the kettle as he was speaking and I let it drop into the sink with a clatter.

'It's all over?'

'We're separating – we have separated.'
'You and Sophie?'
'Sophie and me.'
'When?'
'Two or three days ago.'
'Oh, my poor Callum.' I rushed over and sat down beside him and put my arm round him. He leaned his head against my bosom, and then, silently and purposefully, bit off one blouse button and then began nibbling at my bra.

'Don't, my love,' I said, 'you'll bite off more than you can chew.'

8
Kept Woman

I told Grace that I was sure I would plough my finals, and she said: 'You can't plough, not in Cambridge, they're sure to give you *something*,' and, a little to my surprise and that of my tutor, I got an upper second. More surprising still, I got a research grant to work for a post-graduate degree at the London School of Economics. I had applied for the grant, not because there was any particular line of research which I wanted to follow, but because I wanted to live in London, and I was not quite sure what I could do with an economics degree otherwise.

Both Stevie and Uncle Willie kindly offered accommodation, but I wanted to have a flat, or at least a room, of my own, and I found furnished rooms in Bloomsbury. Visitors were surprised that I could afford anything so spacious on a mere research grant, and presumed that I was being helped out by father, but I felt that I had imposed on him long enough and would not have taken a penny. The flat was, in fact, paid for by Callum, and I, Ducks Courlander, BA (Cantab), was, at the mere age of twenty-one, a kept woman.

Shortly after I had settled in, Vida came to supper (after assurances that everything on the table would be kosher). Unlike other members of the family, I was not at all disturbed by her reversion to Judaism. What did disturb me, however, was her apparent belief that dowdiness was next to godliness. She was basically a handsome girl, with a fine figure, good legs, high cheek-bones and large lustrous eyes, but the sort of appearance she projected came to a good deal less than the sum total of her parts. She wore a woollen hat like a tea-cosy, clamped down about her ears, a long, shapeless coat, and a thick, brightly coloured woollen scarf of the sort normally worn by football supporters – of which perhaps she was one – but worst of all was a pair of huge glasses which made her look owlish.

She sensed my situation at a glance or rather, at a whiff.

'Have you acquired a passion for brandy and cigars – or is Callum keeping you? Presumably he is. The moment I heard Sophie had left him, the first thought which came to mind was, "Oh my God, Ducks." '

'Why? Do you think Callum wasn't up to this sort of thing while he was with Sophie?'

'No doubt he was, but I don't think you'd have been a party to it while she was around. We may not have received a religious upbringing, but we still harbour traces of Jewish puritanism. Well, as I feared, so it hath come to pass. You accused Vesta of picking up poor Weedy as her good deed for the day, and Weedy wasn't quite the *nebbish* we thought he was, but in fact you're doing the same for Callum. Poor, poor Callum. You fell in love with him, we all did. Falling in love with him was part of growing up, but if one continued to grow one couldn't help seeing through him. He's a broken shell of a man, discarded by his wife, treated with contempt by his children, laughed at by his employees – and finally come to rest in your ample bosom.'

'What makes you think I haven't seen through him?'

'I'm sure you have, that's why I call him your good deed, but perhaps you also cherish him as a memory of childhood – though I would have thought that at twenty-one you were a bit young to start looking back.'

There was something in that, though I sometimes wondered if I was not kept by Callum as a cherished memory of his heroic years, for he could look into my eyes and see at least traces of the adoration they used to reflect when I was younger. I'm afraid he got little else from our relationship. He came to see me two or three times a week.

We usually – if I had my way – ate at home, nothing elaborate, a chop which I put on the grill, a salad, and a fruit salad. He generally had two or three whiskies before the meal, a bottle of claret, or sometimes two (of which I had my goodly share), with the meal, and a very large brandy after. He talked from the moment he arrived, his rate of speech gathering velocity with the flow of liquor. By the time he reached the brandy he was generally incomprehensible, and sometimes in tears, and I would undress him, put him to bed, tuck him in, kiss him goodnight, and return to my work. Occasionally he would get into my bed in the morning and snuggle up against me, but it was not something I could encourage for I liked to be at my desk in college by nine in the morning. We also arranged that he should limit his visits to certain fixed evenings, for although I was not ashamed of our relationship, or my situation, I had no wish to flaunt it, and would have been embarrassed to entertain friends while he was around.

Grace came to see me one evening, and the half-amused look on her face as she entered told me that she knew all about it. I was afraid she would materialize sooner or later, and I dreaded the thought of the visit, for I was very close to Grace, and there is something slightly indelicate in living in quasi-concubinage with the father of one's best friend. It made her a step-daughter of sorts and the whole relationship began to look and feel incestuous. She knew about my feelings for her father when I was younger and she would laugh at it. 'My God, what do you see in him? It's the missing arm, I'm sure, like Dayan's missing eye. If someone should materialize short of a right arm, a left leg and an eye, he would have the whole of womenfolk at his foot.'

However, when she finally did arrive, our meeting was strangely free of embarrassment.

'I could always envisage the old man as a sugar-daddy,' she said, 'but to be honest I never quite imagined you as the sort of thing sugar-daddies went in for. I don't mean your looks – don't misunderstand me – but your personality. You've also struck me as far too formidable for that sort of thing. Let me give father his due. He has never been afraid of physical hazards and has more than his share of brute courage, but he is deficient in every other sort, and likes uncomplicated relationships – the quick screw so to speak.'

'And you think of me as a slow screw?'

'Not that so much as a complicated screw. Mother, of course, is also complicated, but then she had a fortune to compensate for her complications.'

'Whereas I cost him a fortune.'

'No, it seems to me that he has a weakness for the daughters of Israel. Don't you find him a bit of a bind?'

'Not in the least. I've always loved your father.'

'When he was younger everybody did, but now that he's fat and wheezy and debauched and discarded – that's the thing, discarded. Aren't you afraid of becoming the second Mrs Roscoe? My God, I'll have to call you mother.'

'I can't see that happening, can you?'

'When it comes to father, anything can happen, and almost anything does. But in any case, don't you find him in the way of something better? We're all keen on mature men when we're a bit under-ripe ourselves, but we are getting on.'

'You're beginning to talk like a Yiddisher mama.'

'Don't forget I'm the daughter of one.'

Callum never mentioned Sophie, as if he had vowed not to do so, which made me suspect that he missed her, but I certainly missed her, especially on those occasions when I went home for weekends. She had a tough, brittle personality, but she glittered and was a font of good sense, though I could not help wondering even in my younger days how someone so sensible could have married Callum, and I put it down to her main, perhaps her sole, weakness: snobbery. It was, of course, perfectly possible that she had fallen in love with him, but one of the things I admired about Sophie was that she had her emotions carefully under control, and I couldn't imagine that she would ever, even as a young woman, have allowed her affections to push her into an otherwise imprudent marriage. No, she was a snob; her father had acquired money and she, in time-honoured fashion, had used it to acquire pedigree. But her divorce did not quite fit the theory, for had pedigree been all that important, she would have continued to suffer Callum for another few years till she had seen her children married. And in any case, his pedigree was not all that exalted.

She had taken what she called a bijou residence in Hampstead, which was not in fact all that bijouish, but was tiny compared to Roscoe House. She had sent me a printed card mentioning her change of address, and had scrawled on the back: 'Hope I'll see more of you in London than I did in Essex,' which I took to be a standing invitation and I often dropped in for tea on Sunday afternoons after a walk on Hampstead Heath.

She had one large room in the house which I loved, for it was full of Victorian furniture and bric-à-brac, including a bell-pull by the fireplace which actually worked, and at a tug of which a small, dusky-skinned Fillipino maid appeared in a white cap and apron. Sophie herself, apart from her South African accent, could have been a figure out of Jane Austen, for with all her underlying toughness, there was something olde worldely, dignified and refined about her, though the impression may have been enhanced by the fact that her coats and dresses seemed to have a vaguely Regency look about them.

She was a cultivated and well-read woman, knew a great deal about music and art, and played the piano beautifully, all of which confirmed my belief that her marriage to Callum had been something of misalliance. There was nearly always someone of interest to meet in her house, though I met no one quite as interesting as herself, and she seemed to surround herself with guests to prevent anyone getting too near her; but one afternoon I did find her on her own and we talked with an intimacy and ease of which I had not thought her capable.

'I gather you're living with Callum,' she began in a matter-of-fact way, 'a very attractive man, though not without defects. He's like your father in many ways, which, I suppose, is part of the attraction.'

'Callum like father?'

'The same sort of overblown, debauched good looks, the same sort of breezy charm, the conviction that every woman they address is, or is about to fall in love with them. In a word, the same narcissism.'

'I don't see father like that at all.'

'You wouldn't. I knew your father before I knew Callum. I met him on a Union Castle liner. He had a very grand manner, the typical English milord, I thought, and he quite swept me off my feet. Father in particular was keen on him. "That's the man you should marry," he kept saying to me, "that's the man you should marry – an English gentleman." And then your father introduced me to Callum.'

'*Father* introduced you to Callum?'

'You sound surprised.'

'I am surprised. Callum told me how he met you while he was convalescing in South Africa –'

'After he'd lost his arm?'

'Yes.'

'Not true. Did he tell you his arm was bitten off by sharks? He's got all sorts of fantasies about it. He sometimes describes how he lost it in a tiger hunt, or how it was bitten off by a lion. He's an incorrigible liar. To do him justice, he never – or hardly ever – tells lies to get himself out of difficulties, or to aggrandize himself, it's just lies for their own sake to round off a good story. I sometimes think he should have been a writer. He lost his arm in 1942, Grace and Robin were born in 1941, and we were married about the same time as your parents, shortly before the war. In fact, I was to have been at your parents' wedding, but we were held up by something or other. No, your father introduced me to Callum. He more than introduced me, he sold him to me. "You must meet him, handsome, dashing, father's a baronet, vast estates." In retrospect, I think your father was merely trying to suggest how grand he was by proclaiming the exalted status of his friends, but I saw Callum through his eyes and when Callum proposed – which he did at our second meeting – I thought it would be churlish to say no, especially as he was in uniform and we were on the brink of war.'

'I can't imagine you falling for a uniform.'

'Ah, but it was a dress uniform, tight-fitting with scarlet tunics and golden buttons, and I was from Johannesburg, you know, which is very provincial, the only daughter of a Lithuanian immigrant.'

'Did the fact that he was not Jewish matter?'

'Oh, it was something in his favour. In South Africa in those days – and perhaps even today – if a Jew made money he could transcend his Jewishness. My father would never have converted to Christianity – he had too much self-respect for that – and there might have been some difficulties if Callum had insisted on marrying in church, but, as he was the son of a lapsed Christian and I the daughter of a semi-lapsed Jew, he was the ideal suitor. We in fact married in a registry office here in London. I dare say the children will marry in church, but that's inevitable.'

'It doesn't worry you?'

'But my dear, why should it? Nothing I know about Christianity suggests that it's harmful or pernicious, and there is much about it that I find attractive. I went to an Anglican prep school in South Africa, and loved the hymns and carols, even though they had a vaguely northern tone and didn't quite go with the blue skies, the bright sunshine and the exotic vegetation about us. I don't think I would want the children to become Catholic any more than I would want them to become Orthodox Jews, because I don't care too much for smoky rituals and sacramental wines, but once they have settled down and become accepted in some established faith, they should be less troubled by the sort of questions which have been troubling me: Who am I? What am I? What am I trying to be?'

'You surprise me.'

'In what way?'

'Because, well, you seem so composed that I just can't imagine you agonizing over any such problem.'

'Agonizing would be too strong a word, my dear. It's really a sort of disquiet. Everyone brought up in South Africa has labels thrust upon him. One is black or white, English or African, Christian or Jew, and one of the reasons I left South Africa is that I wanted to leave the question open, to be anyone I liked.'

'Though not black to be sure.'

'To be sure, but by leaving the matter open I've left my children with options which I did not have myself.'

'Would it bother you if they opted to be Jewish?'

'Of course it wouldn't *bother* me, but I think it would delay the inevitable, for even if they did become Jewish I cannot imagine, given the sort of world in which they would find themselves, their children remaining Jewish.'

The matter was not entirely academic, for the relationship between Rocky, who was now seventeen, and Robin, had reached the stage where he was regarded as a member, and a welcome member, of the family, especially by Tilly, who seemed almost to cringe when he was around, like an unctuous draper in the presence of gentry. He had also become more talkative, and could even be vaguely amusing, but he had acquired a disconcerting habit of leaning over and nibbling at Rocky's ear-lobes during breaks in conversation, like a hungry horse nibbling at thatch, and I once asked him if they didn't feed him in the army. I also wondered how anyone could want to be a regular soldier, especially in peace-time.

'Haven't really thought about it,' he said, 'family tradition I suppose.'

I couldn't see Rocky as an army wife and neither, I suspect, could she.

'He doesn't have to be in the army for life, you know,' she said. 'He can resign his commission after four or five years.' She obviously already had her eye on the estates and the title.

'I can't see anything coming of it,' Grace said to me

several times, with rather excessive insistence. 'He's intelligent, well read, interested in what's happening around him. She wouldn't know how to hold a book and is interested only in herself. He's far too good for her' – which broadly speaking was true, but I somehow resented her saying it. They made a handsome pair and were very happy – or seemed very happy – together, and I rather liked the thought of my baby sister being the future Lady Roscoe and châtelaine of Roscoe House. And in any case, Rocky was only a child; she could mature, change, improve. Grace, I felt, was judging her prematurely and showed a censoriousness which she rarely applied to herself.

Then two things happened. Robin was badly injured in a training exercise and was invalided out of the army. He was left slightly disfigured, with a scar on his neck which extended to under his chin, and he no longer felt that he was a fit and proper consort for someone as unblemished as Rocky. She, for her part, did not attempt to persuade him otherwise.

The second was that Vesta took his rehabilitation in hand. I don't know whether it was his disfigurement which drew her to him, or the fact that he had become once again rather silent and withdrawn, but about a year later I was greeted with news of their engagement. I could see it happening, but was not too pleased that it had, indeed, happened, for I regarded Vesta as one of the wonders of creation. She had perfect, if austere features, a perfect, if somewhat undernourished figure, and the soul of a saint. I felt that she deserved someone better, but I could not recall ever meeting anyone whom I would have regarded as even remotely suitable, and if she hadn't taken Robin she might have landed up with someone like Weedy. Moreover, I knew father was delighted with the direction their relationship had taken, and I drew gratification from his gratification. He clearly felt that the House of Courlander was being finally grafted on to Olde England, and not only on to Olde England, but on to his olde friend. It was, I suppose, about the nearest thing to being married to Callum himself. It was, I felt, his happiest and proudest hour.

Sophie gave me the feeling that she did not quite share his gratification, for she had substantially the same social ambitions as father. If the engagement represented a leg up for the Courlanders, it presumably meant a leg down for the Roscoes, but possibly I was doing her an injustice, for she claimed that she had always adored Vesta. As a prospective Lady of the Manor, Vesta looked, sounded and acted the part – as if to the manor born, English country-style with a slight touch of pre-Raphaelite chic.

The wedding was a surprisingly small affair. I had expected something large enough to pack the mock-baronial hall in Roscoe House and to spill over into the surrounding park, but perhaps after the disastrous coming-out ball both Sophie and father had decided to invite only people they actually knew, and their range of acquaintances was not as vast as I had imagined. There was a large contingent of prosperous-looking South Africans with tanned hues and elegant outfits, who more or less dominated the affair; a lot of old soldiers with red faces and stern-looking wives; and some grandams from Italy, who I gathered were Callum's relatives. There were few guests from our side of the family, for grandpa had fallen out with his brothers and nephews and there had been no attempt to restore links, though father came across their names from time to time in the columns of the *Financial Times*. Stevie arrived in a black velvet outfit which made her look even older than she was, awash with perfume and tears.

'I love all my nieces, but Vesta's my favourite, well she's everybody's favourite, she's a goddess, and I'm so happy to see her happy, that's why I can't stop crying,' though it was quite obvious that she was crying for herself rather than her niece. She had once asked me if I had a boyfriend and, when I said I hadn't, she added, only half-jokingly: 'That's just as well; don't you *dare* get married before your aunt.'

Callum greeted guests with Sophie on his arm and it was

difficult to believe that they were separated or about to divorce. Everybody in the room must have known about my relationship with Callum, and if they didn't know they must have learned something from the pains he took to avoid even glancing in my direction, for usually at such gatherings he would pinch my cheek or my bottom, or put his arm round my waist, or prod me furtively on my nipples, and always showed a keen awareness of my presence. I decided there and then that I did not at all care for being the other woman, even where the principal woman was bowing out of the scene. It would mean moving out of my lovely Bloomsbury flat into some bleak little garret. Better a garret . . . and what therewith? Loneliness? I had had some taste of it in Cambridge and hadn't liked it one bit, and I could imagine that one could be very much lonelier in London. Callum was not only the rent, he was company of sorts.

Uncle Willie said I could have the run of his flat. He had acquired a small place in the country and was spending less and less time in London, but whether he was in his flat or not it retained something of his presence, and his presence was that of an old man. British bachelors don't wear well, especially if their innards have been ravaged by malaria, and, although not yet sixty, Willie had the bearing and air of a man who had drawn from life the little it could offer and had entered upon a gradual phase of decomposition. All the colour in his face was to be found in his nose, everything else was a mottled grey, except the whites of his eyes which were an ivory yellow. He wore well-cut suits which kept their shape, but he himself was sagging.

He had a woman who came in daily to clean the flat and prepare an evening meal, but otherwise he was on his own, and Vida felt that we were neglecting him. I thought the charge was directed principally at me and I said, 'If you feel that way, why don't you stay with him?'

'He lives in South Ken', she said, 'and it would take me two hours to get to college, but that's the least of it. He's troubled by my Jewishness. You'll notice he offered *you* the run of his flat. He's made no such offer to me.'

The obvious solution would have been for Stevie to move in, especially as she kept complaining about the impossible cost of maintaining her own flat, but there had been some sort of difference between her and Willie which no one spoke about, and they were never on the best of terms. They never actually quarrelled, at least not in our presence, but they had little to say to each other.

The wedding coincided with my twenty-second birthday – an event which, I'm glad to say, almost everyone overlooked. The approach of my birthday over the past year or two always left me pensive, and the day itself almost suicidal; this day was no exception. I watched Vesta and Robin and would have liked to have basked in their joy rather more than I did. I was probably envious. I had never experienced the ecstasy which they seemed to radiate, and had an unhappy feeling that I never would.

Shortly after the wedding I told Callum I was moving out of Bloomsbury. He seemed neither pained nor surprised. If anything, he was relieved.

'Lost your taste for old men? Don't blame you. It's time you found yourself someone young, attractive and solvent. You will invite me to your wedding – won't you?'

He drove me and my possessions across town to Uncle Willie's flat and Willie, who was shortsighted, mistook him for a removal man and tried to tip him.

Willie was semi-retired and used to spend about half the week in a tiny cottage on the edge of the Sussex Downs, but once I moved in he rarely left town and was clearly delighted at the prospect of company. Instead of having something on a tray in front of the television as was his custom, he prepared a fairly elaborate meal with wine, which we ate in the dining-room.

I have never particularly cared for meals as a form of social intercourse, largely because I find eating a demanding occupation in its own right. I don't eat and talk if I can help it, though I'm prepared to eat and listen, which was substantially all that Willie required of me, and he was content to drone through one long monologue after another, though from time to time he tired of his own voice and tried to draw me out. I was writing a thesis which touched on the economies of the Baltic States between the wars, and he said to me:

'The Baltic States? Who's interested in the Baltic States? They don't even exist any more.'

'The Baltic States in general terms, but Latvia in particular,' I explained, 'and I suppose I picked on it, partly because the period is compact and so is the area, partly because most of the material is in German and I understand German, and partly because I feel there's a family connection.'

'Strange that,' he said, 'when I was a young man it was the old who were forever sniffing around for family roots – doing the Soames Forsythe I called it – now the young are up to the same thing. Shouldn't read too much into the name Courlander – it's no proof we're from the Baltic. Had a grandmother who was a great one for family histories and she said we've been Pomeranians for generations, centuries. There was a time when people were content to be Englishmen and that was the end of that, but of course England isn't what it was. Everyone is twisting its tail or poking its ribs or tugging its mane, and it doesn't as much as raise a paw in protest. The last man to stand up for England was Eden, and see what happened to him, poor chap. Made me ashamed to be British, the way we pulled out with our tail between our legs, though the fact that we had to go into it with the French didn't help – never trust the French, not in business and certainly not in war. Perfidious pack. I'm glad the Jews kept their ground, for a while at least, and gave the Gypos what for. For the first time in my life I was proud to be Jewish.'

'*You* were proud to be Jewish? I had no idea you even thought of yourself as a Jew.'

'I still don't, not when it comes to prayers and incense and that sort of thing, no time for it at all, and I can't stand the sort of kosher capers Vida gets up to, splendid girl though she may be in other ways. No time for them at all, but I've never tried to hide my origins. During the First

World War it was something of a hazard to have a German-sounding name like Courlander and everyone urged the old man to change it, but he had the same answer for them all: I am what I am, and whatever happens I shall not try to pass myself off as something I'm not. I was proud of him. If I should ever get a knighthood that would be my family motto: I am what I am. Being Jewish is part of it, a minor part usually, but it comes into prominence from time to time, as it did at Suez. It was a joy to see them racing across Sinai in a matter of days. The Anglo–French lot hadn't moved thirty miles.'

His monologues often consisted of a monotopic – the continuing rise in prices and the decline in everything else: manners, service, literacy, business ethics, personal honesty, civic mindedness. 'You may laugh,' he said, 'but while the pound kept its value, people still had principles, but that's all finished with. The currency is the temperature of a nation – now you can put that in your thesis. When the old man was in business people didn't bother with papers and documents. Your word was your bond. Now you have everything in writing, and in lawyers' writing at that. When a country becomes a paradise for lawyers, it's hell for everyone else.'

I wondered whether it was age or isolation which made him sense decline everywhere, but it was not long before I began to yearn for the feckless geniality of Callum. I had thought I was lonely in Cambridge, but at least during the working day, when there were lectures and tutorials, there was company of sorts, people one could nod to or exchange a thought with. As a research student in London I hardly saw anyone except my supervisor: a tall woman with a large, white, expressionless face and long, lank hair, who would listen impassively and, I thought, impatiently, to what I had to say and would, as far as possible, avoid saying anything herself. She was a prolific writer and did not care to spend more time on her students than she could help. I did not even see people at mealtimes, for as I often had a substantial meal in the evening, and as I was putting on weight, I tried to avoid having lunch altogether.

One evening I was alone in the house, when there was a ring at the door. In those days Londoners were not afraid to answer the door at night, even if they were alone, but for some reason the ring made me apprehensive, as if it represented somebody very unwelcome. Nevertheless I opened it and found myself face to face with a good-looking young man, with a cleft chin and polka-dot bow-tie. He seemed surprised to see me.

'Is Mr Courlander in – the name's Mackeson.'

'Is he expecting you?'

'I hope he is.'

'He's not in, I'm afraid.'

'Oh dear – can I use your 'phone?'

I let him in and as he dialled, he scrutinized me with an amused look on his face, obviously thinking that I was part of Willie's secret life. I was not sure if I was flattered to be thought of in such a context. He was very good-looking. His hair was a dark red, the colour of dried blood, and was carefully brushed back, without a hair out of place. His face was freckled with light-blue eyes. He was smartly dressed, in a well-cut tweed suit and waistcoat, and his shirt cuffs, which seemed rather too large, were kept together by gold clasps. He exuded ambition, confidence, success.

'The old man doesn't seem to be in his Sussex place either. Any idea where I can get hold of him?'

'None. He's not usually in London on a Sunday night.'

'Neither am I, but something rather important's cropped up. And he said he'd be here.'

A few minutes later Willie appeared, full of apologies. He'd had trouble with his car. 'Had my old car for fifteen years and never a moment's bother. I've only had this one for six months and I've had nothing but bother. The British have forgotten how to make cars. I should have bought something Japanese. I will do next time – if I live long enough. Have I introduced you, by the way? This is my niece, Henrietta.'

'Ducks,' I corrected him, 'nobody calls me Henrietta.'

'I do, I can't stand this silly family nickname habit. This is Mr Troy Mackeson, works for my stock-broker.'

They were closeted together for about two hours. When he left, Willie said to me: 'Very conscientious young man. You wouldn't get many people coming out on a Sunday evening just like that. He's put me on to Far Eastern stock – Shanghai, Hong Kong, Tokyo. They're doing a damned sight better than the local stuff I can tell you. He'll go far that young man.'

The next evening Troy 'phoned to ask me out to the theatre. I was so surprised to hear from him at all that I almost said no, and I spent a sleepless night marvelling at this unexpected turn of events and wondering if it was possible that I, Ducks, of all people, had at the mature age of twenty-three fallen in love at first sight. I had experienced something similar as a child when I fell for Callum, but there was something dramatic and dashing about him, especially with that missing arm. Troy didn't look as if he had a hair missing and, on the whole, I tended to find good-looking men banal.

We went out a few days later and, as we were hurrying along Shaftesbury Avenue, we bumped into Stevie and a woman colleague. They both eyed him with warm approval.

She 'phoned me the next day: 'Who is he? What is he? He's beautiful.'

'Oh, just somebody I know.'

'Nothing more to it than that?'

'I'm afraid not.'

'Pity.'

But in fact I was allowing myself to believe that there possibly was much more to it than that. I suspect that the main reason why I thought I was disinterested in good-looking men was that I did not really believe that good-looking men would be interested in me, but Troy evidently was.

He asked me out again the next evening and we began to see each other two or three times a week. My work began to suffer, which did not worry me for I had never looked on it as an end in itself, but something to do in the absence of anything better – Troy's company was well worth a PhD.

One Sunday we decided to take a run to Burnham-on-Crouch, on the east coast, where he had a boat, but the day was hot and the roads were jammed, and we decided to drop in at 'West Wynds' for lunch instead.

The family were dining *al fresco* under the awning on the back terrace. Stevie was there and Callum had brought along an exotic piece of goods with long red hair and long tanned legs. There was also a young man with hairy legs and long black hair, who, I presumed, was Rocky's latest escort. Rocky herself was in the shortest of shorts, which exposed half her buttocks, and the briefest of bras, which just about covered her nipples.

Father had been engaged in an argument with Callum about stocks and shares, into which Troy was drawn almost as soon as we sat down, and the company divided between the gentlemen at one end of the table and the ladies at the other. The exchanges among the latter tended to be desultory because Callum's red-head either had nothing to say or regarded her function in life as looking beautiful and said nothing, and her ostentatious silence put something of a dampener on the rest of us.

After lunch they all drove off to Callum's for a swim, except Stevie, who had put on weight and presumably did not feel her best in a swimsuit. I was dying for a swim, but my period had just started and I was afraid that if I should take to the waters they would turn red. I had hoped, when I said that I didn't care for a swim, that Troy would stay with me, but he didn't even try to cajole me into going. All he said was: 'Sure you don't want to go?'

'I'm quite certain.'

'Pity,' he said, and was off.

Stevie turned on me as soon as we were alone.

'You lying bitch. I thought you said there was nothing in it.'

'There was nothing in it when I said it. I'm not sure there's much to it even now. We're only friends – if that.'

'He's the most heavenly young man I have ever set eyes

on. What does he do?'

'Investment counsellor. Give him your money and he'll look after it.'

'I would give him every penny I had, if I had a penny to give. He's perfect, perfect. Every feature. The mouth, the teeth, that lovely cleft chin, and that tiny cleft on the tip of his nose, I so wanted to kiss it.'

'Why didn't you? I'm sure he'd have appreciated it.'

Father and Tilly returned in time for tea. It was dark before Troy and Rocky got back and she was without her escort.

'Pity you couldn't come,' he said, 'you'd have loved it.' I didn't answer.

I asked Stevie to drive me to the station, but she said she was going back to London in any case and drove me all the way home. Neither of us had much to say, and I could feel in her silence the thought – there goes Stevie, a generation on.

I was not too heartbroken by it all, for I had never felt that I had entered upon a lasting relationship and had anticipated that something like this would happen, but was sorry about the circumstances in which it had happened. The only thing I couldn't understand was how a man who had shown an interest in me could be interested in someone like Rocky.

They became engaged a few months later and I was not surprised to hear that they were to marry in church.

She wanted a white, traditional, English wedding. Father brought us together to impart the news. It was clear he was not happy about it, and as soon as he finished all eyes turned to Vida, but her eyes were averted.

'I know how you must feel,' he said, 'but the fact is I'm an agnostic like my father before me, and, I dare say, his father before him, but I'm not a devout agnostic and I don't feel that I have any God-given right to impose my non-belief on my children.'

Willie was beside himself when he heard the news. 'It's an outrage,' he shouted, 'an outrage to the family, an outrage to the church. People shouldn't be able to get away with that sort of thing. I'll cut her out of my will, I shan't go to the wedding.'

'But Uncle Willie,' pleaded Vesta, 'Troy is a practising Christian.'

'Then he should marry a practising Christian. That sort of thing shouldn't be allowed. What would his family say if he married in a synagogue?'

'Would you want Rocky to marry in synagogue?'

'I didn't say I did, but this is England, damn it. There are such things as registry offices – you married in a registry office.'

'He's a silly old man and he'll get over it,' said Stevie, but he didn't. He left without a further word, drove back to London and took to his bed. When I got back to the flat the next evening, the place was in darkness, which surprised me, for I had expected to find him busy in the kitchen. I took off my coat, put on the kettle, and had an odd feeling that I wasn't alone. 'Uncle Willie?' I called. There was no reply. I ran to his bedroom, switched on the light and found him in bed, his head thrown back, his mouth wide open, his eyes staring, dead. I marvelled at my composure, but recalled that I was rather good with dead people. I closed his eyelids, opened the windows, 'phoned the doctor, father and Stevie, and sat down and made myself a cup of tea. Rocky might have taken Willie's sudden death as a stern admonition had he not left instructions to be buried in the village churchyard near his cottage in Sussex.

9
Grace

Well, at least I got my PhD, a little later than planned, but I got it.

I had completed my thesis in a furious burst of work through which I hardly ate and barely slept. For a time the sheer relief of having it off my shoulders kept me fairly cheerful, but once that went I was desolate.

It may be a reflection on the sort of people who get doctorates in economics that I entered upon the project and brought it to a successful conclusion without a thought of what I would do next. I suppose I may have had the feeling that before the three years were over I would be married, or that my future would otherwise be settled. It was only after my graduation that I began to circulate universities and government departments with my curriculum vitae in the hope that I could be of use to them, but few of them even invited me for an interview and none of them offered me a job.

'In my day,' said father, 'if you had a BA you could walk into any job you wanted, now even a PhD doesn't get you anywhere.'

'Don't forget she's a woman PhD,' said Tilly.

'There's always teaching,' said Vida.

'The last resort of the unemployable,' I said.

Uncle Willie had been overtaken by death unexpectedly and much of his estate went in death duties. He hadn't even had time to cut Rocky out of his will and left each of us five thousand pounds, which was a useful windfall. He left me the lease of his flat, which still had twenty-seven years to run, and this I promptly sold, providing some useful income, but I was still unemployed and, it seemed, unemployable. There was no point in remaining by myself in London. Vida, who was now teaching in school, had suggested that I share her flat, but she lived in the gefilte-fish zone of north-west London, which I found rather unattractive. There was nothing for it but to return to the family hearth at 'West Wynds', and try to make myself useful round the farm.

Father had lately brought in a new manager, a soured-looking young man, called Nigel, straight from agricultural college, who had urged him to uproot hedges and trees, and organize the farm on a prairie system with huge fields of cereals; but father was attached both to trees and hedgerows and wouldn't hear of it. There were three acres of woodland, which provided some of the firewood we used for fuel, but Nigel reckoned it would be cheaper to buy logs ready felled; again father found great pleasure in walking through his wood. It was the same with the dairy. Father liked the neat configuration and the brown and white colouring of Ayrshire cattle. 'They may be good to look at, but you sell your milk by the gallon,' said Nigel, 'and you get more milk from a Friesian, who are less fussy about their food.' He, in any case, regarded the breeding of pedigree cattle as a rich man's hobby, which had nothing to do with real farming. 'He's running a show-place here,' said Nigel, 'not a farm, not a *real* farm.'

I for one was happy with the show-place, and especially the pedigree herd. There were about fifty milking cows and as many heifers who at first looked alike to me, but I gradually got to know them all by name and appreciate their distinct needs, characteristics and idiosyncracies, and spoke of them as fondly as a mother might speak of her children. I enjoyed the work while the working day lasted, but it was over all too soon and I found the evenings very long, especially in the summer. I writhed with undefined longings which, once I began to think of them, were not all that undefined.

I remembered a conversation I once had with Vesta before she was married when she spoke about the 'moral satisfaction' she derived from working on the land, and I said to her: 'What about physical satisfaction?' She had looked at me with her large eyes.

'What sort of physical satisfaction?'

'The physical sort.'

'You don't mean –'

'I do.'

'You would. The way people go on about sex and fornication one would think the world would stop without it.'

'The world *would* stop without it.'

'But it doesn't mean that one can't have self-fufilment without it.'

'But don't you ever feel when you're alone in a cold bed on a cold night –'

'Of course I do, but clearly not half as much as you do. I don't know what makes you think that wants are necessarily there to be satisfied. A little bit of self-denial does you good.'

I hated to sleep alone and was conscious of an aching void between my thighs, which, on winters' nights, I thought was due to the cold, but which, in fact, became more pronounced in the spring and summer. There were times when I was living in Kensington, when I had to grasp hold of myself to stop myself from trotting across the corridor and climbing into Uncle Willie's bed. It was even worse in the country. Perhaps the country air is an aphrodisiac, or the inherent earthiness of farm life gives greater rein to one's primitive urges, but there were nights when I was steaming with discontent, and one morning I woke with the grim determination to obtain satisfaction from someone, somehow.

We had a herdsman on the farm called Hughie, sandy-haired, green-eyed, apple-cheeked, gap-toothed, who looked like a schoolboy but who was, in fact, a married man with three children. I went round to the cow-shed and asked him if he could show me how to milk cows.

'Any time you like. There ain't nothing much to it.'

'Don't they kick out or anything, the cows I mean?'

'No, not unless you come on them suddenly.'
'Don't they mind having their nipples pulled?'
'You don't touch their nipples, machine does that.'
'Does the machine hurt them at all?'
'No. They just suck, and gently at that. It's like feeding a baby.'

The top two buttons of my blouse were undone and I could feel myself swelling at the conversation, but he seemed oblivious to my state.

'Will you be feeding them?'
'Feeding them?'
'Don't you give them hay?'
'Not at this time of the year. They've got the pasture.'

I wanted to get him into the hay barn and it didn't seem as if it could be done without leading him there by the hand. I decided to get straight to the point.

'Hughie, I want a romp in the hay.'
'A romp?'
'In the hay.'
'You mean . . . ?'
'I do.'

He put down the bucket he was holding, looked around him as if afraid that somebody might be listening, wiped his hands on his overalls, and followed me at a trot to the barn.

He might have taken his cap off, and maybe his wellington boots, but otherwise it was heavenly. Hay, I decided, was the natural location for such an act. It absorbs any lingering feelings of guilt one might have. It is soft, springy, noiseless and with an earthy fragrance which, I suspect, could be nature's own aphrodisiac. No one knows what an orgasm is who has not fornicated in hay. A bare floor is passable, a carpeted floor better, a sofa better still, and one might think that beds, especially between clean, crisp, cotton sheets, were best of all, but there is nothing to compare with hay. If there was a Richter scale for orgasms, hay would come top.

I returned to the hay barn almost as a daily routine and Hughie said to me: 'You're very good, *very* good, better even'n Rocky.'

'Better than Rocky? Who else have you had in the barn?'

'Oh, just about everybody and their mother.'

My summer idyll was broken by the unexpected arrival of Grace. Grace had been working in New York for the past three or four years and, to judge from her letters, life there, especially among the literati, was one long orgy. 'They're all Jews,' she added, 'or nearly all – haven't seen a foreskin in years.'

She kept urging me to come over on a visit: 'You'll have a ball. A ball? You won't be able to see Manhattan for balls. But be quick about it – before you've had your change of life.'

I was not averse to the sort of pleasures she promised, even though the way she described them had a mildly off-putting effect. When Uncle Willie left me the money, I had arranged to spend Christmas with her, but she wrote back to say she would be spending Christmas with her mother in South Africa. I then planned to come over at Easter and she drew up an elaborate programme of entertainments for my benefit.

'I take it you're not on the pill,' she wrote. 'It's not worth starting just to carry you over a week or two, and I would therefore suggest a Dutch cap. Bring several, because you can't imagine the wear and tear.'

Then came a letter so calm in tone that it might have been written by a different person:

Dearest Ducks,

Have you ever woken in a darkened room filled with sunbeams and luxuriated in the sheer sensation of being alive? For that's how I feel and I'm wondering if I could be in love. You'll get a shock when you meet him, I certainly did. He's British, an actor and is the spitting image of Robin. In fact at first I thought it was Robin. He is slightly older and a good deal more self-assured, but I still can't get over the likeness, and I keep wondering whether what I've really been looking for all these years is a permissable form of incest . . .

I was happy for her, but in the circumstances I felt I would be in her way and cancelled my plans to go to New

York. Now, four months later, and without a word of warning, she was on my doorstep.

We dived into each other's arms, and to my astonishment I found her heaving with sobs. I had never in my life seen her shed as much as a tear. What astonished me even more was that I found myself in tears. What the hell did *I* have to cry for, except the fact that I had nothing to cry for.

I've often heard women say that they felt good after a good cry, but they rarely looked good. I daren't think what I must have looked like, but poor Grace was a mess. Her eyes were swollen and her whole face seemed raw and sore, but it didn't take her long to recover her spirits.

'He wasn't single,' she said, 'which in itself wouldn't have worried me, but his consort was another man, and he wanted us to set up a *ménage à trois*. I have, as you know, an appetite for complications, but that was too much even for my tastes, especially as his partner was a hideous creature, with a face like raw meat, and he would sit up between us reading his poems aloud. I can laugh at it now, but at the time I nearly went out of my mind. What I'm looking for now is a dull, semi-literate, heterosexual Englishman with ten thousand a year.'

More immediately she wanted a holiday and she insisted that I come with her. I protested that the harvest was due to begin in another few weeks and that father would need all the help he could find, but as the weather was wretched and as it was years since I had had a good holiday myself, I succumbed to the brochures she kept pushing in front of me and we went off for a few weeks in Greece.

It was some years since Grace and I had been away together. We both had changed more than we realized and I was surprised how irritated we became with each other. I wanted to see the sights, she wanted to rest. She tended to blister and get blotchy in the sun, and preferred to keep in the shade, whereas I tanned easily and painlessly and liked to be in the sun, so that she kept under the awnings, while I stayed out in the open. I liked white wine and she preferred red, so we ordered both. We couldn't finish the two bottles in one meal, so they were brought back for the next, and they had both plainly been got at. But these were minor troubles. A major one was soon to surface.

Grace's bright colours, her red hair, her pink complexion, her rather flamboyant manner, attracted attention wherever she went, whereas I almost blended in with the natives. The locals, in particular, laid siege to her and offered to take her here, there and everywhere by scooter, by car, by boat and, on one occasion, even by private plane, and they hardly seemed to be aware that I was there at all. At first she loyally insisted that I had to come with and, at first, *dumkopf* that I am, I went, but her new-found companions took no great pains to make me welcome and no pains at all to make me comfortable. I had never thought of myself as a particularly large woman, but found myself hemmed into the back seats of the tiniest cars. Once when about a dozen of us piled on top of a tiny motor-boat, someone gave me a playful jab with his elbow and I fell into the water, which was possibly part of the fun, but if Grace had not dived in to get me they would have been disposed to leave me there. I also fell off the back of a scooter, which may have been a genuine accident, but the driver went on his merry way, oblivious of the fact that he had lost his passenger. After other minor misadventures, I told Grace to go on her own, for I was perfectly capable of amusing myself. She put up token resistance to the idea, but it was only token resistance, and although I am rarely averse to my own company, I weary of it when I hear the sounds of pleasure on every side. I had brought a stack of books with me in case of such an eventuality, but I found it difficult to read when I had come braced for non-literary pleasures, and after a week or so of this I decided to fly on to Israel for a few days.

'What for?' said Grace. 'Aren't you enjoying yourself?'

'Me? I'm having the time of my life, but you can have too much of a good thing.'

'Seriously though, have I been neglecting you?'

'No, but I've had a sudden urge to return to Zion. By the

waters of Babylon we sat –'

'Shut up, I'm trying to be serious.'

'I'm being serious. I want to go to Israel.'

'Then I'm coming with you.'

'You don't have to.'

'I want to.'

She had been to Israel before (she had been everywhere before), but this was my first visit and I was bowled over. I liked the colour, the vivacity and briskness of the place. It was as hot as in Greece, yet the heat did not bring the same feeling of lethargy, but that may have had something to do with the fact that here I was almost as much in demand as Grace and rarely had a free minute to myself.

One evening Grace and I were taken to a concert, and during the interval I noticed a lean, boyish figure, with cropped hair, staring at me with a surprised look on his face. There was something vaguely familiar about him, but before I could place him, he came over to me and said:

'What's the matter? Don't you recognize me, or don't you want to recognize me?'

'Good God,' I said, 'Otto. It is Otto, isn't it?'

I would never have recognized him. He had shaved off his beard, was tanned to the point of being swarthy, had lost weight and, in his sandals and shorts, looked hardly more than a schoolboy.

'Why didn't you write to say you were coming, and why didn't you 'phone me when you came?'

I was going to say that I didn't think he'd be interested, but said that we had come on impulse. In fact I had toyed with the thought of 'phoning him and would certainly have 'phoned him if I had been less in demand.

He invited us to the Weizmann Institute and we travelled down by taxi the next day. At first glance it seemed more like a garden suburb than a world-famous research establishment, for it was beautifully landscaped, with lawns, trees, shrubs and a riot of exotic plants.

Otto had a well-appointed flat, with a balcony overgrown with bougainvillaea. He showed us around his laboratory, which consisted mainly of metal hardware, like a very elaborate and very expensive hi-fi set, full of dials and knobs and loud with sinister pinging noises. He explained its function and both Grace and I made appropriately appreciative noises. I, for one, had only the vaguest understanding of what he was talking about, though already then, during moments of silence, he and Grace were exchanging glances which made me feel a trifle out of place.

As we were preparing for bed that night, Grace said to me: 'He looks very young, your friend Otto.'

'He's almost exactly my age, but in what sense do you speak of him as *my* friend?'

'In the sense that you're friendly. He's obviously warmly disposed towards you.'

'Though not half as warmly as he's disposed towards you.'

'No, chuck it, Ducks. You're trying to make me angry.'

'Why should I do that? We were friendly at Cambridge, but all that petered out after he left. I have no claim on his affections, and he has none on mine.'

While I was in the bathroom the 'phone went. Grace answered, and I could hear by her delighted tone that the call was a surprise and a particularly pleasant one, and I presumed from the way she immediately lowered her voice, that it was Otto. What would he have done if I had answered? Asked me to pass him on to Grace? Didn't he know that we shared a room?

I waited in the bathroom till they had finished: I could have had a bath and washed my hair, and perhaps shaved my legs in the time.

'Who was it?' I said, trying to sound innocent.

'Theo – you know, with the huge teeth, from Corinth.' As far as I knew it was the first time she had lied to me. 'It was very nice of him to call. He misses us' – I liked that *us* – 'and wants to know when we're going back.'

'When *are* we going back?'

'Any time you like.'

'Tomorrow?'

'Wouldn't that be rushing things a bit?'

'You can stay on if you want, but I want to get back tomorrow.'

'Ducks, what *has* got into you?'

'Nothing. It's just that I never particularly enjoy holidays, and I'd like to get back to work.' She sighed and went into the bathroom. I put out the lights and tried to go to sleep, and eventually fell into a sort of weary stupor.

I woke early the next morning. I dressed quietly, threw my things into my case, scribbled a note which I left by her bedside, and tiptoed out of the room. It had one word: *Mazeltov*.

— 10 —
Woman of Letters

Sophie came to see me shortly after I got back.

'Who is this Otto? What's he like? Who are his people? Can she be serious?'

'She can be,' I said, 'and I'm sure she is.'

'I shouldn't sound so anxious, but you do know she hasn't been herself lately. She's short-tempered and querulous, morose. I wouldn't like her to get caught up in yet another preposterous liaison.'

'There's nothing preposterous about Otto. He's brilliant, ambitious, perhaps ruthless, but he's got his little feet solidly on the ground. You should be very happy for her, I certainly am.'

A little later we were joined by Callum.

'I hear my daughter's marrying a bloody Jew-boy.'

'What can you expect if you marry a bloody Jew-girl?' I said.

'Yes, but can he support her? I know he's a scientist of some sort, but what does he do?'

'He's in nuclear physics.'

'Bombs, that sort of thing, eh? Ah well, you're always safe with bombs.'

I didn't go to the wedding, but it was apparently held in the open air on the grounds of the Institute with the ceremony performed by a bearded rabbi. The irony of the situation appealed to me. About a year ago, my sister, who was Jewish (after a fashion), was married in church; now Grace, who was Christian (after a fashion), was being married in a sort of open-air synagogue. It all seemed a little bit crazy to me. Vida, who was the authority on such matters, made it seem even crazier.

'As far as the Jewish law is concerned, if the mother is Jewish, the child is Jewish. That's all there is to it. So Grace is a Jewess.'

'Even though her father is not?'

'Her father's a detail.'

'And she was effectively brought up as a Christian.'

'That's also a detail – though as you well know, we were all brought up in a spiritual no man's land. Nothingness may be tenable for a generation, but one can't build a dynasty on it.'

But that was not the only ironic part of the situation. Stevie said to me: 'You know what you are, Ducks, a sort of emotional catalyst. You arrive with this heavenly boy, Troy, and presto, you have found a husband for Rocky. You meet up with Otto, and before you know it, you've found a husband for Grace. Perhaps you can do the same for me.'

It wouldn't have surprised me if I had. I only had to show an interest in someone for him to fall into the arms of the nearest woman. I wasn't at all sure that if Otto had proposed to me, I would have been disposed to accept, for he seemed too young and small, and made me feel large. I imagined that we would eventually look like a pair from a McGill postcard, but that notwithstanding I felt terribly pained at the course which events had actually taken. I kept telling myself that I had no grievance either with Otto or Grace. I had no claims on the one, or against the other, and I was – or at least I told myself that I should have been – happy for both, but yet I could neither face them, nor anyone else, and I committed a sort of semi-suicide.

It is useful in such a situation to have money. I went to Rome and blew a good part of Uncle Willie's legacy on a completely new outfit in an impossibly expensive shop. My hair at the time was shoulder-length. I had it cut short, almost cropped. I am not sure if my new outfit and hairstyle actually suited me, but when I looked in the mirror, I saw a different person, which was all that I wanted.

But having done that, I wasn't at all sure what to do next: the matter, as such things often are, was settled for me. When I got back to 'West Wynds', I found a letter waiting for me, offering me a job as Assistant Professor of Economics at Hurstfield University, near Chicago.

I had applied for the job almost nine months previously and had been invited to meet the head of the department, a white-haired figure with floppy jowls, in a London hotel. He was sunk into a chair, mopping his brow and talking of jet lag, and hardly seemed to be aware that I was in the room with him. I wasn't invited to any further interview, received no further communication and had concluded that that was the end of that.

The offer was almost the answer to my prayers. I accepted at once, and a few weeks later I received a letter with the printed heading: FROM THE DESK OF THE PROFESSOR OF ENGLISH, written in a small crabbed hand, welcoming me to Hurtsfield, advising me of the joys awaiting me, and warning me of some of the perils. For a moment I thought that by some dreadful error I had applied for and been given a job in the wrong faculty, until I looked down at the signature and found it was from one J. R. K. Reed, otherwise Weedy.

The thought that I would have Weedy as a colleague did not cause me to miss a heart-beat, on the other hand it was nice to know that I would have at least one acquaintance in what would be an entirely new world.

I flew straight to Chicago, and he was there at the airport to greet me together with a member of the economics faculty. I hardly recognized him. He had filled out, his face had become rounder, his eyes brighter, and he had lost some hair and his hang-dog expression.

He took me out to dinner the next evening.

'You're going to go down big here,' he said. 'Your name alone is an asset. Most of the people round here originate from the Baltic States and your thesis has been selling like hot cakes – and, of course, it's going to be a set book. I'm no economist, but I'm tempted to use it in my English course, it's so beautifully written. All my experience of economists, social scientists and, indeed, unsocial scientists, is that they are semi-literate, either because they lack the capacity to communicate or because they are afraid that, if they write intelligible English, people may discover that they have nothing to say.'

He was right about the impact of my book, for although something like sixty students had enrolled for my course, the number attending my lectures was over a hundred, and I was frequently invited to appear on local radio and television.

Unmarried members of the faculty lived in a block of flats, rather like an hotel, on the campus. There was a restaurant on the ground floor and a swimming-pool in the basement. My flat consisted of a sitting-room, bedroom, study, small kitchen and a large bathroom, and I enjoyed a degree of comfort I had never known in my life.

I had a number of graduate students, one of whom was preparing a thesis on the Latvian timber trade and I was asked to be his supervisor. He was short, with broad shoulders and short reddish hair, which stood up like porcupine quills. His name was Kreiger. He was a bright student, with a good analytical mind, but a little over-zealous, and he tended to call on me at all hours of the day and most hours of the night to discuss some issue which puzzled him, or some discovery which seemed to contradict the available wisdom on the subject. I had warned him to beware of 'discoveries', for they were generally based on misapprehension; as a result, almost every time he chanced upon something new he would be at my door and I finally had to put it to him that if the world had waited goodness knows how many million years to hear of his discoveries, it could possibly wait another few, at which he collapsed in a flood of tears. I wiped his face and made him coffee, but he would not be comforted till I put an arm round him. He began to nuzzle my breasts like an infant looking for his mother's milk and, before I knew what he was doing, he had unbuttoned my blouse, heaved one of my breasts out of its holder and was sucking my nipple. His tongue was on the rough side, and I didn't care for the smell of whatever it was he put on his hair, but it was otherwise not an unpleasant sensation.

He grew bolder in the course of subsequent visits – which I limited to two a week – and I ended up conducting tutorials in bed.

In the meantime Weedy began displaying a degree of virility which I had not thought he harboured. He had a sizeable house in its own grounds a few miles from the campus, which struck me as extraordinarily spacious for a mere professor, and he also had living-in help, and I said that the English department must be paying extravagant salaries.

'They pay so little', he said, 'that I'd be embarrassed to tell you what I get.'

'But the house, the grounds, your servants.'

'Well, fortunately my mother was killed in a car crash a few years ago. Had she lived to a ripe old age she would no doubt have cut me out of her will, but she died intestate so that I inherited a fortune, which has confirmed my faith in natural justice.'

I did not sleep with him the first time we went out, but the second time he prepared a meal so elaborate, with wines so superb, that I felt it would have been churlish not to do so. His performance was not quite in the Otto or Hughie class, but it was more than adequate, and I found my stay in America satisfying in more ways than one.

'We're fortunate in Hurstfield,' said Weedy. 'It's a backwater, so that it's the sort of place the trendies avoid, and it's untouched by the turmoil which has shaken other universities. The fees are high, grants are few, and most of the students here have to earn their keep and they work too hard to get into mischief. This is not California, thank God, or even the Ivy League. You can measure the stability and tranquillity of a campus by the hair count: I'd guess that we have fewer beards and shorter hair in Hurstfield than in any other university of equal size in America.'

He was, as far as I was concerned, touching on the one

great disadvantage of the place. One felt the world was passing one by. What was more to the point, I missed my family and 'West Wynds' more than I imagined. Stevie wrote to me every few weeks, but from the others I heard hardly anything at all.

'Once people start having children their lives become too full for correspondence,' she wrote, 'at least if my experience is anything to go by. You're a good letter-writer for the time being, but wait till you're married and your correspondence will be reduced to Christmas cards.' She had little news to impart apart from the fact that Vida had found herself a 'not-so-young young man'.

When Vida wrote she made no reference to any such liaison. I asked Stevie for further details, and she wrote back:

'His name is Norbert, which should tell you something about him. He is well kempt, with a small black beard and large glasses, and wears well-cut suits and a waistcoat like your father. I gather he's an accountant and I believe he's very, very kosher. But what, WHAT, if anything, is happening to you, and by happening, I mean HAPPENING? It is good to hear that you are making progress in your work. I have never had any doubt that one day you will become a fully fledged professor, but these are trivialities. What I really want to know is how is LIFE treating you – if at all?'

I thought if I mentioned Weedy it might give her the wrong idea. I was, by now, spending most weekends in his house, but was not unhappy to return to my own flat and my own books and papers on Sunday nights; nor was the thought of having young Kreiger between my legs from time to time entirely displeasing. Perhaps I was too promiscuous to accept the possibility of a stable relationship, though there was one married couple (with two young children) of whom it was said that they slept with everyone on campus and sometimes came to bed with each other by accident. I could not claim to be a believer in the sanctity of marriage, but I did regard marriage as a form of resignation and I wasn't ready to resign – at least not yet. In any case, nobody had as yet given me cause to resign. Weedy was by now regarded as my regular escort and, if he or I were invited to a party, we were generally invited as a couple. Weedy was content, and I was not discontent, with the arrangement.

Then came the summer. I said I was going back to England for a couple of months. Weedy said he would also be in England, and for a painful moment I didn't know how to react. Should I invite him to 'West Wynds'? He had, of course, stayed there before, but everyone regarded him as one of Vesta's lame ducks. What would they think if I came back with him now? He was not the Weedy that he was then, but did he represent the best that America had to offer?

There was the widow of a former president of the university called Mrs Sokol, who lived in a large house on the campus and regarded herself, and was generally regarded, as the matriarch of the university. She kept a motherly eye on all single members of the faculty and, wherever possible, tried to get the single paired. She began by trying to introduce me to Weedy and, when she found that we had already met, she thought her work was done. But then as term succeeded term and she noticed no startling developments in our relationship, she took him aside to ask what, if anything, was happening.

'I think you'll have to ask the young lady,' he said, upon which I was summoned to her presence, offered coffee and her own home-made ginger biscuits, and asked what I thought of Weedy.

'A fine scholar and a nice man,' I said, 'but what makes you ask?'

'My dear,' she said, 'you're far, far too clever to ask that sort of question. But can I ask you another? It's a rather personal, and perhaps even an impertinent question, but I'm an old woman and I think we old women should be forgiven for not minding our business, don't you?'

I waited for her question before answering.

'We may be fairly far from the East coast, and even further from the West, and, as I said, I *am* an old woman, but I do know what is going on in this world – to my sorrow – and I am aware that there are young ladies who, how shall I put it, are not interested in men –'

'And what you want to know is whether I'm a lessie.'

'A what?'

'A lesbian.'

'You do have a way of getting to the point. Are you?'

'Not yet, but I'm willing to try anything once. Is there anyone in particular you would like me to meet?' After which I was barred from chez Sokol. I told Weedy about the exchange and he said:

'She finds it difficult to understand why you and I aren't married.'

'Do you suffer from the same difficulty?'

'It would seem to be the most sensible thing to do, don't you think?'

'Is that a proposal?'

'Yes, I suppose it is.'

'You don't seem to be sure.'

'I hesitate about everything, you should know that.'

'In which case I hope you'll forgive me if I hesitate before giving a reply.'

I suppose if there had been an equivalent of the Samaritans for people contemplating marriage (which perhaps there should be), he would have phoned them that night.

When I met him the next day he looked as if he had spent a sleepless night, and he said to me:

'It strikes me that I have been singularly ungallant. Would you like to marry me?'

I almost said yes there and then, for I had only that morning received a letter from Vida to tell me that she was about to become engaged and it would have been nice to cable back: CONGRATULATIONS. ME TOO, but that did not strike me as a good enough reason for rushing into marriage. If Stevie could turn down Arnold at forty, I could turn down Weedy at twenty-six. Not that he was unattractive, but I hadn't even had a Nick in my life as an excuse for turning him down. In fact the main reason I felt I couldn't say yes was precisely because I hadn't yet had my Nick. Grace used to insist that there was no such thing as ecstasy, but she had found it more than once. I had had my Callum, perhaps I should have been content with that, except that I had loved my Callum only when he was unattainable – attained and he wasn't Callum. I recalled the words of Byron: 'In her first passion, woman loves her lover. In all others all she loves is love.' Perhaps I was an incurable romantic, and I promised myself that I would seek a cure in the course of the summer, when I would be returning home.

'There's no hurry,' he said, 'take your time.' He saw me off at the airport, gave me a peck on the cheek and walked off without a backward glance. His walk was hurried, but it was the hurried walk of an anxious man rather than a purposeful one, as if he had left something on the gas – which may have been precisely what he had done. His shoulders were slightly hunched and his head was slightly on one side. It was, I thought, a sad back, and I wanted to run after him to tell him that I had, after all, decided to marry him. By the time I reached London I wished I had done so, if only to get the matter out of the way. I hated indecision. Yet the moment I saw Vida I was glad that I hadn't, for she had the glow that I was seeking. The sensation I was looking for was difficult to define, but I recognized it the moment I saw it in others, and Vida shone with it.

I remembered Norbert, or Norrie, as she called him, as soon as she introduced me. He had been at Cambridge in my year, a quiet, unassuming student, who I recalled mainly because of his well-tailored suits.

They were married two months later in a north-west London synagogue before a vast congregation. Vida asked me if I would be maid of honour and I agreed without knowing fully what was involved. I found myself on the great day in a long canary-yellow dress, with a small bunch of posies in my gloved hands, trying to keep five or six bridesmaids – likewise in canary-yellow, though in tulle rather than satin – in line, like a mother hen trying to keep her chicks in order.

And then there was one. Stevie drove me back to 'West Wynds'. I was glad of her company, though I was not too happy with the way she was beginning to regard me as a contemporary. I was, at twenty-six, exactly half her age, but she seemed to feel that I was reliving her experience and she tried to comfort me with stories of her contemporaries who had married, but had separated or, worse, were still chained to one another. I felt tempted to interrupt her with the news that I was on the brink of marriage myself – except, of course, that I wasn't – and I wondered how many nieces had rushed into marriage in order to silence garrulous aunts. In one respect, though, we were alike: if Stevie had merely wanted a husband, she could have married a dozen times (or so she assured me, and I had no reason to disbelieve her). I couldn't quite say the same for myself, but here was a man, perhaps a year or two older than I, fairly presentable, some might even say good-looking, a university professor in a fairly respectable university, and with private means. He hadn't exactly gone down on his knees to me, but he had asked me to marry him (after a fashion) so that I could claim, like Stevie, that my spinsterhood was voluntary rather than enforced.

I didn't even mention Weedy. Why didn't I? Because I didn't really want to deprive her of the comfort she drew from the fact that, for the moment at least – and a wedding is a painful moment – she had a companion in her spinsterhood, and because I should imagine she still had the vision of Weedy she first received when Vesta brought him down from Oxford. Stevie often irritated me, annoyed me and sometimes even bored me, but I was fond of her and I knew that she was fond of me, and to have mentioned that I was even having a liaison with Weedy would not only have lowered me in her esteem, but she would have felt I was letting the whole family down. She thought I was special and would not have been happy to see me settle for anyone less than special, and special Weedy was not. Vesta had, after all, married the heir to a baronetcy, and goodness knows how many acres; Rocky had married a financial wizard; and even if Vida had settled for someone fairly commonplace, her religious beliefs had limited her choice. I could do better. Damn it, I would. It was, oddly enough, not his face – which was fairly attractive – which had confirmed me in my decision, but his back: it was the back of a broken man.

I sat down to explain my decision in a letter so that I could have the matter out of the way before I returned to Hurstfield, but when I drove into the village to post it I changed my mind. Uncle Willie had about a dozen precepts which he was fond of quoting over and over again, and the one I remembered best was: 'Never act on a decision made late at night.' I would wait till the morning before I posted it, but when the morning came I didn't post it. I still have the letter.

My second year in America was the year of the great freeze. The snows descended early in January and remained on the ground till March, and during all this while the skies were leaden and a shrill, biting wind whirled across the open plain on which the campus was built. There were no hills or woodlands to break the force of the blast and one walked doubled up against the wind, so that by the end of March I found it difficult to straighten up. When the snows first came, the campus, with its red-brick library and lecture halls and its white timber houses, looked like a Christmas card. We revelled in it. We made snowmen and had snow fights and took photographs, but long, long before the thaw set in one's soul began to ache for the sight of lawn and greenery and flowers and sunshine.

When Christmas came, almost everyone on campus vanished like migratory birds to the warmer climates of the south. Weedy offered to take me to Florida, but I had been commissioned to write a book on the Baltic States which I had promised to deliver by the summer. I had made a desultory start and the untrammelled three weeks of the Christmas holiday would give me the chance to get my teeth into it, though another reason why I didn't go was that I wanted to see how I felt living in a place like Hurstfield without Weedy.

I didn't like it at all, but that may have been due to the fact that I had deprived myself not only of Weedy's company but of all human contact. Then one glorious day Callum 'phoned. He was in New York for a few days – would I like to see him? Would I like to see him! I changed into a frock, put on my new fur coat (which I had bought with the advance on the book), and was on the next plane to New York.

We had drinks and went to the theatre, and returned to the Waldorf, where he was staying, for a late meal. As we were going up in the lift to his room, I caught a glimpse of myself standing beside him in the mirror and we did not look at all an improbable pair. Perhaps my fur coat had something to do with it – or maybe my title of Assistant Professor. I was also approaching an age in which only women grew old and men seemed ageless. And he was as formidable in bed as he had ever been, but that may have been due to the fact that he was drinking less. He had had two whiskies before the meal, two brandies after, and but one bottle of wine with the meal itself which, for someone with his intake, verged on total abstinence. Had he proposed to me that night, or the following morning, I would have accepted like a shot. I wouldn't have at all minded being the second Lady Roscoe, even though it would have meant that I'd be my sister's step-mother, but there was no chance that he would propose to me, and as I lay staring at the ceiling in my post-coital wakefulness (while he snored like tearing canvas), I toyed with the idea of proposing to him. I had a feeling he might have accepted, for one of his most appealing features was an irrepressible streak of gallantry; he would have found it difficult to say no to a lady or, at least, to the daughter of a friend, though he would probably have fobbed me off with some excuse like: 'What me? I'm sixty and I've only got one arm. A girl like you could marry a man of thirty, with two.' To which I would have said: 'You've got two balls, which is all that counts.'

In the end I did not propose, but the encounter did for me what Nick had done for Stevie, it settled one question: I could not and would not marry Weedy. Yet when he told me that he had become friendly with a divorcee whom he had met in Miami, I received the news with dismay; my safety-net had come apart. Here was I struggling with my conscience on how to let him know that I could not after all accept his proposal of marriage (for the time being at least), while in fact the proposal was no longer on offer.

'Is she the right woman for you?' I asked. 'How old is she, what does she do?'

'I can answer the second and third question,' he said, 'as for the first, it remains to be seen.' She was ten years older than him, a psychotherapist, which suggested that she probably was the right woman. When I eventually met her I was quite taken aback by her striking good looks, though on closer examination her complexion was so smooth, while her arms and hands were so wrinkled, that I suspected she had had a face-lift and was possibly even twenty years older, but they seemed very happy together and I was very happy for him. I was rather less happy for myself.

If the meeting with Callum helped to settle one matter, it had an unsettling effect in other ways. Leaning against him I smelt, or thought I could smell, the hay and straw of England, the trees and hedgerows, and the soft, moist air. It was, he told me, every bit as cold in England as it was in America, but that was not the England that came wafting back to me. The Hurstfield beyond the university was a parking lot rather than a town. The nearest centre of civilization was Chicago, a two-hour drive across a treeless, hedgeless, featureless wilderness, which could look quite striking in the spring when the corn was green, and at harvest, with great combines advancing majestically across the fields like galleons in sail. But the winter – or at least that particular winter – was so endless and severe that it banished all memories of spring or summer, and one felt the sun would never shine again on this godforsaken wilderness.

In March I had to make the crucial decision whether to stay on for a third year or not. If I did not, where would I go and what would I do? I had been contemplating vacancies in other universities – including one or two in Britain – and found none which were particularly attractive, but I did seem to have acquired a facility for writing. I received a commission to write a third book before I had even delivered my second, and I could write anywhere, as long as I was within reasonable reach of a good library.

While I was thus dithering (or possibly because I was known to be dithering thus), I was summoned by the head of the faculty for what I presumed, from the beaming expression on his face, to be good news. And in a way it was. I would be raised from the level of Assistant Professor to that of Associate Professor, with a small rise in salary, and I would be given tenure, which meant that the job was mine for life. I should have been gratified by this unexpected advance in my fortunes, but it helped to settle the issue, for it was clear that if I did not decide to leave there and then, I would indeed remain in Hurstfield for life.

And one could tell at a glance those who had reconciled themselves to a lifetime in Hurstfield. The junior staff, people of about my age or even older, still had the bearing and stride of individuals, who thought they were getting somewhere; but those with tenure, people like Weedy, had the resigned air of men who had taken the measure of their circumstances and were learning or had learned to live with them, people who hadn't made it and knew they weren't going to make it and who sought and, in some cases found, consolation in honorific title – Professor, Dean, head of this or that school – minor perks and illicit liaisons. What, I wondered, did failures do to compensate themselves for failure before adultery was invented?

In the meantime I was discovering that writing was more satisfying even than sex – or was I growing old? But the fact was that for my last six months at Hurstfield I was leading what was an almost celibate existence and it didn't trouble me a bit. Weedy was preparing himself for marriage; Kreiger had had a nervous breakdown and had left the university, and I was on my own. I was able to complete opus two on time and, about a month after I had sent off the manuscript, I received a cable from my publisher to say that it was the greatest thing since the Resurrection, if not before, by which I took him to mean (I had been in America long enough to take the measure of American enthusiasm) that he was reasonably satisfied with it. What was rather more gratifying was the fact that he was prepared to offer a generous advance on another book. With two such commissions in my kit, I felt there was no need for me to look around for another job. I would return to England and set up shop as a woman of letters.

11
Rustic Idyll

I had planned to get myself a small flat in London, but father thought I was crazy even to think about it.

' "West Wynds" is almost empty. The girls are all married, Josh is at Harrow, Mrs Donelly has left, there's only Tilly and me. It's not as if you have to be in London, and when you do, you're an hour away by train or car. And you can have all the space you want: a room, two rooms, a whole suite. Quite frankly, I'd feel offended if you lived anywhere else.'

I had rarely heard him express himself so forcibly on any topic and, when I arrived at 'West Wynds', I thought I could see why.

His marriage had never been idyllic, but that was because he seemed to fear intimacy of any sort and he liked to have a buffer of children and friends between him and Tilly. At first we crowded the house, but then we went off one by one until he was left with Josh, and, as Josh was a good bit younger than any of us, he was around for quite a time. I thought he might be around for good, and was surprised when they sent him to Harrow, but I suppose they felt that people in their position could do no less. And now they were on their own, amid the many rooms and winding corridors of 'West Wynds'.

At first Tilly had tried to busy herself in county politics and to cut a figure in county society, but she had been rebuffed. Father was, or seemed to be, content enough with the mere role of farmer, but Tilly had been content with the role of farmer's wife for as long as she believed it might lead – in social terms at least – to something higher.

She once appeared in a glossy magazine in animated conversation with lady something-or-other at a hunt ball and that was about as far as she got. What I think had happened was that both father and Tilly had depended on the Roscoes for their entry into country society, but the Roscoes, though titled and rich, were not really part of it. Their money was new, their title was not old, and Callum was too much of a maverick to be fully accepted. In any case, it seemed to me that once Sophie had settled in as Lady Roscoe and had got the measure of her neighbours, she was not particularly interested in acceptance. She was prepared to fall in with their ways – hence the Grace–Vesta coming-out ball – but had very little time for their company. 'The men talk of cattle,' she said, 'and the women of the expense of everything, and both complain about what the government is doing to the country, and that's about it. Where are the Roger de Coverleys or the Emmas or even the Lady Bracknells?' I suspect her boredom with country life was one of the reasons why she had left Callum, and once the Roscoes had broken up, father and Tilly lost their link with what Tilly, at least, regarded as the higher England. She now spent most of her time at home, morose, fractious and embittered, and she made no attempt to hide her look of resentment when I appeared.

Father said she had been ill, without specifying the nature of her illness. She had certainly lost weight. Her face was thin, even haggard, and her long fingers were skeletal. There had been times previously when I had disliked her, but now I was almost afraid of her.

I was anxious to keep out of her way as much as possible and to get down to my books in earnest. Father had given me two rooms for my own private use, and at table one evening I asked if I could have a communicating door built between them. At this she interjected:

'At whose expense?'

Father seemed more taken aback than I was.

'At mine, of course,' he said.

'Do you know what these things cost?'

'I've got some money,' I said. 'I shall be quite happy to pay for it.'

'It's not only the money. You already have one communicating door with the bathroom. If you have another with the room next door you'll have more doors than a French farce. Don't forget you're not the only child in the family. Josh will eventually want a suite of his own, the others are often here at weekends, to say nothing of Stevie and sundry other relatives and friends. You can't have three rooms for your exclusive use just like that.'

'She wouldn't be having three rooms,' said father, 'she would be having two, and I already told her she could.'

'You told her? You never said anything about it to me.'

'I didn't feel there was any need to.'

That did it. She gave him a venomous look and flew out of the room. We had dinner in silence, which is what I expected. She was not down for breakfast the next morning, and I was not in for lunch, but when we met again for dinner the silence persisted and I wondered for how long it would continue. When the meal was over I said to father,

'You know this can't go on, I'd better leave.'

'You're not leaving, and that's that. Give me a rough sketch of what you want done and I'll ask the builder to come in and have a look at it.'

'I don't want to cause any difficulties.'

'You're not causing any difficulties, they've always been there.'

I had arranged to go away for a few days, and he said he might have a happy surprise for me when I got back.

'You're not going to have the builders in, are you?'

'Why not?'

'Because Tilly may have a point. I don't know how long I'm going to stop here and I can't expect you to start knocking holes in walls for my benefit.'

'I'm not doing it for your benefit. I happen to like your suggestion and want to bring these rooms together into a suite.'

'I don't think you should.'

'Now don't *you* start telling me what to do with my own house.'

Rocky had acquired a house in Chelsea (she had another by the sea) which, according to all reports, was the eighth wonder of the world and I decided, after some hesitation, to spend a weekend with her.

It was like the set of a Hollywood musical to look at and much too dazzling to live with. As a matter of fact it did not quite go with Rocky, who romped about the place in a floppy jumper and faded jeans – though she did change for dinner.

'It's the last word in vulgarity,' she said, 'but I love to make a splash. Damn it, what's money for?'

'New money,' I said, 'but your money is fairly old, isn't it?'

'Nothing of the sort. Troy is to all intents and purposes a self-made man. The few thousands we got from father and his parents was so much petty cash. He handles millions. In fact I handle fortunes myself.'

She had her own investment portfolio, which she handled quite independently of Troy and which had quadrupled in value in the few years since she married.

'No, my dear,' she said, 'we are decidely *nouveau riche*, and it's only us upstarts who know how to enjoy our wealth.'

Here was I, the economist with a BA and a PhD, who, comparatively speaking, did not have two pennies to rub together. She hadn't even finished school and had accumulated a fortune. So much for academic training.

While I enjoy having money and spending it, I find it extremely tiresome as a topic, but Rocky, who in the past, could be depended upon for a ready flow of malicious gossip, didn't seem to be interested in anything else. I had expected her to sit up when I told her about my exchange with Tilly, but all she had to say was, 'I always thought that woman was a bitch,' and led the conversation back to money.

Troy's conversation was less limited, but he had become plump and pompous and gave the impression that he was on first-name terms with half the Cabinet. Moreover, I was not amused by the frequent jokes he and Rocky made about father, especially as father spoke of him with great pride as a genius. He had taken over father's investment portfolio, had doubled its value in a matter of months, and it had continued to appreciate, if at a less dramatic rate, ever since.

'Your father', said Troy, 'was brought up to believe that any share whose movements are actually discernible to the naked eye should be shunned as adventurous, and he rarely touched a company which had been in business for less than two hundred years. Hudson Bay, that was his sort of thing. Woolworth, Great Universal, too volatile. If it weren't for me, he could have foundered by now. The farm, as you know, is losing money. It's his shares which keep him in clover.'

I noticed that when I was speaking, he wasn't paying attention to anything I said, but had his eyes fixed firmly on my cleavage. I wore a low-cut dress which hadn't been particularly daring when I bought it, but I had put on a good bit of weight since, and the food Rocky served was hardly calculated to reduce it. I wasn't, to be honest, quite sure what the food was, for it was all chilled and served on floating beds of ice; the only things I recognized were the caviar at the beginning and the strawberries in brandy at the end. A white-coated manservant brought the dishes and cleared them away. The third baronet Roscoe, with all his acres, did not live in such style.

Troy became less pompous as the evening progressed, or possibly seemed less pompous because the wine was abundant. Rocky became tipsy and giggly.

'Troy doesn't like it when I drink because I make a fool of myself.'

'You don't make a fool of yourself, my love,' he said, 'but you become impenetrable.'

'Im – what?' I asked.

'He means in bed,' said Rocky. 'Isn't it the same with everybody?'

Troy turned to me: 'Is it the same with you?'

'I haven't thought about it.'

He lit a cigar. 'Would you like' – puff-puff – 'to try?'

The idea was fairly appealing, but I wondered if Rocky had heard. Was this how they wound up every meal?

'I would like to think about it.'

Rocky slumped forward, with her head on her arms, asleep.

'She wouldn't mind, you know.'

'But I might.'

'Beautiful girl, your sister, quick, bright, but sex isn't her strong point. It is yours.' He stubbed out his cigar and hurried over to my side of the table and put his hand on my thigh. 'If there was an index for orgasms like there is for shares, you'd come near the top.'

'Only *near* the top?'

'*At* the top. Look at me. With Rocky I'd need splints to get it this hard.'

I rose with my face averted, rushed to my room and dived on my bed convulsed with laughter. A moment later there was a knock on my door.

'Ducks, I didn't upset you, did I? I hope I didn't upset you, did I – Ducks?'

'No, you didn't.'

'Promise?'

'Promise.'

'Ducks?'

'Yes.'

'Can I come in?'

I didn't know what to say, for I was moved more by pity than passion.

'I'm very tired, Troy, and want to go to sleep.'

'Tomorrow maybe.'

'Maybe tomorrow.'

'God bless. You're a good girl, Ducks.'

When I came downstairs the next morning, Troy had left for his office and Rocky was still asleep. I left a note to thank her for her hospitality and left.

There were various things I had to see to in London and when I got back to 'West Wynds' late on Monday night the household was asleep. I let myself in quietly, unpacked, got into my nightie and went into the kitchen to make myself a cup of tea. I heard the creak of floor boards above me and a minute later father appeared.

'I thought you kept farmer's hours,' I said. He looked bleary-eyed and haggard.

'There's something I think you should know,' he said. 'Tilly's gone.'

The cup of tea fell from my grasp and crashed to the floor.

'When?'

'This morning. She's been on the brink of doing so a dozen times during this past year.'

'So what finally made her go?'

'The builder. The moment he came in, she walked out.'

I was aghast.

'There was no hurry, you know. It could have waited. I could have worked somewhere else.'

'No, no, on the contrary. I was happy at the thought of someone in the family wanting to stay here. You should know me by now. I may be slow in reaching decisions, but I am not slow to act on them. In any case the builders were already here on another job.'

'Where has she gone to?'

'I've no idea, but no doubt I will hear from her lawyer, and no doubt it will cost me a packet. But in the meantime, my dear, you are châtelaine of this mansion.' With which he kissed me on the head and went to bed.

In an odd way I was sorry. I should have liked to like Tilly and, on the odd occasions when she went out of her way to be approachable, I liked her very much, but at most other times she was on guard, distant, abrasive, brittle, though that may have been because – with the possible exception of Vesta – none of us in our heart of hearts felt that she was nearly good enough for father. We were all, in our different ways, critical of father, and there was much to be critical of, but we felt that with all his faults, he was basically a good sort, gallant, chivalrous, generous, a gentleman, whereas Tilly, with all her qualities, was never quite a lady.

The following Sunday, Vesta, Vida and Rocky came down to 'West Wynds' for a sisterly get-together or, as Vida called it, a witches' coven.

Vesta thought that we were all being unfair to Tilly (she would), that we were snobbish and couldn't suffer the thought of an ex-governess presuming to act as father's wife. 'A governess isn't a kitchen-maid, you know, and even if she was, she would deserve to be treated with greater understanding than you've shown.'

'You don't know what she's been like,' I said. 'Ask father. She's only been away a week and he's already a different man.'

'Why did he marry her in the first place, I wonder?' said Rocky.

'She was a striking and intelligent woman whom any man would have been glad to marry,' said Vesta. 'He loved her. And he'll miss her, you'll see. I wonder if one could bring them together again.'

'You dare,' I said.

'Do you think he'll marry again?' asked Vida.

'Never,' said Rocky. 'Twice bitten, thrice shy.'

'Wouldn't it be nice if he married Sophie?' I said. 'I've half a mind to write to Grace about it.'

'Why write to Grace?' said Vida. 'Vesta could speak to Robin.'

'You're all being very silly,' said Vesta.

'Not only that,' said Rocky, 'you're out of touch. Sophie already has a boyfriend.'

'I'm beginning to find this conversation a bit much,' said Vesta rising, and we quickly changed the subject.

Father had been out during the day, but in the evening he joined us for dinner. It was seventeen or eighteen years since we had been together like this in a Tilly-less household, and we almost felt as if the intervening years had not happened.

I had planned to start on my new book as soon as I settled in but, now that I found myself in charge of the household, I had to postpone any such plans. In any case the builders were in my room putting in communicating doors, bookshelves and so on, and I couldn't start before they were out. It took them nearly a month to put in two doors and a wall of shelving, by which time I was not disposed to start on the book at all.

It didn't take me long to learn how to run the household. Mrs Doyle from the village came in every day. She prepared lunch and dinner and saw to the cleaning, so that there was very little to do. But Tilly had also helped in the dairy and it took me rather longer to become expert in its mysteries, but once I had learned the craft, I found it rather more exciting than the Baltic States. I turned my mind to my book only in the evenings and I was happily surprised by what I could pack into a day. It was not that I had found new energies, for I was always fairly energetic, but my activities complemented one another.

I rose at about five in the morning, had a coffee and toast, and was in the milking-parlour by five-thirty. We now had one of the most up-to-date units in the county, a carousel, so that instead of moving from cow to cow to wash down the udders and fix on the milking units, the cow, so to speak, came to me, moving slowly on the merry-go-round. Hughie used to have pop music on, but I changed that to Vivaldi and Mozart, and I think the cows preferred it. They seemed to swing their tails in time with the music and, what was more to the point, gave slightly more milk.

We used to have a milking engine and, when I was younger, we would wake to its spluttery chugg-chugg, chugg-chugg. The new machinery was almost soundless and the loudest noise was the plop, plop of the cow pats, which came in rapid succession with each cow seeming to set the others off. I loved the smell of the cow pats in the straw and of the cattle feed, and of the raw milk, and even of the disinfectant with which I washed down the udders, and the sight of the cows steaming on cold winter mornings.

One hardly saw the milk itself, for it flowed along pipes straight into a refrigerated tank from which it was collected by tanker later in the morning, I would help clean out the milking-parlour and steam down the utensils, and then go home for a shower ready for a second breakfast at half-past nine, by which time the post and the papers had arrived. It was my favourite time of day. Mrs Doyle prepared an abundant meal of sausages, kidneys, sweetbread and eggs, which we ate in leisurely fashion, with papers propped up against the tea and coffee pots. It was then also that we went over the various things that had to be seen to that day. I had learned to drive a tractor and was able to perform a host of small jobs around the farm, such as harrowing or muck-spreading, which kept me busy till lunch. Father used to have a fairly substantial meal at lunch-time to keep Tilly company, but now he preferred a sandwich and a beer, which we either had at home or at The Dog and Duck, a pleasantly ramshackle pub near the end of the farm lane.

Mrs Doyle had dinner ready for us on a hotplate in the evening and we ate about six. Father liked wine with the meal and I felt tempted to join him, but I preferred to have my head clear for my writing and I would spend three or four hours at the typewriter before turning in for the night. I rarely had more than five hours sleep, but it was as much as I needed.

The cows – Thelma, Bella, Cleo, Dinah, Elsa, Freda and the rest – became real people to me, and I sometimes even found myself in conversation with them. The one chore which troubled me a bit was the artificial insemination. It was so cold and unceremonious, a mere matter of poking what looked like a drinking straw up their vaginas. I felt that cows, or at least our cows, deserved something better. Artificial insemination was less awkward and messy, and infinitely less expensive, than keeping a bull, but it didn't seem right to me – all the pains of motherhood without the compensations. Father said there was no room for sentimentality in stock-breeding, but I felt that milk produced by such methods could not be nearly as tasty or nourishing as milk produced in the old way, and that one way or another nature would have her revenge. Still, the calving season was exciting, and for the first time I began to understand why so many maiden ladies I had met were content with their situation, for they nearly all lived on the land and were engaged in one way or another with agriculture. It was not necessary to give birth oneself to be fulfilled; one only had to be a party to the process of regeneration and farm life gave ample scope for that. When I was twenty-six or twenty-seven, I thought I would kill myself if I was thirty and still single, but now, at twenty-nine, I approached my next birthday with equanimity. Perhaps it was resignation, but I genuinely felt that these were the happiest years of my life. I don't know if I would have been as content had I been engaged in farming and nothing else, but farming and writing taken together were the ideal occupations, for though both were in their different ways exacting, one turned from the plough to the pen with a refreshed mind.

I had been under the impression that rustic life predisposed one to the most basic of rustic pursuits and I feared that once I had settled in at 'West Wynds' I would reduce poor Hughie to a frazzle. But either because I was getting older or because I was too busy, our romps in the hay were infrequent, and my one regret was that I had not turned seriously to farming sooner. But time seemed to be gathering velocity like a train gathering speed. 'Unto everything its season,' especially on the farm, and the seasons turned with increasing rapidity, and one morning I woke up and I was thirty-two. The age was a significant one to me because I remembered a party which Stevie made for me when I was five, and I thought it would be nice if I could grow up to be like her, a grand and beautiful lady. She was thirty-two at the time and I still have a photo of the occasion, taken shortly after the war. And here I was, thirty-two. I didn't feel particularly old and I don't think I looked particularly old, and Hughie was kind enough to say to me after one brief encounter: 'Funny you shouldn't have a man, you're the best-looking of the sisters by far, and you've got more meat than any of them' – which gave me some idea what he meant by good looks.

I travelled very little during this period, which was in itself a measure of my contentment, and I was disinclined to go away even for weekends, though Vesta, Vida and Rocky all tugged at me to stay with them. I had not yet as much as set foot in Rocky's seaside place, with its tennis-courts, swimming-pool and sauna.

I would have liked to have seen Vesta rather more often than I did, but she kept having children at almost annual intervals and now had three of them. She looked wonderful with an infant at her breast, like a nordic Madonna, but I was amazed at the extent to which childbirth brought her down to earth and her talk was all of rashes and teething and breast-feeding and bottle-feeding. This changed as the children – two girls and a boy – grew older, yet though I was fond of my nieces and nephew, I was perhaps excessively on guard against becoming the Aunt Stevie of my generation.

Vida didn't talk about children, for she had none, but she couldn't stop talking about her attempts to have them. 'Be fruitful and multiply' was, apparently, the first of all the commandments, and when two years passed and she failed to bring forth, and showed no imminent signs of doing so, she and Norrie subjected themselves to an almost continuous succession of tests, but there was apparently nothing wrong with either of them. As I believe they were both virgins when they married, I asked if Norrie knew his way around, to which she retorted – a trifle infelicitously, I thought – 'You don't have to go to America to know where the Grand Canyon is.'

Rocky, to do her justice, never touched on the subject of children or childbirth, but then I couldn't imagine her being a mother, and I suspected that her innards were rather like her kitchens and bathrooms, all lined with ceramic tiles.

If I saw little of my sisters, I began to see rather more of my half-brother.

We adored him when he was small, because he was small and unexpected. We were all so much older than him and treated him as an animate doll, but as we grew older we felt rather ambivalent about him because we – or at least I – felt rather ambivalent about his mother, and also because he became large, importunate, podgy and tearful. He didn't talk, he whined, and I might have poked his pretty, little eyes out if they weren't half-obscured by his blubbery face. Childbirth had done something to Tilly: she was as indulgent as a mother as she had been strict as a governess, and she let him have the run of the house. The Miracle Child was turning into a monster and Rocky, who saw rather more of him than we did and suffered most from his tantrums, threatened to drown him in the village pond. What saved him from becoming utterly impossible was the fact that he suffered from frequent ailments, and Tilly regarded sleep as a panacea for them all. Up to about the time he was eight, the refrain which constantly echoed through the house was 'Shh, the child is sleeping.' It was possibly because he slept so much that he didn't seem all that wakeful even when he was awake, and if we, in our different ways, were all bright, he was downright thick, a fact which pained Tilly, for she took it as a reflection of her own intelligence. The house was filled with a constant succession of tutors, who coached him in English, arithmetic, French and even elocution – for he had developed something of a stutter – and somehow he managed to scrape into Harrow.

At first I took this to be a measure of the decline of one of England's foremost public schools, but Harrow wrought miracles in the boy. For a start he lost weight and out of the bulk there emerged a rather smart-looking lad with his mother's handsome features. He also lost his whiny, doleful manner, became almost amiable, and could engage in an intelligent conversation. I suppose he merely grew up, but as we only saw him at infrequent intervals, the changes seemed sudden and dramatic.

He was sixteen when Tilly and father separated, and his first remark was: 'Ah, well, that should put me on par with the rest of the chaps.' His mother had a flat in London, and he dutifully spent part of his holidays with her, but he spent most of his time in 'West Wynds'. He liked country life and, in particular, he had known the cows since they were born and was anxious to see how they were developing. He frequently helped me with the cows and in the dairy, and was good company. I once asked him if he planned to be a farmer himself.

'Well, it's something I haven't mentioned to anyone yet, but I rather think I should like to work on a kibbutz.'

He had been to Israel with father and Tilly for Grace's wedding, and had fallen in love with the place.

'One of the chaps in my house has a brother on a kibbutz. I spent a week with him, and it seemed to have only one drawback: they have no pasture for the cattle – all the feed is brought in. Otherwise it has everything. I'm going back this summer.'

'Does your mother know?'

'She does, and is not very happy about it, but I haven't told her that once I finish at Harrow I intend to go back for good.'

'She's not going to like that.'

'No, nor will father.'

'I dare say you'll grow out of it.'

'I somehow don't think I will, but they might both remarry by then so they'll be less preoccupied with me. It's awful being so much younger than the rest of you. When I was small I thought I had five mothers – six if one counts Mrs Donelly – and for years I felt like an only child.'

I also hoped that Tilly would remarry, for she was the one cloud to my otherwise sunny existence. For the time being she was keeping her distance, but they were not yet divorced and I had the unhappy feeling that if she ever took it in mind to resume her position as mistress of 'West Wynds', father would be too weak to refuse her. I wasn't even certain that he would want to refuse her. Stevie once told me that she had seen her crossing the road recently while she was driving through central London and she had been tempted to accelerate and run her over, to which I blurted out quite involuntarily: 'Oh, but why didn't you?' I felt that I would never be safe until she was exorcized, and one day I returned from work and found that my fears had assumed material shape. She was in the drawing-room talking to father.

She must have recovered from her illness, or perhaps she merely benefited from being away from father, for she looked stunning, steel sheathed in silk, and for the first time I began to wonder if I had a lesbian disposition, for I couldn't take my eyes off her. I couldn't imagine father refusing her anything, but it soon became clear that she had not returned to reclaim her position. Josh had finally announced his intention of settling on a kibbutz, and she had arrived for an emergency conference.

'I don't see how we can do anything to stop him,' said father. 'He'll be eighteen by the time he leaves, so he'll be his own master, and it's not as if I can disinherit him, for he's virtually disinheriting me. One of the reasons he's attracted to the kibbutz is that he wants to live in a moneyless society. Remove money and what authority have you got over a child?'

'There's such a thing as moral authority,' she retorted. 'You see far more of him than I do, you could have been more assertive.'

'But he only sprung this on me last week.'

'And you treated it as a *fait accompli*?'

'What else could I do? It's not as if he's running off to join the French Foreign Legion. He's going to a civilized country, among civilized people, and there's every likelihood that he'll lead a happy and useful life.'

'Can't I ever depend on you to back me up?' she said through clenched teeth.

And the Miracle Child had his way and went off to join a kibbutz in Israel. Grace was asked to keep a motherly eye on him and Tilly went off to sulk.

At about the same time I became aware of an increasing traffic in legal documents and legal-sized envelopes and the gigantic sheets of expensive stationery favoured by lawyers, as if the stationery used by ordinary mortals was too meagre to contain their expensive torrents of expensive words, and I took it that the machinery for a divorce was now at last in motion. This should have reassured me, but then I thought, if a divorce comes, can remarriage be far behind?

12
Atonement

Ever since Tilly had left 'West Wynds', I had harboured the dream that Sophie might take her place. I was not put out by Rocky's insistence that she already had a boyfriend, for Rocky believed that everybody had boyfriends; but now that I was securely established as châtelaine, I was not at all sure that I would welcome the intrusion of even someone as attractive and urbane as Sophie. Apart from other considerations I was afraid she would convert 'West Wynds' into a stately home and father into a stately person, and much of the farmland into parkland, but more than that, I feared she would disrupt my happy routine and put an end to the second breakfast, which I regarded as my golden hour. There was a certain relaxed atmosphere to the house and to the day. I couldn't define its exact elements, but I was happier now than I had been at any time in my adult life, and it was inevitable that a person as formidable as Sophie would bring changes, and change, as far as I was concerned, meant deterioration.

But time passed and it seemed to me that I was worrying about nothing, for father seemed to be as happy with his routines as I was with mine, and at his age – and after his experience – he must have been even more averse to change than I was. Then one Sunday as I was having lunch with Callum, he said to me:

'How would you like to have my wife as a mother?' I had just taken a mouthful of food and almost choked.

'What makes you ask?'

'Doesn't your old man tell you anything? He wants to

marry Soph.' He must have noticed my look of dismay, for he added quickly, 'Oh, it's all right, she wouldn't want to marry him, not unless he becomes a baronet or a knight, at least – which he might, for he's been giving away fortunes to all the right charities. Soph likes to be a lady.'

I thought of taking up the matter with father right away, but Grace was due on a visit (a shopping expedition in fact) the following week and I decided to wait till I spoke to her.

'Oh, mother would do anything for a title,' she confirmed, 'but honestly, I can't see her marrying your dad, affable and charming though he may be. He's too bland for her tastes and too Jewish.'

'Too Jewish? Father?'

'Well, he *is* a Jew, you know, and I think she's mortally afraid of being sucked back into the fold. She wasn't too happy about my marriage to Otto, even though he's a thoroughgoing atheist, and she was pained to hear us talking in Hebrew. "Have you forgotten your English?" she asked. "No," I said, "but I'm trying to learn Hebrew." Then we're fairly friendly with a religious family. They and their children were in our house with their little skull-caps on their heads, which I suspect gave her nightmares – and what with a Jew as a son-in-law, I don't think she would risk another as a husband.' All of which I found vaguely reassuring, but I was still afraid that even if they didn't marry, they might live in sin, and Sophie could still move in.

'You really don't know my mother if you think she could go in for that sort of thing. I wouldn't say she's a puritan, but she acts like one, and she would not be found living in open concubinage. In any case she and father aren't divorced, they're only separated. They might come together again.' All of which put my mind at rest, and I was able to turn my untroubled attention to my beloved cows.

One day my American publisher, who was on a visit to London, invited me to lunch. He loved Olde England and all things appertaining thereto, and we met at Simpsons in the Strand for a lunch of roast beef. It was Callum's favourite restaurant and I had eaten with him there a number of times. We had a couple of drinks in the bar before the meal – dry martinis, which was the most comforting habit I had picked up from my sojourn in America. We weren't in any particular hurry and, as we sat drinking and talking, we became aware of a commotion in another part of the building, with waiters rushing in all directions. A minute later I heard the sound of an ambulance approaching and, as we walked towards the dining-room, we were just in time to see the prostrate form of Callum being carried out on a stretcher. He had collapsed over lunch.

I rushed down the stairs and out into the street, stopped a cab and managed to get to the hospital immediately behind the ambulance. Callum had had a heart attack and was taken into the intensive care unit. I waited on a bench in the corridor and was joined half an hour later by Sophie. She had 'phoned Grace, who was catching the first available plane and expected to be in London by the morning. Robin and Vesta were on the way and we were joined a little later by father.

Sophie was allowed in to see him and came back to say he was still unconscious, and that they did not hold out much hope for him.

'It'll have to be a complete recovery or nothing,' she said. 'Callum will not be prepared to live the life of an invalid.'

He died during the night without regaining consciousness. He was sixty-three.

He was buried in the village churchyard next to his father. There was a large gathering of old soldiers who didn't look as if they had worn nearly as well as poor Callum, and although father was in black and in a bowler hat like them, he decidedly wasn't one of them. Neither for that matter was Robin, who towered a head above everybody else, eyes downcast, lips tight. Vesta, in black, her face very pale, looked like the figure of a youthful and benign death, and death in this instance had been benign, painless, swift and dignified. Callum would not have grown old gracefully. He had not even grown middle-aged with particular grace.

'A wasted life,' said Sophie. 'So much promise, so many advantages, so much ability, so much energy and all put to such little use. I think if he had been born penniless he might have done something with himself.'

'He was an excellent soldier, fearless, a natural leader of men,' said father, 'and with great presence of mind, even under stress.'

'The war was his finest hour,' Sophie agreed, 'but you cannot keep the world at war to keep the Callums of this world usefully employed. If you ask me his wartime experience rendered him unfit for anything else. He didn't have the patience to run the farm or the estate. "Everything takes years before you see any results," he complained, and he said to me only last week: "You know, if it wasn't for Robin and Grace, none of us would have been the worse off if a bullet had gone through my head." '

I was surprised at my self-possession. Sophie and Grace, Grace and Vesta, Vesta and Sophie were on each other's shoulders for hours on end. Vida and even Rocky both wept bitterly, but I did not shed a tear, and then, one afternoon about a week after he died, I was alone in the farm office when I was overwhelmed by a grief so intense that I thought I would choke. I staggered to my room, threw myself down on the bed and let loose a catharsis. I felt as if my body and soul were dissolving in tears. I must have cried myself to sleep. When I awoke it was dark, and I was shivering with cold. I didn't try to find out what time it was or if there was anyone else in the house. I washed my face, brushed my teeth, changed into my night-clothes, went into bed and fell asleep the moment my head touched the pillow. I was awakened by father.

'Hughie told me you weren't at milking either last night, or this morning. Are you all right?'

'What time is it?'

'Nearly ten.'

I had a shower, dressed and tried to have breakfast, but

could not eat. Father – although he didn't say so at the time – must have been startled by my appearance, for he called Grace to come over, and as soon as she appeared I began to cry again.

Nearly a month passed before I felt I was myself again, and even then I didn't look myself. I caught my reflection in the hallway mirror one day and noticed the face of a middle-aged woman. Up till that moment I had still thought of myself as a girl. Perhaps I had looked like that for some time, but I hadn't felt like that and had certainly not thought of myself as being that. I had, whether I knew it or not, been mourning for myself rather than Callum, the self when young. Callum had represented my first experience of love and, looking back on it, I didn't think it had been wholly unreciprocated. I was fourteen or fifteen when I first became aware of him as a man, and he was dashing, handsome and, I thought, wicked. I had no grounds for my belief, and I suppose I must have thought that wickedness was a necessary companion to his other qualities, that men who were handsome and dashing and war heroes couldn't possibly be – or perhaps preferably shouldn't be – good, but apart from passing infidelities connived at by his wife, which was part of his larger tendency for self-indulgence, he was, like father, a man of almost insufferable goodness.

He was not, however, very responsible. His wife's fortune had got him used to a very high standard of living. When she moved out, he made no attempt to adapt himself to a lower one. He left his affairs in great disorder, and Vesta said it looked as if they might have to sell the estate to pay for the death duties.

'I can't imagine the Dowager Lady Roscoe letting Roscoe House pass out of the family's hands,' I said.

'You don't know the Dowager Lady Roscoe,' she said. 'Besides, even if she was disposed to help, most of her money's in South Africa and can't be brought out. In any case I doubt if she's as wealthy as everyone thinks she is. Callum certainly was not nearly as rich as he thought he was. Most of the family money is tied up in trusts and the only people who seem to get anything out of it are the lawyers.'

'What about the paintings?' I said. 'Can't you sell any of them?'

'I'd love to. They're ghastly. They're pseudo pre-Raphaelites by a consummately untalented painter discovered and befriended by the first baronet. He could cover large canvases with great gusto, but he was hardly more than a house painter. I suppose we'll have to convert the house into a sort of poor man's Woburn Abbey, with teas and one-armed bandits in the conservatory. Horrible thought, but there's no alternative.' She was almost in tears.

We were soon in the middle of the harvest, which was my favourite time of the year, and I regained something of my old equanimity. We had about three hundred acres under cereals in four large fields and I loved the sight of the scarlet combines munching their way through the yellow fields, the haze of dust which surrounded them, and the flocks of birds which swooped on the clouds of insects sent up by the blades.

'The combine's all right,' said the farm manager, 'but you should have been around during the harvest in the old days. First there was the mowing, then the binding, then the stooking. You're probably too young to remember what a sheaf of corn even looked like. They'd be stalked together in the fields, the sheaves, in little groups of five or six, one against the other, to let the winds blow through and dry them. A beautiful sight a field full of stooks, as if the sheaves were bowing to one another. And then the stacking. I don't suppose you've seen a stack, have you, like thatched cottages, a golden brown. And finally the threshing. Well, the combine does all that in one, and it's corn out at one end and straws at the other, but it's a lonely job. In the old days, come the harvest, the fields were full of people. Men brought out their wives and children, aye, and their mothers, to give a hand, with beer by the barrel at break, and the things that went on behind the hedges, and sometimes inside them, was nobody's business. Now you're out on your own without even a horse to talk to.'

He taught me how to work a combine, and I didn't in the least mind being out on my own. I was up high on the platform, which felt like the bridge of a sailing ship, with a commanding view of the surrounding countryside. The days were hot and hazy, so that one couldn't see all that far, but I was monarch of all I surveyed. There were swallows swooping around every side, and I could almost reach out and touch them. Then one afternoon, looking towards 'West Wynds', I could see father's Land Rover coming down the drive. He seemed in a great hurry, but instead of continuing towards the road, he turned and bumped his way across the fields, towards me, as if on some urgent errand.

'Guess what?' he shouted. 'It's Vida, at last.'

Vida had been married now for nearly five years and had finally become pregnant about a year ago only to lose her child in the seventh month, which had left her in a parlous state – and it looked as if she might never give birth. When I last saw her she looked as if she had put on weight – she wasn't the only one – but she had said nothing about being pregnant, so there was nothing to prepare me for the news.

I jumped from the combine, washed my face and hands and, without even changing out of my working clothes, drove straight into London. Vesta, Rocky and Stevie were already by her bedside, as well as several womenfolk from Norrie's side of the family.

The baby was of considerable size, with a head as round as a cannon-ball and a black mop of hair. Vida was sitting up, radiant.

'Now it's your turn,' she said to Rocky.

'I'm saving motherhood for my old age,' said Rocky.

'Actually,' said Vesta, 'it's going to be my turn next.'

'What another?' said Rocky. 'Have you turned Catholic?'

'I like children,' said Vesta.

'So do I,' said Vida, 'and now that I've started, I'm going to have lots and lots.'

'What are you going to call it?' I asked.

'Ah,' said Vida, 'You'll have to wait till the circumcision.'

'Oh, that should be nice,' said Rocky. 'I've always wanted to see a real circumcision.'

'Josh was circumcised,' I reminded her.

'Yes, but he was nipped in the bud in hospital when nobody was looking. This is going to be the real thing, isn't it, in public?'

'Very public,' said Vida. 'It's going to be done in synagogue.'

'Are they always done in synagogue?' asked Vesta.

'No, but he was born on Saturday, so the eighth day will be Saturday. As next Saturday is *Yom Kippur*, the day of Atonement, synagogue is the only place where you can have it – because that's where everybody is going to be.'

And so for the first time in our lives, we were in synagogue, not for a wedding or a funeral or a memorial service, but for an actual festival.

We arrived shortly after eleven and the place was packed in honour, we thought, of the circumcision, but it appeared that synagogues were always packed on *Yom Kippur*. Someone had reserved places for us in the front row of the ladies' gallery and had provided us with prayer books. Father was downstairs in his regimental bowler hat, looking as bewildered as we felt. It was nearly one before the circumcision took place, and Rocky, believe it or not, had brought a pair of opera glasses in her handbag so that she could watch every stage of the operation. When it was all over, Vesta, Rocky and I left, though, to our astonishment, father remained in his place. He presumably felt it would have been indelicate to walk out in the middle of the service.

Rocky was picked up in a chauffeur-driven Daimler, while Vesta came home with me. As we were driving out of London I put on the car radio and was listening to some music, when the programme was interrupted by a news flash that Syria and Egypt had attacked Israel, and that a full-scale war had broken out. I got such a shock that my hands began to shake and I had to pull into the side of the road to take it all in.

'Josh. He's in the army, I hope he's all right,' said Vesta. I felt oddly helpless.

'What do we do?' I said.

'What do you mean? What can we do?'

I drove on. It seemed wrong to go back to the farm and continue with the milking as if nothing had happened, but cows had to be milked and people had to be fed whatever happened. I tried to continue with the routine as best I could, though instead of Vivaldi on the loud-speakers, I had a continuous flow of news which seemed to become more depressing with every passing hour. Shortly after six father 'phoned to say that he would remain for the time being in London.

'To do what?' I asked.

'To be honest, I'm not quite sure, but I'm going to see in what way I could be useful.' A little later Vesta 'phoned. Robin was on his way to London and was hoping to get on a plane for Tel Aviv.

'Why? What can he do?'

'He's a trained soldier. It should count for something.'

She came over after supper and we spent the night together glued to the television.

Robin was unable to get to Tel Aviv, but he got to Cyprus and the next day he 'phoned to say that he and several others had got hold of a boat and would be making for Haifa.

For the next day or two I went about my work in a daze, with the radio plugged into my ear ('What are you listening to?' Hughie asked me, 'they can't be playing cricket this time of the year.').

I couldn't understand why I felt so personally affected by events in a faraway place with which I had hitherto felt no personal connection. I remembered the Six Day War, but it seemed to be over before it started. I was immensely cheered by the brilliant victory, but I could not recall experiencing any anguish or concern when the fighting broke out. Was it simply because I now had a half-brother in the Israeli army? Or was it that during the few hours in synagogue on *Yom Kippur* I had allowed Jewishness to seep back into my soul? Vesta felt equally concerned, but then Robin was now in Israel as well as Josh, and was probably doing his best to get into action.

'He looks meek, even timid,' she said, 'but he's like his father in some ways and he always kept moaning that it was very unlikely that he would ever hear a gun fired in anger. Now's his chance. Men never grow up, do they?'

The reports from the front were contradictory and it was uncertain which side was winning and which was losing, but by the end of the week it was clear that the Israelis had taken the initiative and were advancing on both fronts. But then, on the day the cease-fire was announced, we received a cable to say that Josh had been seriously wounded in action.

Father made immediate arrangements to fly out, and I drove him to Heathrow, wondering if I shouldn't go with him and uncertain as to what use I'd be if I did.

'No, no, you stay where you are. Somebody's got to be around on the farm.'

Tilly was waiting at the check-in desk. She seemed sombre and gaunt and looked at me almost without recognition. They walked through passport control arm in arm; I was rather afraid they would come back the same way.

Robin 'phoned in the evening. He had seen Josh in hospital.

'He's comfortable,' he said. He'd been shot in the stomach and the bullet had lodged in the spine, without, however, severing the spinal column. He had been in danger because of loss of blood and was on the mend, but it was too early yet to attempt to remove the bullet, and they wouldn't be able to offer a prognosis until after the operation.

A few days later I got a 'phone call from Troy.

'Where can I get hold of your father?'

'He's in Israel.'

'I know he's in Israel, but where? It's important. People

are unloading shares by the million, and there are fortunes to be made.'

'I'm not sure if father would have a mind for the market if you ask me.'

'Will he be in touch with you?'

'Probably.'

'Tell him to get in touch with me without delay or, better still, give me his number.'

'I haven't got his number.'

'What do you mean you haven't got his number? Where's he staying?'

'I've no idea. He's not there on holiday, you know.'

'All right. If and when he 'phones, tell him to get in touch, at any time of the day or night. How's Josh by the way?'

I had the feeling that he was listening impatiently as I told him.

'He'll pull through,' he said reassuringly, 'he's as tough as they come and in good hands. But don't forget, any time of the day or night.'

Father 'phoned that night. I forgot to give him Troy's message and, to judge from his tone, he wouldn't have been interested to hear it if I had. They had tried to operate and the operation was proving trickier than they had anticipated. Josh was being moved to another hospital.

Troy 'phoned the next morning. Had I heard from father? Had I given him the message?

'Yes and no.'

'What do you mean yes and no? What fucking game are you playing at? Do you know what's happening here? Does your father know?'

'I don't think father cares.'

'Give me his number.'

'I haven't got his number, he's rushing round all over.'

'Look, let me get something into your fucking head. The market's gone wild. Do you know what that means – you're supposed to be a fucking economist.'

'I'm not that sort of fucking economist,' I said, and put

the 'phone down.

He was on the 'phone again in the evening and we had an even more acrimonious exchange. After that he left me alone. I later learned that he had been on to Grace, who did pass on his message to father. Vesta 'phoned the next day. She had just spoken to Robin. They had managed to operate, the bullet had been removed, and Josh was expected to make a complete recovery. She was crying as she told me the news and I also broke down.

Father returned about two weeks later and to my relief he was on his own. I was half afraid he would be with Tilly, but she had been taken ill herself and was remaining in Israel to recuperate. He had lost weight and seemed to be under strain. His plane had landed shortly before midnight and it was nearly two before he got home, but he rushed to his office right away and was on the 'phone for nearly an hour. I didn't want to weary him further that night, but the next morning I said to him, 'Don't you think I have a right to know what's happening?'

'With Troy, do you mean?'

'He's been on the 'phone to me almost every day since you left. Where were you, where could he get hold of you.'

'He's been going through an anxious period, poor chap.'

'And you haven't?'

As he drew breath to answer, the 'phone went. This time I followed him into the office and sat on his desk as he spoke. My presence made him uneasy for he clearly felt that one's womenfolk should be sheltered from a matter as indelicate as money. I could hear Troy's high-pitched and insistent voice at the other end, but all father could say was 'Yes . . . yes . . . I see what you mean . . . yes . . . no doubt . . . well, if you say so . . . yes . . . yes.' He wanted to draw the conversation to a close, but Troy wouldn't let him. When he finished I said:

'Are we going bankrupt?'

'We could be – or if Troy's prognostications are right, we could be very, very rich, but the odd thing is, it doesn't seem important. I remember during the war my father tried to cheer me up with reports of how well the company was doing, the defence contracts he was receiving, the record output he managed to achieve with a depleted work-force. The letters arrived in a batch during a heavy battle along the Arno. The shelling was so intense I thought the whole earth might crack at the seams, and here were these letters on the triumphs of Courlanders Castings. It was the same with Troy. I got to Israel after the worst of the fighting was over, but the casualties were pouring in from the field stations, young boys with limbs shot off and faces burned beyond recognition, and there was Josh himself, lying white-faced and helpless, with hardly a breath in his body, and with no certainty that he would ever walk again, and everywhere I went there were messages: " 'phone Troy Mackeson, urgent; Urgent, 'phone Troy." I naturally presumed that something had happened to Rocky, and 'phoned, but what was it? This was my great chance to make a killing. Prices were toppling and I could pick up whole companies for petty cash. I told him simply do what he thought best, and left it at that. His whole strategy was based on the conviction that the market would level out, but it hasn't levelled out and for all I know it could fall through the floor.'

'And if it does?'

'We've still got the farm.'

'Why have you never talked to me about these things before? I was trained as an economist, you know.'

'This has nothing to do with economics – it's all a matter of having the feel of the market, it's something in your blood. Troy has it, or at least had it, and I didn't. Most of my shares represent palpable assets and, if they could be liquidated at book value, I would be fairly well off. Until a few months ago I was, in paper terms, very well off, but it looks as if my paper has turned to paper. Troy feels I should hold tight even if I have to mortgage the farm.'

'Not the farm,' I said, 'whatever you do, don't touch the farm.'

'I have no intention of doing so.'

I was still uneasy and puzzled by the course events had

taken, and in particular I felt that he had vested excessive faith in Troy. I asked if I could see the books.

'By all means,' he said, 'but I don't know if you'll be able to make head or tail of them. I know I can't.'

Father had come into a substantial sum in the mid-fifties and, after buying the farm, he invested the surplus into gilt-edged and a number of blue-chip concerns, which yielded steady if undramatic profits. Then came Troy, the Wonder Boy, at whose bidding he reorganized his portfolio and moved into new issues which, with few exceptions, were concerns of third or fourth rank, which rose rapidly and which for a time yielded considerable capital gains, but which had slumped almost as quickly and were now virtually worthless. That much even I could see, but there were deals within deals, and purchases through nominees which I could not quite fathom, and I asked father if I could bring in Norrie to guide me, for I was not an accountant.

'If you must,' he said.

Norrie came and, after spending the better part of a night on the books, said: 'A lot of this doesn't make sense. We had better see Troy.'

' 'Phone him now,' I said.

He looked at his watch: 'It's after two.'

'Troy isn't a respector of time.' I picked up the 'phone and dialled his number. There was no reply.

'He's asleep,' said Norrie.

'If he is, he's going to have a rude awakening.'

I got into the Land Rover and, with Norrie muttering uneasily beside me, I drove into London there and then. But when we got to Chelsea the house was in darkness.

When I tried his office in the morning, I wasn't at all surprised to learn that he hadn't come in and that nobody knew when he would be in or where he might be contacted. I tried his place on the coast, and again there was no reply. Finally I tried his parents in Warwickshire. They sounded as agitated as I felt. They had been trying to get hold of him for the past two days, and no one knew where he was.

In the meantime Norrie sent two of his assistants to work in Company House and gradually pieced together quite a story. It was extremely complicated, but in essence it was this. Troy specialized in volatile shares in which comparatively small dealings could give rise to comparatively sharp movements, up or down, and before buying for clients in one name, he would buy on his own behalf in another, which was all right as long as the market was rising. When it was falling the operation became more complicated, and before unloading shares on behalf on his clients, he would unload his own (again, of course, through nominees) which he would then repurchase after they had fallen. But latterly he had been too clever, for the market had continued to fall and he had landed himself with a mass of shares which were almost valueless and, in a desperate attempt to save something from the débâcle, he had unloaded them on to father and fled.

'Who's going to tell father?' I said.

'Not me,' said Norrie, 'but before you do we might still be able to salvage something from the wreck. I'll be down tomorrow with a lawyer.'

When we came together the next day, father's voice sounded curiously slurred, as if he had been drinking, which may indeed have been the case, for he seemed oddly oblivious to all that was going on around him. When Norrie put out some papers for him to sign, he found he couldn't control the pen.

'Good grief,' he said, 'what's happening to me?'

Norrie and I exchanged troubled glances.

'We could come back tomorrow,' said Norrie, 'but it's rather important we deal with this matter without delay.'

Father tried again, but could hardly make a line on the paper, let alone write his name.

As soon as they were gone I called the doctor who examined him at length.

'Is your father a drinking man?' he asked.

'No, not to that extent,' I said.

'I thought not. I'm going to take him into hospital.'

A neurologist examined him some time later and told

me that he had suffered a slight stroke.

He recovered the full use of his hand and his voice and was back to normal by the following day, but the neurologist explained that even a slight stroke could have serious consequences. 'It's like a tiny pebble being removed from a large pile – it may be tiny in itself, but it could unsettle the lot. I'll give him some tablets which he should take three times a day, but he'll also have to learn to take things easy.'

'These things tend to go with the farming life,' said our family doctor. 'You see, there's always something to aggravate a farmer. If the weather's good for the cereals, it's bad for the root-crops. If they have a good harvest, it could mean a glut. If they have a bad one, it could mean disaster. If they get a good price for their corn, it means they have to pay a high price for their feed. There's always something to aggravate them. Half my patients come down with strokes.'

Norrie managed to salvage about ten thousand pounds out of an investment porfolio which only a few months before had been worth nearly two million, but father took it all philosophically: 'I suppose you know how I came by the money in the first place.'

I didn't, and I reminded him that when I asked him where it came from he had told me off for being impertinent.

'My late father-in-law owned a small bank which was seized by the Nazis and, about twenty years ago and as sole heir to the estate, I was offered about a million pounds in reparations. After all the Germans had done to us I hesitated to touch their money, but Tilly prevailed upon me to accept, which I did, but I've always felt vaguely uneasy about it all, and now it's all gone. Naked I came into this world, and naked shall I go.'

It wasn't that bad, I told him, for there was still the farm, but as Norrie continued to work his way through father's books, it became doubtful if even the farm was safe.

'The trouble is', said Norrie, 'the farm's been running at a loss since the day he bought it, but while there were profits from investments, there were almost benefits to be had from the losses. But now?'

'Could we sell off some of the land and farm the rest?'

'Would that be a good idea? He's in his sixties, you know. If he sells now, he should be able to live in reasonable comfort for the rest of his days. If he continues to play the farmer, he may end up on social security.'

The following day Norrie and I had a meeting with Robin and Vesta to see what, if anything, could be done to save the farm. I was hoping that Vesta, as a dutiful and hitherto generous daughter, might come up with the suggestion that Robin take over the farm and let father work it, or at least remain on it, for the rest of his days (which I rather feared would not be all that prolonged), for our whole farm, though not small in itself, could have been accommodated comfortably in a corner of the Roscoe estates. Both she and Robin were very sympathetic, and brought in their lawyer and steward but found they could do nothing. I have never been able to understand the peculiar English system of land-owning which left people heirs to great fortunes and vast estates, but deprived them of ready cash.

A few days later, when we were already meeting with auctioneers, a large Mercedes pulled up outside the house with a loud crunch of gravel and Sophie emerged. She had been visiting her father who was very ill in South Africa and had only just heard of our difficulties. She had a plan which she had already discussed with her lawyers and which seemed to have everything to commend it. She would buy the farm and everything on it, and lease it back to father at a nominal rent.

I had always admired Sophie for her many qualities, but had never regarded generosity as one of them, if only because I somehow did not associate generosity with great fortunes, and because I had had the impression that in financial terms she had always kept Callum on a tight rein. Norrie was with me and I looked over to him wondering if there was a catch to the offer which I might have overlooked, but there was none. We were saved!

I threw my arms round her with such force that I dislodged her earrings and rumpled her coiffure, and rushed out to find father. He was not in the house or any of the farm buildings, and I couldn't find him in the fields. The Land Rover was in the garage, so I presumed he was somewhere about the place, and I eventually found him wandering aimlessly in the woods and looking rather lost. I told him about Sophie's offer, but he seemed unable to take it in. I wondered if he had had another stroke or if he had quite got over his first one.

Sophie hadn't seen him for some time and was startled by his appearance. She quickly collected herself, however, and embraced him warmly, but he stood there unresponsively with his hands hanging limply at his sides. I made him lie down and called the doctor, but by the time he came he was fast asleep.

'That's all he really needs,' said the doctor, 'complete rest. I wouldn't really bother him with business details for the time being.'

'I suppose it's the delayed shock,' said Sophie.

'Losing two millions just like that is enough to blow anyone's mind,' said Norrie.

'It wasn't the money he invested in the shares so much as the faith he had vested in Troy,' I said.

'What about your naughty little sister?' asked Sophie. 'Wasn't she a party to all this?'

The odd thing was that I had hardly given her a thought. Of course she must have been, and the very fact that she had vanished along with Troy confirmed her guilt, yet her name had never cropped up once in the many exchanges I had had with father since his return, as if we had subconsciously surpressed the thought that we had been harbouring a Goneril in our midst.

I was devoted to all my sisters, though rather less so to Rocky than the others, for although she had a sparkling personality, she tended to exploit her charms too readily. I thought of her as predatory, egocentric and corrupt, and a certain distance developed between us till that bizarre evening when I had dinner with her and Troy, after which

I began to feel a little sorry for her. One is always ready to forgive people one is sorry for, but what she had done now was beyond all forgiveness.

'If I should ever set eyes on her,' I said, 'I'll strangle her.'

'That won't help anyone, least of all your father,' said Sophie, 'and perhaps she'll have some sort of explanation.'

'I have no doubt she will. I'll strangle her first and listen to it after.'

Norrie had to rush back to town, but Sophie stayed to keep me company and I was glad of it. She was obviously fond of father and spoke of him affectionately, but then, as we were having tea, she said something which startled me.

'You know, of course, that he's had a breakdown before.'

'Father?'

'During the war. Perhaps you were too young to remember.'

'I knew mummy had breakdowns.'

'Your mummy, poor child, was broken down, which is, I think, why your father married her. She was also very pretty in a pale, ethereal way, and of a good family, but she had to be propped up for as long as I knew her –'

'And you think she may have caused father's breakdown?'

'No, no, it was quite different. A friend of Callum's once told me that your father was the bravest man he'd met, which surprised me and which, I dare say, would have surprised you, and I blurted out that that wasn't the impression most people had of him. Exactly, he said, that's what made him so courageous. He was a mild and timid man, who was determined to conquer his fears and nearly killed himself in the attempt. His trouble was that he worshipped Callum, of all people, and tried to model himself on him. But Callum wasn't courageous, he was merely fearless and lacked the imagination to know he was in danger. It's always harmful to try to be the person you're not. But anyway he got over it, and if he got over that breakdown, he'll get over this one.'

I was less sanguine, so was his doctor. He came round again in the evening, but father was still asleep.

'He'll have to go into hospital for a check-up,' he said, 'but if you ask me, he's no longer up to running a place this size.'

13
Prodigal Daughter

When I first contemplated the possiblity of having to leave 'West Wynds', I thought it would be the end of the world. What, I kept asking, would I do with myself? But now it had actually happened, the question uppermost in my mind – in our minds – was: what was to be done with father?

With three married daughters, including one who was châtelaine of a forty-roomed mansion, there was no problem of finding a roof for over his head. It was decided he should go to Vesta, who provided him with a beautifully appointed suite of rooms, but he spent much of his time sitting in an armchair gazing out of the window at the park, and could not be induced to turn his hand to anything useful or even to switch on his television.

I urged him to see the doctor recommended by Sophie, who had been so helpful to Vesta, to which he said with a slight flicker of a smile: 'Why? Do you think I'm mad?' I wasn't sure. Perhaps I did.

The thing about him which troubled me most was the inane smile which hardly ever left his face, as if he was enjoying the impenetrable little world in which he now found himself.

'I wonder how he would feel if Rocky came back?' said Vesta.

'I know how *I* would feel if Rocky came back,' I said.

'She could be the medicine he needs.'

'To finish him off.'

'He was so devoted to her.'

'That's why he's like this.'

'I'm sure something must have happened to make her

go off like that – perhaps Troy forced her.'

'You should know your sister better than that. Nobody could force Rocky to do anything she didn't want, or prevent her from doing something she did want.'

'You're harsh.'

'You're innocent.'

'She's our sister, you know.'

'I know, that's what makes it so hard.'

'I'm worried about her, aren't you?'

'Not in the least. If she needs us, she'll turn up.'

And as I spoke, so it came to pass, for a few days later we received a letter without an address, but with a French postmark: 'I hope you won't think too unkindly of us – though I wouldn't blame you if you did – but I have an explanation for everything. Troy hopes to repay all his creditors, and certainly father, a hundred pence in the pound. We hope to be back in another few weeks. PS. I've had a miscarriage.'

I did not believe the postscipt and was convinced it was added to elicit sympathy. I didn't even believe she had a womb, and if she did it was only capable of bearing hard currency. And I did not for a minute believe that they would be back in a matter of weeks, or even months, but one evening, while I was with Vesta, Rocky turned up in a battered Mini, looking so pale, thin and distraught, that Vesta fell upon her in a flood of tears. I must confess, however, that my own tear ducts were not overwhelmed.

'I'd better tell you before you ask anything about Troy, that we've separated,' she said.

I waited till she had eaten and had a good night's rest before I asked her anything at all, and then only because she was singularly unforthcoming with information herself.

'Where is Troy now?'

'God knows. Spain possibly. It's more than a week since I saw him last.'

'How is it that he urged father to keep buying at a time when everyone else was selling?'

'That's the best time to buy,' she said, putting some

bacon onto her fork and popping it delicately into her rosebud of a mouth. 'That's how fortunes are made.'

'He must have known that his own company was on the brink of collapse and yet still kept loading shares on to father –'

'He didn't know. He floated the company at a pound a share and was buying them back at a penny – who can resist a bargain like that, especially if he is convinced the market must turn? You seem to think Troy's a crook. To be a crook in the City you have to have more than an ordinary level of competence. Troy is merely an incompetent megalomaniac.'

'How long did it take you to find that out?'

'I've suspected it for some time.'

'Why didn't you tell father?'

'He wouldn't have believed me, I doubt if he would believe me even now. He worshipped Troy.'

'Father's been ill, you know.'

'I know.'

'You know?'

'I felt it instinctively, that's why I've come back.'

Father was still asleep, and I was uneasy as to how he would react when he saw her.

When he came downstairs Vesta took him by the hand and said, 'If you had a wish, what would you wish for?'

'If I had a wish?'

'What would you wish for?'

'What would I wish for?'

'Yes.'

And he thought for some time with furrowed brows. The matter seemed to be giving him genuine concern.

'You know I can't think of anything that I do want.'

'Wouldn't you like to see your baby daughter?'

'My baby daughter?'

At which point Rocky materialized and his smile gradually broadened and his eyes brightened.

'It is Rocky, isn't it?' he said. Rocky and Vesta broke down, and this time I couldn't keep back my own tears.

Vesta was right. Her effect was therapeutic and he

gradually emerged from his private world. He ate with gusto, he began to take wine with his meals. He joined us in walks and began to take an interest in the running of the home farm, and especially Robin's prize herd of Channel Island cows. His memory had lapses and he kept referring to dead people, and especially Callum, as if they were still alive, and to living people, like Tilly, as if they were dead (from which I drew some reassurance).

Rocky's two homes were seized by the official receiver, but she acquired a flat near Hyde Park whose size and furnishing suggested that she was not entirely penniless. She confessed that she still had 'a bob or two', and had not lost the knack of making them multiply.

As for myself, I moved in with Stevie (who made me very welcome) and divided my time between writing occasional articles for the financial press and looking for a full-time job. It wasn't easy, and even the papers which were happy to accept my articles and commission new ones were reluctant to take me on their staff.

One day there came an unexpected letter from Weedy enclosing a lengthy and glowing review from a learned journal of my latest book (which had been published more than a year previously). I wrote back to thank him and to say that my royalties, alas, suggested that my books were no longer getting through to the general public, and he wrote again to say that they were getting through 'to the people that count', and that the economics chair at Hurstfield would be vacant at the end of the year and that he was fairly certain that I could have it if I wanted it. I weighed his suggestion seriously but finally concluded that, if I returned to Hurstfield now, I would be there for the rest of my days. I hoped that even at my advanced age, life had more to offer than that.

I had for long been aware that idleness was the mother of mischief and now that I was only semi-employed, my thoughts turned longingly to Hughie and the hay barn. I began to find my celibate state painful. One day I had an angry exchange with a sub-editor who handled my copy on one of the papers. He invited me over for a drink so that he could explain his difficulty, which was that he had to fit a quart into a pint pot.

'Your prose is far too good to re-write it,' he said, 'so the only thing I can do is cut.'

I was not completely mollified, for he generally cut what I thought of as the most important parts of the piece, but we became friendly and he asked me home for 'a bite'. I had a fairly clear idea of what was to be bitten and who would do the biting, but that didn't worry me. What did worry me was the fact that as soon as I came through the door I saw on every side the frayed furnishings of family life. There was a picture of the Pope on one wall and of a stern-looking woman, who I took to be his wife, on the other, and vicious-looking children. They were presumably away for the night, or a week, and he was taking the opportunity to live a little. He helped me off with my coat and pulled out a bottle of Spanish wine to offer me a drink, which I politely declined.

'Do you prefer spirits?' he asked.

'No, but I find if I drink it takes me longer to come, and if I drink a lot I don't come at all.'

At which he put down the bottle and tore off his clothes.

A frayed sofa is not a hay barn, and he was no Hughie, but on the whole it was a fairly satisfactory experience, and he 'phoned me the next morning to ask if I was free that night. 'We can't come to my place,' he added, 'the wife's back. Can we go to yours?'

'No,' I said, 'the husband's back,' and put the 'phone down. He must have described me in appreciative terms to his colleagues, for I was subsequently invited out by the night editor, the managing editor, the chief sub, the foreign editor, a layout man (an aptly named calling), the head electrician, and the doorman (who had a wooden leg which tended to jack-knife at crucial moments). I was still not offered a job and concluded ruefully that even though I was not on the staff of the paper I had had the staff of the paper on me.

The encounters all took place in their homes, or hotels, and in one or two instances in the back seat of a car. I never brought anyone home. When Stevie invited me to stay with her, she had made but one stipulation: 'Please knock on my bedroom door before you enter,' which made me think that the place might be quaking with orgies, but in fact no man was suffered to cross the threshold. She was sixty and said: 'The least you can be at my age is respectable,' and I therefore felt it inappropriate to offer flagrant evidence of my lack of respectability.

Vida was worried about the fact that I was still single and frequently invited me to meals and, almost as inevitably as the gefilte fish, I would find some 'young man' (as she called them) at table. Some were in fact in their late twenties or early thirties, but others were divorcees or widowers in their forties or fifties. All were nice Jewish men from nice Jewish families – successful accountants, lawyers or dentists – and clearly Vida was hoping to coax me not only into marriage, but into the fold. None of the men, however, were my type and I dare say I wasn't theirs, and even if love had begun to burgeon, it would, I am sure, have wilted in the atmosphere created by Vida's small, attractive, but restless and noisy infants (the birth of her first child had fructified her womb: another infant had followed and there was a third on the way). I loved Vida and had grown fond of Norrie, but I could not take young couples with young children.

One day Rocky asked me to lunch at the Savoy Grill (where else?). She had cut her hair short and dyed it grey. Her skin was tanned, and she looked delicious in a crisp light-yellow linen suit. As soon as she sat down she complained that I was neglecting myself, that my clothes were dowdy and my hair unkempt, and that I was allowing myself to drift into premature middle-age.

'Why premature?' I asked. 'I'm thirty-four, you know.'

'Thirty-four. For Christ's sake, that's nothing. I know women twice your age who are being poked twice nightly in every orifice.'

'I don't think I should have liked that at even half my age.'

'But seriously, Ducks. I don't think you should be

staying with Stevie. People living together soon begin to resemble one another. Why don't you come and stay with me?'

'Why? Do you want to resemble me?'

'You are basically a handsome woman, but don't know how to make the best of yourself. Look, can I treat you? I would love to fix you up with a new outfit and a new hairdo. Can I please? Just for fun.'

It was like the Rome experience all over again. We went first of all to her hairdresser, who not only gave me a hairdo, but what felt like a face-lift. The whole operation took nearly two hours and I daren't think what it must have cost. We then took a taxi and bought up Knightsbridge – not only new dresses and shoes, but new underclothes (my old ones, Rocky felt, weren't nearly sexy enough). I kept the new clothes on, and she grabbed my old attire, which I had been carrying in a bag under my arm, and rammed it into a dustbin. She came back with me to Stevie's, rang the bell and hid round the corner. Stevie opened and looked at me for a moment without recognition. Then she put her hands to her face.

'Ducks! It isn't Ducks, is it?' at which point Rocky emerged. 'I would never have recognized you, never. Rocky, you must do the same for me. I know I'm older, but I want to be transformed. I'm going on a cruise shortly and I would like to be a new woman – especially for the cruise.'

A week or so later Rocky invited me to a party. I had been to her parties before, when she was still married, and hadn't cared for them at all: gallons of champagne and tiny little canapés in plastic coating, and company that reminded me somewhat of the canapés – glossy young men in mohair suits and unseasonable tans – and the conversation was all about keeping second homes in Corfu or Montego Bay, and I would quietly slip away after about half an hour. This time I wanted to try out my new *persona* in public, and stayed for rather longer. The fare was much the same, but the guests somewhat less cocky; one or two of them looked as if they had lately undergone some chastening experience and stood around with glasses in their hands and rueful expressions on their faces. One of them with a lock of hair over one eye and a longish nose bore down towards me.

'You must be Rocky's sister,' he said.

'How do you know? Do we look alike?'

'No, not in the least, but she said you'd be the one with the big tits.'

His conversation did not at all go with his appearance – which was sober, even grave – or his voice, which was rapid and donnish.

I asked him if he carried a measuring rod.

'No, no, my dear, I can size them up at a glance. Years of training, you see. I'm obsessed with them, I'm afraid.'

'You sound as if you were neglected by your mother.'

'That's one theory. I've heard others. Goes back to prep school. Our matron was well endowed and let me fondle them. Haven't looked back since, or up, or down, for that matter. It's left me with a bad memory for faces, women's faces, that is. Gives one a crick in the neck too. Not so bad in England or America, where the women are fairly tall, but I was in Italy for a while and came back with a stoop.'

'Are you a tit-fancier by profession?'

'Wish I was. I'm an economist, I'm afraid, with an international agency. Well paid but frightfully dull. I gather you're an economist yourself.'

'Did Rocky tell you that too, or can you tell from my tits?'

'No, no, most women economists I know are as flat as Norfolk. Do you practice? Teach?'

'Neither, I'm afraid. I scribble.'

'Under what name?'

'Courlander.'

'Ah, the Baltic States. I reviewed it in the *East European Economic Digest*.'

'Then you must be Conan Maitland. Oh, you *are* a nice man.'

'It was a nice book, if I may say so, and beautifully written. Not at all the sort of thing one expects of an economist, but then one doesn't expect tits like yours either.'

'Everything seems to lead back to tits.'

'As everything should.'

'Would it help you to resume normal conversation if I stripped?'

'What? Right here?'

'If it doesn't embarrass you, it won't embarrass me,' and I began to undo my blouse buttons. He watched me as if in a dream. Did he really think I would go through with it? I was tempted to do so, if only to see how he would react. He was already breathing heavily and beads of perspiration were forming on his brow. I undid all the buttons, but let the blouse hang together.

'Shall I go on?'

He tried to say something, but words wouldn't come. He still had champagne in his glass and gulped it down.

'No,' he said hoarsely, 'let's find a room.'

He insisted on having all the lights on as I undressed and, when I took my blouse off, he threw himself on his knees, as if in worship, and grasped me by the waist. I became slightly worried.

'My God,' he said, 'you're self-supporting. What a pair! I should like to have them cast in bronze.'

'Wouldn't that be a bit cold?'

His hands were shaking, as, still on his knees, he began to fondle me. I hitched up my skirt and pushed him over so that I had him between my knees.

'I don't suppose Rocky told you that I was an all-in wrestler as well?'

I sat up in bed and watched him as he dressed. He was a bit heavy and rounded in the shoulders, but otherwise had a fine athletic frame and a most distinguished profile. I was suffused with a feeling of bliss, tempered by apprehension, the apprehension stemming from the near certainty that it couldn't last, if only because it never did. I wanted him to come home with me so that I could sleep snuggled up against him (I didn't know what Stevie would have said and didn't care), but I didn't think I could ask. I felt I had been forward enough – perhaps too forward – for one night. Grace once told me that she felt aggressive after coitus. I, on the contrary, felt shy, and although he wanted to pull the blankets off me for a farewell look, I wouldn't let him, for apart from anything else, I felt sticky and messy and I wanted him to leave the room so I could have a shower.

He hadn't even asked me for my telephone number. Was this the last I would see of him? He had hardly said a thing about himself. For all I knew he was married, and he would now hurry home to his wife with some excuse that he had been late at the orifice. Except that he didn't look, sound, or even smell married, and I was by now old enough and experienced enough to sense wife in a man at twenty paces. He lacked the sly-dog look, the furtive in-and-out-lest-I-be-caught-in-the-act manner, or the post-coital contrition. On the other hand he could be the sort of married man I was yet to encounter, the one with a very, very understanding wife. For all I knew she may have been with him there at the party, for I had barely glanced at the other women and had not spoken to any of them.

When he was almost fully dressed and looking around for his shoes, he said: 'You know, I'm ready for another innings.'

'Not tonight, Josephine.'

'So when do we two meet again?'

'I shall have to consult my diary, but as far as I can recall, I'm free tomorrow morning, tomorrow afternoon, tomorrow evening, the next day, the day after that, and –'

'My God, you do lead a full life.'

'Are you married?' I asked.

'No,' he said, 'would you like to marry me?' He was sitting on the bed with his back to me, as he said this, putting on his shoe. I came behind him, crossed my arms over his chest and pressed myself against him.

'Would you be able to support me in the manner to which I should like to become accustomed?'

'Not if you have your sister's tastes.' And he turned and

rolled himself on top of me.

'Would your sister mind if we spent the night here?'

'I can't. It's too late to 'phone my aunt to say I'm not coming, and if she wakes up and finds I'm not there she'll be worried and upset.'

'You stay with your *aunt*?'

'What's wrong with staying with an aunt?'

'Nothing really, except that you don't behave like the sort of girl who lives with her aunt.'

'Wait till you meet my aunt.'

'Why? Has she also got big tits?'

'Oh Christ, we're back where we started.'

By the time we emerged, the party was nearly over and Rocky was standing with folded arms by the door.

'I was wondering whether I would have to come and winkle you out,' she said, then turning to Conan (whom she called Onan): 'I hope you're going to make an honest woman out of her.'

'It's a bit late for that, I'd have thought,' he said.

When I drove home in the early hours of the morning I felt like dancing, and I must have driven as if I was dancing, for as I turned into the street where Stevie lived I bumped into the back of a taxi. It was in fact a slight bump, but the taxi driver immediately pulled on his brakes and came round to inspect the damage, muttering under his breath about women drivers.

At that moment a woman put her head out of the cab window and immediately withdrew. I only glimpsed her for a second. It was Tilly, and the sight of her dissolved my euphoria and brought me back to earth. I felt like Cinderella when the clock struck twelve, and was convinced that the events of the past five or six hours had been a dream and that I was returning to Stevie after some workaday errand. The taxi driver was berating me for my carelessness and I stood there in a stupor, hardly taking in a word, but he stopped when he saw tears pouring down my face, at which he drew back: 'All right, all right, you needn't take it to heart. Bugger me, you can't open your mouth to some people.'

I was wakened by the insistent shrill of the telephone. I was at first not sure where I was, and had no idea what time it was. I must have drunk more than I realized.

I picked up the receiver.

'Hello – Ducks?'

'Who is it?'

'Conan.'

'Conan who?'

'Conan Doyle.'

And then it all came back to me, like a happy dream invading reality.

Conan, Conan Maitland, or Tits, as I had decided to call him.

'Any chance of meeting for lunch? I'm not particularly hungry and we don't have to eat. We could just hold hands.'

'I feel so groggy. I'm not sure if my legs will carry me.'

'If they won't, I will.'

'All right, Tits, for you, but promise not to look at me too hard because if I look as I feel, I'll be unsightly.'

I met him in a small, overcrowded City pub. I didn't know how I looked, but the moment I saw him I felt fine, and we sat squashed against each other, saying little, and sipping Perrier water.

It was a warm spring day and I walked through Regent's Park on the way home. The trees seemed to sag under the weight of their blossoms and I felt heady with happiness, almost satiated with it. I sat down in a deckchair, stretched out my legs and closed my eyes. Whatever happened between now and doomsday, nothing could erase what was happening now. Love, it occurred to me, was very selfish. Usually when I sat down at a vacant moment, doing nothing, worries crowded in upon me from every side. What could we do with father? How was Josh managing on his kibbutz after his injury? What would happen to Stevie after she retired? But now nothing and no one seemed to matter except him and me, me and him, but this was perhaps one of the joys of being in love; it made selfishness seem forgivable.

I saw him every evening after that, and not infrequently at lunch-time, and we spent entire weekends together, sometimes in London, but more usually in the Chilterns, which he loved, and which we walked across. It often rained and we stomped around in windcheaters and wellington boots. My wellingtons almost symbolized my years at 'West Wynds'. I hadn't touched them since the farm was sold and the moment I pulled them on, their moist, rubbery smell brought back my days in the cow-shed, the cows on the carousel, the cow-pats and the quiet chuff-chuff of the milking units, and tears welled up in my eyes.

Conan looked at me with disbelief.

'You're not crying, are you?'

'I'm not sure if I am or not, I don't always know what's happening to me. Do they trouble you, my tears?'

'In an odd way, yes.'

I suppose they troubled me, or rather they troubled me because I no longer seemed to be in control of myself. I was changing, either because of my age, or because I was in love, or because of the pressure of recent events – perhaps all three – and I was not altogether happy at the thought of changing because by and large I rather liked the person I was. It didn't mean to say that I *approved* of the person I was, but I wouldn't have cared to be anyone else.

I asked him if he thought he was changing.

'Don't we all?'

'I mean personality changes, finding responses and reactions in yourself that you hadn't noticed before.'

'I don't go in much for introspection, you know. I sometimes catch a glimpse of myself in the mirror, and think: "Is that me? Curious-looking bloke. Am I really a tenant of that property?" I don't think of myself as being that tall, and at college there was hardly a day in which I didn't brain myself against the oak beams.'

'Do you mean in every tall man there's a short man crying to get out?'

'In a way, yes. I sometimes feel lost inside myself, but

what I'm really trying to say is that the person you see is not quite the person I feel.'

'Pity,' I said, putting my arms around him, 'because I rather like the person I see.'

We would set out early in the morning and stop at a pub for lunch, by which time we had covered ten to twelve miles. Sometimes, where the pubs were residential, we stopped for more than lunch.

We were lying in bed one afternoon, in a happy stupor when, apropos of nothing, and as if talking to himself, he said: 'I was surprised when Rocky told me her father was a farmer, she doesn't look like a farmer's daughter,' at which the cloud on which I was floating suddenly popped and I hit the ground with a bump. I sat up.

'What made you think of Rocky now of all times?'

'Nothing in particular. I suppose it was something you said.'

'I never said anything which had remotely to do with Rocky.'

'You were talking about your farm and how you loved farming. But why shouldn't I mention Rocky? Is she a forbidden topic?'

'No, but I had the feeling you were comparing performances.'

'Comparing what?'

'Performances. How we perform in bed.'

At which he sat up, and regarded me with a pained expression.

'Christ, Ducks, it never occurred to me you could be stupid.'

'And it never occurred to me you could be insensitive.'

'I've never laid a finger on Rocky, she doesn't inspire me in that way. In any case she's been married for as long as I've known her.'

'What's marriage these days – and, in any case, she's separated from her husband.'

And even as I was speaking I heard my voice in my ear and it had a raucous, acrimonious tone which sounded alien to me.

'I'm sorry,' I said, 'I've never spoken like this before, but then I've never really been in love before. I suppose I'm jealous.'

'Jealous? What have you got to be jealous of? You're not a dolly-bird, but who the hell wants one?' I found this only mildly comforting, for I liked to think that when I made the effort – as I did on the night I met him – I could be a dolly-bird.

We had hoped to cover another five miles before nightfall and we began to dress, but then, as I was slipping on my bra, he stopped and took it off, and we sank back on to the bed.

There is nothing like an orgasm to set doubts at rest – if only for the moment.

When I got back to London, the 'phone was ringing. I was always troubled by the sound of the 'phone late at night and I approached the receiver with apprehension. It was Vesta.

'I haven't woken you, have I?'

'No, but you gave me a fright.'

'I'm sorry, but I've been trying to get you for weeks now, and there's never any reply.'

'Stevie's away.'

'I know that, but are you never at home?'

'I've been exploring the Chilterns.'

'But you're all right?'

'I've never felt better.'

'Thank God, you had me worried.' But she had another reason for 'phoning. Father had taken up genealogy as a hobby and wanted to trace his family background. He had examined all the material available in England, which was sparse, and he wanted to travel to Germany to see what he could dig up there. Vesta – in spite of reassurances from the doctor – was not sure whether father was fit to undertake such a journey on his own and she wondered if I might want to accompany him. 'Of course,' she added, 'you may not have the time.'

'No, time is the one thing I do have.'

'And, of course, I would pay your expenses.'

'It isn't that either.' I wasn't sure why I was hesitant about giving her the real answer. Was I afraid that if I let it be known that I, Ducks Courlander, was happy and in love, old Satan might stick his oar in? But I told her and blushed as I did so. I thought I could hear her dancing at the other end with delight. 'Oh, that's wonderful. I'm so happy. Rocky had said something about it, but you know Rocky, and I didn't give it a thought. Why didn't you tell me earlier?'

'It hasn't been going on for all that long. To be honest I'm not even sure I should have said anything even now.'

'But Ducks, how can you think like that?'

'It could come to nothing.'

'Why should it? He's jolly lucky to find a girl like you. I only hope he's worthy of you. You must bring him down for a weekend. Ducks, you *must*.'

And I did and, as I half-expected, he fell in love with Vesta.

'You two complement each other in the most marvellous way,' he said. 'You're mother earth, and she's –'

'Mother heaven?'

'No, I'm looking for the precise expression, and I'm not sure if there is one in English. You know the German *geistlich*?'

'It means ghastly, doesn't it?'

'Ghost-like, if anything. She's totally of the spirit. I'm surprised she married and had children – in an odd way I'm even disappointed –'

'I could put it to her that in deference to your feelings she should leave her husband and family.'

'Please don't make fun of me, Ducks, I'm serious. Seeing and talking to your sister I felt I was in the presence of something ethereal. What sort of man is your father, what sort of woman was your mother to have given birth to such a daughter?'

'Nothing special, really, but then we're Jewish, and there's no telling what a Jewish mother can come up with.'

I had now known him for over a month without coming upon anything which one could describe as a serious weakness, but I could see one now. He was nuts, not violently so, but enough to make him something I had never imagined he could be, a bore. He was prone to ecstasies: one day it was my bosom, the next my sister – what would it be next? As a matter of fact some of the observations he had made about Vesta were perfectly valid – I had made them myself. She *was* a thing of the spirit, but I didn't care to be juxtaposed as the antithesis, even if this too was valid. When he tried to come into my bed that night, he found a cold and unwelcoming back.

Father had, in the meantime, gone to Germany with Rocky in the improbable role of dutiful daughter, companion, escort and amanuensis, and he returned some weeks later, full of excitement, with a mass of papers, but without Rocky.

'Rocky, Rocky? What happened to Rocky? She's found a young man, a Von something or other and – would you believe it – a distant relative.'

One evening, apropos of nothing, Conan suggested that it was about time I met his mother. The way he put it made it sound as if it was a grim and unpleasant duty, which I suspected it might be. While he had become familiar with most of my family, he had rarely mentioned his, even indirectly, and I was beginning to wonder whether he had been found in a handbag in a waiting-room at Victoria Station. When I touched on his reticence, he said: 'The fact of the matter is, I've got a good deal to be reticent about,' and I braced myself for some startling revelation, but it was nothing like that.

'I've never really hit it off with my people. They spent a lot of money on me, but that was about the limit of it. Can't recall receiving anything in the way of affection. I think they regarded me as some sort of intruder. I don't think they had planned to have a family and, given the disposition of the old man, who was a sort of licensed pederast, it's a wonder I was conceived at all. He's dead now, killed by a drunken sailor he was trying to bed. "Not very discriminating, your father," was the old girl's comment. I see her dutifully every three or four weeks. In old age she is becoming rather more talkative than she used to be, and I'm hoping that one day I shall find her in confessional mood and she will tell me who my actual father was. How different, you must think, from your own dear family.'

'My family's odd,' I said, 'but their oddities are fairly normal. I take it you'd rather I didn't meet your mother.'

'I would rather there was no need to meet my mother, but she's alive so you have to, and we had better get it over and done with.'

After such an introduction I couldn't wait to meet her. She had taken a vow a few years before not to set foot in London to which she had taken a particular dislike, and she lived in a large house, attended by one ancient retainer with a club foot. She was very tall, very thin and very severe, and I recognized her at a glance. I had seen that face at an exhibition in a West End gallery in which Troy used to have a share. It was a self-portrait and a very striking one, for it was a life-sized nude, and the naked picture of a woman in her fifties, painted in almost bluish hues, does not fade easily from the memory.

'Conan never told me you were a painter,' I said.

'I'd have been surprised to learn that he mentioned me at all, he treats me as a dark secret. On the other hand he hasn't stopped talking about you. Do you like my work?'

'It's striking.'

'So is a poke in the eye. I don't go in for the pretty-pretty, if that's what you mean –'

'But you do sometimes go in for the ugly-ugly,' said Conan.

'I go in for *actualité*, and if you can't face *actualité*, that's your problem, not mine. However, I take it you didn't bring the poor child here for an art seminar.'

I drew some reassurance from her dislike of the pretty-pretty, and in fact I took an almost instant liking to her.

At supper she said to me: 'Ducks can't be your real name, can it?'

'No, but that's what everybody calls me.'

'Absurd English middle-class habit. I can't call my daughter-in-law Ducks –' She must have noticed the embarrassed exchange of glances with Conan, for she immediately turned to him and demanded, 'She is going to be my daughter-in-law, isn't she? I take it you haven't brought her here for a quick fuck.' Which is more or less how – or should I say why – Conan and I became engaged.

Vesta and Vida both wept at the news. Rocky was still abroad and could not be contacted. Stevie threw her arms round me and also wept, but I wasn't sure whether it was for herself or for me, and I almost wept with her, though again I wasn't sure for whose sake. My announcement couldn't have come as a surprise to her, for by then Conan was at the flat almost daily, but she had warned me not to vest too much hope in our relationship (as if I needed any such warning) for 'there was many a slip between cup and lip', though I had almost felt compelled to warn her not to vest too much hope in the probability of such a slip, because clearly she had been looking forward to having me as the companion of her old age. I understood her ambivalent attitude to my announcement. I would have felt the same in her place and I hesitated to tell her for that reason. In fact I became rather concerned about her. She still had her sweet, kindly face and luminous eyes, but she was redressing the deprivation in the other areas of her life by over-indulgence in food and drink, and her face was becoming pouchy and her figure bulky. 'You know,' she said to me once, 'it's good to know you're past it. You can relax and enjoy yourself.' But she was neither relaxed nor enjoying herself. She said she planned to devote her retirement to writing a novel, 'a classic, a masterpiece, *millions* of words long.' She certainly made the effort, for often when I returned in the early hours of the morning the light was still on in her room, and her typewriter was clicking away like a berserk cricket. When I asked her to show me what she had done, she said: 'No, no, it's bad luck to show work in progress. You'll have to wait till I've finished. It shouldn't take me more than fifty years.'

When I told father I was about to marry, he said:

'Are you? That's nice. I was beginning to think you were too bright for that sort of thing. Men are a little afraid of bright women, I know I always was.' Then he added: 'I don't suppose your young man is Jewish?'

'No, I'm afraid not, nor, for that matter, is he a young man.'

'But you won't be marrying in church, will you?'

'No, I shouldn't think so.'

I know what had prompted the question. His genealogical research had carried him as far back as the sixteenth century, and he had discovered, or thought he had discovered (from what I could see, the evidence was tenuous in the extreme), that we were descended from a famous Polish rabbi called the Admor of Plotsk and he clearly felt that the descendant (albeit a female) of such an eminence had no right to marry in church. Conan had expressed a complete indifference to religion, though he thought it was 'good for a joke', but he would have been quite prepared to marry in synagogue if I had shown any strong feelings on the matter. His mother announced that she was 'off God' and regarded all religious institutions, whether churches or synagogues, as 'places of ill repute'. Before we had settled the matter, however, we were overtaken by another event. Josh, the wonder child, was getting married. I received the news with an involuntary groan. Vesta looked at me with wonder. I wondered at it myself. I supposed that now, when I was at last the centre of attention and a source of joy, I didn't care to be upstaged by my younger half-brother. It also meant that Conan and I would have to delay our own plans for the time being, and I was nervous of delays.

'I suppose,' said Vesta, 'your're worried at the thought that the wedding will bring father and Tilly together again.'

But that wasn't my only worry.

14
A Woman for all Seasons

We didn't charter a plane, though it might have been cheaper if we had, for we went *en masse* – sisters, brothers-in-law, nephews, nieces. Josh met us at the airport, showing no signs of the injury he had suffered three years before, and looked large, cheerful and bucolic, though he had adopted a curious Afro hair-style which did not quite go with the rest of his personality. We were all keen to have a sight of the bride, but she, apparently, was not to be unveiled until the wedding.

We had booked the better part of a floor at the Dan Hotel in Haifa, which was about half an hour from the kibbutz. Tilly, I was relieved to hear, was staying with Josh at the kibbutz.

We arrived in Israel a few days before the wedding. Conan, who was extremely busy, arranged to join us on the eve of the wedding, and so for a night or two I had a room to myself. Rocky asked if she could move in with me, for she did not like to sleep alone, especially in a strange place. I was not overjoyed at the thought of her company.

'Don't you sleep alone in London?' I asked.

'Not if I can help it, and in any case London is not a strange place. I shan't make a pass at you – promise. I'm neither a lessie, nor incestuous.'

'I'm surprised. I always thought you were in the vanguard of fashion.'

I should have said no. I wasn't even sure that I had said yes, but as I was undressing, there was a knock on the door, and there she was in a flimsy nightie under a flimsy dressing-gown.

'Wouldn't it be nice if Vida and Vesta could join us?' she said. 'It would be quite like old times.'

'Somehow I rather prefer the new ones.'

'Don't expect too much out of marriage, my girl, or you're in for a shock,' she said. 'You're listening to the voice of experience.'

'I shouldn't imagine any two marriages are alike, any more than any two people are alike.'

'Oh, but they are, in basics.'

'Which basics?'

'I don't mean sex, but you experience a sort of transfusion. Something of the other person becomes part of you, and if you're fond of the person you are, as I was – as I am and as I take it you are – it can be an unpleasant experience.'

'Wouldn't it depend on who the other person is?'

'Shouldn't think so. It's the otherness of the other person which is unpleasant, if you know what I mean, and it doesn't matter if he's a shit like Troy, or a goody-goody like Conan.'

I hesitated about putting my next question, for I didn't think I would be happy with the answer, but the matter had always intrigued me.

'Was there anything between you and Conan?'

'Do you mean, did he screw me?'

'I'm sure he did, everbody has, but that's beside the point.'

'As a matter of fact, he didn't, and I'm not just saying so to put your mind at rest. You look surprised.'

'I am surprised.'

'I thought you would be. What you're saying, aren't you, is that if he wasn't out to screw me, what else did he see in me, but as a matter of fact he's been after me for years, only I kept telling him he must meet my sister. She's much brighter and has much bigger tits.'

'How did the tits come up?'

'Well you know Conan, don't you, they come up with everything. He kept complaining that mine were too small.'

'Ah, so you were bosom friends.'

'Not in that sense, but he did say if only I had a bosom, or rather more of a bosom, I'd be the perfect woman.'

'Did he ever propose to you?'

'I told you, he never stopped. Mind you, I'm not sure how serious he was, for he even kept proposing when Troy was around.'

I don't know why it should have done, but the conversation disturbed me deeply, and I spent a sleepless night, half-wondering if I should strangle my naughty little sister sleeping, oh, ever so peacefully, in the next bed.

The next morning I descended rather bleary-eyed for breakfast, and Stevie, who looked refreshed and relaxed, if a bit bulky in a flowing caftan, said to me:

'Hello, somebody's had a hard night, and Conan isn't even here, is he?' And when I didn't answer, she came over and put an arm round my shoulders. 'Ducks, I haven't said anything to upset you, have I?'

'No, you haven't.'

'Then who has?'

I shrugged my shoulders.

'Ducks, something has upset you.'

'It's nothing. I always sleep badly when I'm away from home.'

When Conan arrived the next afternoon I greeted him with such fervour that he nearly toppled over.

'What's the matter?' he whispered. 'Have you been missing it?'

'No,' I said, 'I've been missing *you*.' I rushed him up to my room before he could be waylaid by the rest of the family, and it was only after we had slept together that I began to feel at peace with myself and the world.

That evening we had a festive family meal and father, at the head of the table, was in better form than he had been for years, bolstered up, no doubt, by the sight of his children and grandchildren.

There were sixteen of us round the table, and towards the end of the meal he rose, a trifle unsteadily, to make a toast. 'To my absent son and his absent bride first of all, to my daughters and my sons-in-law, and to my grandchildren or, as I like to see them, to my second and third innings respectively. I don't know how many such family gatherings I can hope to look forward to –'

'Dozens,' Norrie interjected.

'But let me say' – he always sounded vaguely Churchillian when he had been drinking – 'that few men could have had as much joy as I have derived, and continue to derive, from my daughters –'

'And sons-in-law,' Norrie interjected.

'And sons-in-law, of course.' I looked towards Rocky out of the corner of my eyes, but she sat with arms folded and her gaze firmly fixed on her plate. 'I cannot myself claim to have enjoyed many triumphs in my journey through life, but life does not end with oneself, it only begins, and I have always looked upon you, my dear Vesta and you –' I felt apprehensive about what he might say next, and was relieved when a waiter tapped me on the shoulder and said I was wanted on the 'phone.

It was Grace.

'Has the clan gathered?' she asked.

'And how! Father's just in the middle of a speech.'

'Oh, I'm sorry. Did I interrupt?'

'No, I'm glad you did. Father doesn't make speeches often but he's like a French horn when he does, you're never sure what's going to emerge. I'll be seeing you at the wedding, won't I?'

'Have you ever been to a kibbutz wedding? They have thousands of guests, and I mean thousands – it's like a football match. Everybody in the country knows everybody else, and the kibbutz is the one place where you can afford to invite everybody you know, and quite a few people you don't, and in any case, people here don't wait to be invited, they just come. Mother's here by the way, and so is my sister-in-law. We'll all be there except Otto.'

They arranged to call in at our hotel on the way to the wedding and arrived in time for a snack lunch, which we ate out on the terrace overlooking Haifa Bay.

'I don't know why I am living in England when I could be living here,' said father. 'Look at the sea, look at the sky, look at the sun.'

'You should do what mother's done,' said Grace, 'get yourself a place here,' which, coming from Grace, was a tactless remark. Did she not know that father was virtually a kept man? But if father was embarrassed, he gave no sign of it, and said he planned to stay on after the wedding to continue with his genealogical research and, while he was at it, he would look out for a likely place to which he might retire. Did he have money that I didn't know about? Could his fortunes have picked up?

Sophie was a feast for the eye. She could not have been less than sixty, yet the only sign of age was a slight pouchiness at the edges of her mouth and a hint of an underchin. Her neck was so smooth that I wondered if she had had plastic surgery, and she was deeply tanned, which suited her and which somehow enhanced the sparkle of her eyes.

I asked Grace whether Sophie had a lover.

'At *her* age? *I'm* even beginning to feel past it.'

'She's never looked better.'

'That's what everybody says. Whenever we have people over all the men crowd round her – it makes me quite jealous. Poor daddy added years to her life, and now he's gone she's enjoying something of a rebate. For that matter your father's in fine fettle. Last time I saw him he looked ghastly. Perhaps people get a second wind when they reach their sixties. Well, that's something to look forward to at least.'

When we reached the kibbutz most of the guests had arrived, and there were milling crowds everywhere. Josh's wife had been born in Israel. Her grandparents were among the founders of one of the first kibbutzim; she and her family knew everybody and everybody knew them and people had descended by the bus-load. Moreover, both Josh and his bride had served in the army and Israel's frontiers must have been left singularly unprotected that evening, for something like a field division turned up for the wedding – some of them in khaki, some in white shirts, others in cotton frocks – and greeted one another with loud whoops of joy. Swarms of small children on bicycles, pinging their bells loudly, wove in and out of the crowd, and crumpled ancients in straw hats approached one another hesitatingly, wondering if they were who they thought they were. I was watching the scene with bemusement when I turned and suddenly found myself face to face with Tilly.

I had somehow contrived her out of my thoughts since arriving in Israel, as if hoping that by not thinking about her, she might never materialize. But there she was, looking magnificent in a pleated frock with large black polka-dots, and a large, garden-party hat.

'My dear,' she said – her voice was slightly hoarse, which gave it an oddly seductive sound – 'I was so delighted by your good news.'

I wondered who could have told her. It wasn't me, so I presumed it was Josh, but I was mistaken.

'Your father 'phoned me, of course, but I was hoping I might hear from you personally, didn't you think I have a right to know?'

'I don't know if this is the moment to be frank, Tilly, but to be perfectly honest, I didn't think you'd be interested.'

She gave me a pained look.

'I'd have been interested if I had only been your governess, but it so happens that I was also your stepmother. I could understand your resentment when I was still married to your father, because you obviously wanted him to yourself, but now that we're divorced – why? Don't you think you and I should have a long talk sometime? Perhaps while we're here?'

I didn't care much for woman-to-woman confessionals. I am not one for opening up my bosom especially as on the rare occasions that I open up, I open up, whereas I was not sure if I could trust her to do the same, but I was not anxious to prolong the conversation at that moment and I agreed to meet her at the hotel the following evening.

In the meantime, the crowds were continuing to grow

and the air was loud with excited screams as friends who might not have seen each other for as much as six weeks cried their greetings in any of five or six languages, and the English alone came in several accents:

'Rivka, is that you? You look marvellous . . . Brenda, what are you doing here? . . . Masha, it isn't Masha, it can't be, it is . . .'

As the day darkened, a black-clad, bearded rabbi appeared from nowhere, flanked by two burly youths, who looked like police escorts, and the crowds quietened as the ceremony was about to begin.

Josh's bride, Jospa (they were known among their friends as Josh and Joss), was small, dark, satiny and exquisite, with huge black eyes, a tiny, upturned nose and a generous mouth. She wore the usual bridal outfit and was almost hidden behind her bouquet. Josh, in a white, open-necked shirt and white skull-cap, towered two heads above her. Many eyes, I noticed, were on Tilly. Her large hat obscured her heavy make-up, but certainly from a distance she looked quite regal, and she and father made a handsome couple. He had originally thought of coming to the wedding in a frock-coat but we talked him out of it, and instead he wore a light-grey mohair suit and a light-blue tie. He had lost some of the bulk which had weighed him down in middle age and, with his thin, silvery hair, he looked rather distinguished, 'like an English milord' as someone observed.

There was a large open courtyard at the side of the kibbutz dining-hall, which had been set up with row upon row of trestle tables, with garlands slung along them and about them. The whole area was festooned with lanterns and fairy lights and, as the sun set, the lights went on. The surrounding trees and flower beds were floodlit and I felt a sense of enchantment I had not known since childhood. Even Conan seemed moved. 'This is fairy land,' he said. The heat of the day had passed and a gentle breeze wafted through the trees.

I don't remember much about the food, though there was plenty of it, but I do remember the singing, and somehow managed to join in, though I was unfamiliar both with the words and the melodies. There was also a cabaret which took the form of a 'This is Your Life' presentation on both the bride and groom, with their different lifestyles contrasted, and although it was in Hebrew (and Grace offered a translation) it was not difficult to get the gist. Josh was born in a palace amidst plenty, into the home of empire (depicted by the strains of 'Rule Britannia'); Jospa was born in a tent, in a time of austerity in a struggling and beleaguered land; but he was pulled towards Zion and she towards medicine, and they met in an army hospital where she was a physiotherapist and he was struggling to get back on to his feet, and they lived happily ever after.

'Marvellous affair,' said Robin. 'It's worth joining a kibbutz just for the weddings.'

Once the meal was over the tables were moved, and the dancing began to a five-piece band provided by the kibbutz, each dance more exhausting than the one before.

I had come in high-heeled sandals, which I kicked off and danced in my stockinged feet. After the first round the soles of my tights were worn clean away, and I went to a dark corner, pulled them off, threw them into a dustbin, and continued in my bare feet, but after three such dances I was too exhausted to continue further. So was Conan, but looking round I was amazed to see father, who had removed jacket and tie, still dancing away. He was held on one side by Jospa's father and on the other by her mother. Her father was a general in the reserves, a robust man with a huge moustache, and a vast chest (or stomach, for it was difficult to say where the one finished and the other began). If a tank could have assumed human form it would have looked something like him, but father was obviously determined not be outdanced by him, and I was worried about the effect. So was Tilly.

'He wants to show that there's life in the old dog yet,' she said. 'He could kill himself. Why don't you talk to him?' There were other white-haired figures even older than father still dancing, anxious to demonstrate that they still had their youthful vigour. I could hardly approach father while they were on their feet.

'I was once at a kibbutz wedding and two or three of the old crocks dropped in the course of the celebrations,' said Grace. 'If you ask me these dances are a form of tacit euthanasia.'

At which I hesitated no longer and went over to father and, dancing along behind him, tried to whisper in his ear that he had had enough. When he didn't hear me, I shouted my message, at which Jospa's father, who was known to his friends as Katanchik ('the little one') shouted back: 'What do you want from him? He dances beautifully.' Father was too breathless to say anything and seemed borne along by the momentum of the dance, but just as I was beginning to wonder whether I should have to remove him physically, the band stopped for breath and he staggered into my arms.

'That was marvellous,' he gasped. 'Never enjoyed anything so much in my life.' Sweat was pouring in broad streams down his face and neck, and his shirt was drenched and clung to him like a skin. 'Bit different from Vesta's coming-out party, what?'

As we were talking, Katanchik, who seemed to have assumed the role of Master of Ceremonies, announced that in honour of the British guests, the band would play the Lancers, and bowing to Sophie, he took her by the hand. For all his bulk he moved with great elegance and others quickly joined, including Tilly and Josh, Vesta and Robin, Vida and Norrie.

'Come on,' said father, 'let's join them.'

'No you're not,' I said. 'We're sitting this one out.'

When Conan asked me to dance I said I had to keep an eye on father. 'Try Stevie,' I added, 'she's looking a trifle lonely and subdued.' Instead he tried Rocky, who was a graceful and beautiful dancer. The dance seemed to go on for ever and I nearly bit through my lower lip before it was finished.

Finally Katanchik introduced his *pièce de résistance*, an old friend of his who had served in the Black Watch during the war and who, after a fanfare, appeared with pipe and kilt to play the Gay Gordons. This time when father jumped up to join in, I did not attempt to restrain him. I looked round for Conan but he was nowhere to be seen; neither was Rocky.

Stevie grabbed me by the hand. 'Come on,' she said, 'don't you want to join in? Don't you like the Gay Gordons?'

At that moment I hated the Gay Gordons, and pipe music, and Stevie and everybody. I had visions of Conan and Rocky copulating somewhere behind a bush, and as I turned this way and that, I promised myself that if I caught them I would tear his genitals clean away from his body.

I must have looked fairly distraught, for Katanchik's wife, a sweet little woman, came up to me and said:

'You sick?'

'Sick?'

'No good, no well? Sick?'

'No, I'm fine, really fine,' and just then I felt Conan's hand on my shoulder and I almost cried with relief.

'Where were you?' he said. 'The dance is almost over.'

It was soon quite over, but by popular request the piper played an encore, a fairly feeble one as it happened, for he was not a young man, but we joined in with gusto.

When it was over Katanchik grouped a large circle of chairs round a table and called for refreshments.

'Here, sit down, drink,' he ordered, and one could not but comply.

I was surprised to find that Robin and Katanchik had already met.

'He was in my brigade headquarters during the war', said Katanchik, 'and wanted to volunteer for service. I told him he would have to forget everything he had learned in the British army before I could use him.'

'What's wrong with the British army?' said father. 'It hasn't lost a war yet.'

'But it has lost many battles. We can't even afford to lose a battle. Even with the so-called greater Israel we have not time or room for manoeuvre. A Wellington or a Montgomery would have been no use to us. We have no time for build-ups. When there's full mobilization there is no one to drive the buses and bake the bread, and, in any case, half the buses are also mobilized. No, all our campaigns are based on *chutzpah*, audacity, on not doing the expected thing, even on not doing the sensible thing.'

'I would agree with that,' said Robin, 'some of the things I saw made my hair stand on end.'

'You should have seen some of the things you didn't see,' said Katanchik, 'your hair would have turned white. I was at Camberley, you know, and I admire the tradition and discipline of the British army, we could do with some of it here.' He put his hand on Robin's knee. 'Why don't you settle here and become a regular soldier? You'd be on the general staff. I would see to it.'

Robin turned to Vesta: 'What do you say to that?'

'Can't see Vesta being an army wife,' said father.

'Wives here aren't confined to barracks,' said Katanchik. 'Israel's a small country. You could live in Tel Aviv and be at GHQ in twenty minutes.'

'I don't know if I could live here,' said Vesta. 'We smoulder quietly up in the grey north. People catch fire here and burn brightly. Perhaps I'm getting old, but I don't think I can take the colour, the vigour, the pace.'

'I have got old,' said father, 'but could live here quite happily.'

'So could I,' said Tilly, at which Vesta and I exchanged looks. She had taken her hat off and let her hair down. Her reddish period was behind her and her hair was now a sort of blue-black, which rather suited her – almost the same colour as Sophie, but Sophie never looked anything other than cool, whereas Tilly was sweating heavily. Both her blouse and her bra were soaked, and the dark-red of her nipples stood out like small, contained bloodstains. I daren't think what I must have looked like.

Katanchik put an arm round Sophie:

'Why don't you come here?' he said. 'There's not enough beautiful women in Israel. I know them all.'

'There's your wife.'

'Her I know too well. Besides, now that she's a mother-in-law she wants to retire.'

'I'm also a mother-in-law, in fact I'm a grandmother, so that I've retired a long time ago.'

'Then it's time you came out of retirement. I'm a general, retired, but in the reserves, and wherever there's a war I'm back on duty.'

'But I'm not in the army, *mon général*, and I'm too old to come out of retirement.'

'Too old? Too old? Years is nothing. I am older than anybody here –'

'Not than me, you're not,' said father.

'Or me,' said Tilly.

'Or me,' said Sophie.

'Or me,' added Stevie hesitantly.

'All right, not in years, but experience. I fight in four wars, I am wounded five times, but I can pack in more in a day than any two young men I know. It's not years that's important, it's – spirit. You, my dear, have got spirit.'

'Not at this moment I haven't,' she said, suppressing a yawn. 'I'm ready for bed –'

'That's what I mean by spirit,' said Katanchik, rubbing his hands, 'so am I.'

'You must have a very understanding wife,' said Stevie.

'I haven't,' he said, pinching his wife's cheek affectionately, 'but she doesn't understand a word of English.'

He later commandeered an accordian player and his accordian and entertained us to a medley of Israeli songs in a deep baritone voice. 'Wars may be bad for everything else,' he said, 'but they're good for songs. Every tune brings memories of a different campaign.' Father then continued with British war songs and we all joined in with 'Lili Marlene'.

'Where do these chaps get their stamina from?' Conan whispered to me. 'I'm ready to drop.'

I was tired myself, but was reluctant to break up the party, especially as father seemed to be enjoying himself so much. But when Sophie and Grace rose to leave, I said it was time to take father back to his hotel.

'What is it, is your father a piece of baggage who can't move on his own?' said Katanchik. 'He's a young man, the night is young. He sleeps here. You all sleep here.'

'There's a lot of us,' said father.

'There's always room in Israel. It's a small country with lots of room, specially for pretty women. The women all sleep in my room, for the men I find room also.'

'Seriously, it's getting late,' I said.

'But I'm serious, you can all sleep here, even if I sleep in the open.'

Conan was expecting an early morning call from London and he managed to persuade him that he for one had to get back.

'All right then you can go, but your father, he stays. He is my personal guest.' It seemed as if we mightn't be able to extricate him without the use of force, and as he was beginning to look very tired, we agreed to leave him as a sort of hostage.

I was sorry we did, for the minute we were in the car I had visions of father spending the night with Tilly. When they arrived at the hotel the next day I felt sure they had done so.

At father's request she joined us at supper and entered into the conversation lightly and cheerfully as if she had never left the family circle. She looked at me from time to time, but even when she didn't she could not have been unaware of the looks of sullen resentment I was casting in her direction. What added to my resentment was the fact that no one else there seemed to mind having her around. I took it for granted that Vesta wouldn't mind, for in that respect she was mindless, but didn't Vida or Rocky resent her – didn't Stevie? Conan turned to me once or twice in the course of the meal and asked if anything was troubling me.

'Everything,' I said, out of the side of my mouth. Finally I could stand it no longer, jumped from my seat and strode out, not only out of the dining-room, but out of the hotel. Conan came after me, his napkin still under his chin.

'What's the matter? What's got into you?'

'I need some fresh air.'

'I still don't understand.'

'I'm going to have a great, big, dirty showdown with that bitch, and I want you to be with me while I'm at it in case I explode.'

'Not on your life I won't. You're not going to bring me into your family quarrels, but if you don't mind my saying so, if you take such violent exception to a person, part of the cause must lie in yourself.'

'Look Conan, it's perfectly straightforward, that woman's a witch and she's been casting a spell on father.'

'If she's cast a spell on anyone, it's you. You're not normal when she's around.'

What he said may have been true, but I didn't like to hear him say it. As a result we had our first serious quarrel, which confirmed my suspicion that that woman was created to cast a blight on my life. I was to have seen her that evening, but I was not in a mood to see anyone. I complained of a headache and went to bed.

I must have dozed off for a while, for when I opened my eyes, Rocky was sitting by my side.

'I got you a pot of tea and some sandwiches,' she said, 'in case of night starvation. You went to bed without supper.'

'Who sent you?'

'Did anybody have to send me?'

'Rocky, I'm not in the mood for games.'

'Stevie put it to me that I'd done something to upset you. I don't know what it could have been, but if so, I'm sorry.'

'Stevie said? The woman's a silly bitch.'

'She said I shouldn't have danced with Conan last night, and that you were casting daggers at my back with every step I made, but damn it, if a girl can't dance with her prospective brother-in-law, who can she dance with? I danced with Robin, I even danced with Norrie. I danced with –'

I didn't know what was happening to Stevie, or rather I did, and I was rather afraid that if I didn't keep a firm control of myself I might say something to her which would leave us both sorry. I wondered whether the defects which I had charitably ascribed to her disappointments and age hadn't always been there.

'Look,' I said, 'I've always been aware that I was never as graceful as you, or Vesta or Vida, but it never really mattered until I saw you and Conan dancing together last night.'

'It would have been unfair, Ducks, if you had grace on top of everything else. You're brighter than any of us, you've got more guts than any of us, more character –'

'More tits.'

'Don't laugh at tits, they also count for something. I thought of getting a pair made.'

'You'd look squat with big tits.'

'Which is why I didn't get them.'

'Rocky, look me straight in the eyes, I want you to be perfectly honest.'

She looked at me, with her large green eyes, flecked with brown, at once so innocent and so mischievous.

'Why are you trying to butter me up?'

'Butter –? For Christ sake, Ducks, don't you know I've always been envious of you?'

'Don't make me laugh. What did you have to be envious of? There are only two things which have ever counted in your life, men and money, and you've never been short of either.'

'Which shows how little you know me. I settled for them because they were the only things I could get.'

'Look, if you're hoping to provoke tears, for poor little, sweet little, misunderstood little Rocky, you're working on the wrong person. It may be that father having sired three diligent, hard-working daughters was prepared to indulge the fourth, and that even Tilly was easy on you, and yes, you may have been spoilt, but the way you've developed cannot be put down to mere indulgence. You're rapacious, predatory, selfish, inconsiderate, venal, vicious, corrupt, scheming, devious, a liar, something of a tart, and more than something of a –' I was cut short by a knock on the door. It was father.

'Hello,' he said smiling, 'am I interrupting a sisterly *tête-à-tête*?'

I was grateful for the interruption, for I was getting carried away.

'Are you feeling better?' he added.

'Words tend to fail her,' said Rocky, rising, 'otherwise she's fine.'

I took father's hand and he sat down on the bed.

'Sorry for the way I behaved,' I said.

'We hardly had any sleep last night, you must have been very tired.'

'Not half as tired as you should be, you danced us all off our feet.'

'I wasn't dancing. I was borne along by Katanchik.'

'Father, a candid question.'

'Oh dear.'

'Why the "oh dear"?'

'Because you'll presumably want a candid answer.'

'Do you intend to remarry Tilly?'

'I was waiting for that. We had a child together, you know, and when that happens you never become entirely unmarried. She was a bit difficult about the time of the divorce when she thought – indeed when I thought – I was rich, but she was marvellous after everything collapsed.'

'You mean once she found you were no longer worth holding on to she decided not to hold on.'

'You do see things in a peculiar way, my dear. No, she was very reasonable and very sympathetic, and then, of course, there was Josh's injury, which naturally brought us together, and now, there's the wedding.'

'But you haven't answered my question. Do you intend to marry her?'

'I'm too old and too poor to contemplate any such step. My insurance policies have matured and that gives me just about enough to live on, but I'm not in a position to take on responsibilities. Besides, I suspect Tilly has a young man.'

'A *young* man?'

'I don't know how old he is, but I've had to 'phone her from time to time and on more than one occasion a man has answered the 'phone. He sounded quite young.'

That mollified me a little, but as he went on I was becoming increasingly aware that it was getting late and that Conan had not yet come to see me. I had said I was very tired and wanted to rest, but he might at least have popped his head round the door to see how I was doing. Instead he kept resolutely away. Was he angry, or was he too engrossed with the company downstairs to think about me?

Father continued to talk in an unusually open way about Tilly and himself, but I was no longer listening, and he only broke off when he heard me sobbing.

'What's the matter? Have I said something to upset you?'

'No, no. I suppose I'm tired and want to sleep.'

I didn't want to sleep, and couldn't have slept even if I had wanted to. I tried to read, but couldn't concentrate, and I put out the light and sat upright in the darkness, waiting for Conan to appear. We had adjoining rooms with a communicating door.

It was after midnight before he came upstairs. I was certain that he would at least put his head round the door, if only out of curiosity, but he didn't. I could hear his radio playing, and then the water gurgling in his bathroom, and for a moment I thought I could hear a woman's voice, but I was mistaken. The gurgling stopped, and so did the radio, but his lights stayed on which suggested that he was reading in bed – or was he perhaps waiting to see if I would come in? He had come into my bed last night, and I had said I would be coming into his tonight. Did he still expect me to keep my promise after he had left me on my own all evening?

I continued to sit upright in the darkness, and after about an hour he switched his light off. I looked round my room for a blunt instrument and had I found one I would have been tempted to use it. For a moment I seriously contemplated stabbing him with my nail-file. I could imagine the headlines: LONDON WOMAN STABS LOVER IN HOLY LAND HOTEL. 'Tells police: "He had it coming." '

I must have eventually dropped off. When I woke there was light streaming in through a chink in the curtain and I could hear the movement of traffic outside. I looked at my watch. It was just after five. I got up, had a bath, dressed, packed, took a taxi to the local bus station, and arrived at the Weizmann Institute in Rehovoth just as Grace was seeing her children off to school. She was still in her nightie.

'Ducks? Where did you spring from at this hour of the morning?'

I opened my mouth to speak, but couldn't and collapsed in tears on her shoulder.

She took me into the house, made me a strong cup of coffee, and listened with her hand over her mouth as I described what had happened. When I had finished, she poured me another coffee and said: 'Don't move, I'll be down in a minute.'

I sat for a time gazing ruefully into my cup, feeling as if my world had come to an end. I rose and wandered into the living-room. Two walls were lined with books, a third was lined with photographs, mostly of children at various stages of development. There were also photos of Sophie and Callum outside Roscoe House, and Callum himself in tropical kit, fair-haired, smiling, his chest lined with medal ribbons, and then, surprisingly, a photo of Vesta and Grace at their coming-out ball. I gazed at it for a long time hardly believing that there was a time when I was part of that world, how distant it seemed and how unreal. There was a family group taken at the same event, and there I was with all the properties of a fully grown, indeed a somewhat overgrown, woman, twenty years ago. There was another, taken in Oxford, of Grace, Vesta and me, with Weedy scowling in the background. Looking at the photographs eased my feelings of desolation slightly. I suppose they reminded me that no matter how hopeless things looked, life had had its moments.

Grace came down after about twenty minutes, fully

dressed, but without her make-up.

'You're coming with me,' she said.

'Where to?'

'A magical mystery tour.'

But it was soon clear that we were on the way back to Haifa.

'You're quite mad, do you know that Ducks? Quite mad. Conan's a man in a million: intelligent, witty, urbane, successful –'

'Insensitive.'

'He didn't strike me as being insensitive.'

'Nobody does at first encounter.'

'Has it ever occurred to you that you could perhaps be too demanding?'

'Demanding? What have I demanded? He could see I was upset –'

'From what you told me, you weren't so much upset as having a tantrum.'

'A tantrum?'

'You're prone to tantrums, you used to have them at school all the time. Wasn't leaving your hotel at the crack of dawn a tantrum?'

'It was not a fucking tantrum,' I screamed, 'it was an act of despair. I couldn't stand the thought of facing them.'

'All right, you're not having a fucking tantrum.' Her mouth tightened and she drove on in silence. I began sobbing, which seemed to catch her by surprise, and she pulled into the side of the road and put my head on her shoulder.

'What's happening to you, Ducks, this isn't you.' There was no point in answering, for I wasn't sure that I knew either. She seemed on the brink of tears herself.

'Look, you're about to get married to the most marvellous man, you should be on top of the world. Why are you acting in this way?'

'Perhaps because I can't see it happening.'

'Why shouldn't it happen? Is it because you think it shouldn't?'

'Why should I think that?'

'You know what Jewish puritanism is.'

'I know what puritanism is, but what's it got to do with me? You're not going to tell me that I'm one of those sub-conscious puritans.'

'You are in the sense that you disapprove of yourself, and you may feel that you don't deserve to be happy.'

'I disapprove of everybody –'

'But of yourself particularly. I suspect you would feel there was something wrong with the world if, in spite of all your short-comings, you married a fine chap like Conan and lived happily ever after.'

Conan was waiting outside the hotel. He had obviously been expecting me and greeted us with a smile.

'Feeling better?' he asked.

'If I am, it's not thanks to you,' I retorted.

'She's all yours,' said Grace and, quickly reversing the car, she shot down the hill. He took my hand and we walked slowly down towards the harbour.

'I'm sorry,' he said, 'but I thought you wanted to be left alone.'

'I did at the moment I went upstairs, but it didn't mean I wanted to be left alone for ever. Father had the sensitivity to understand, why didn't you?'

'Possibly because I'm not your father, and to be perfectly frank, your conduct reminded me a little of my mother.'

'Your mother?'

'Irrational conduct always reminds me of my mother. Father made the mistake of giving in to all her whims, but it wasn't particularly important because he had his own little place in town, and she was in the country, and each lived their own lives, but I take it that that's not how we're going to go on. I can be reasonable and understanding when I'm dealing with reasonable people.'

'And you thought I was being unreasonable?'

'Let's be frank: weren't you? We were in a room full of people, enjoying an evening meal and each other's company, when, for no reason that I could understand, you flounced out. I went after you to humour you, which was a mistake, for you weren't in a mood to be humoured, but having done it once, I was determined not to do it again, and I would have thought you knew me well enough not to expect it a second time. I regard myself as a rational man and think of you as a rational woman, and your tantrums took me completely unawares.'

'Tantrum did you say? That's Grace's word.'
'I spoke to Grace this morning.'
'And she said that I had tantrums?'
'I asked her if you were prone to tantrums.'
'And supposing I am?'
'Then chuck it.'

At that moment I began to realize how hot it was, and how tired I was. We went into a café and he ordered cold drinks.

'Look,' I said, 'I'm normally rational and rarely have tantrums, but am rarely in love. I was dying to see you last night and to have you beside me in bed – not even necessarily inside me in bed – but just to rub against you. I'm so used to having you around that bed doesn't feel like bed on my own. I hardly slept a wink.'

He pushed his hand between the buttons of my skirt and grasped my thigh.

'I didn't sleep much either.'
'Don't,' I said, 'not here, or I shall start to undress.'
'Tired as you are?'
'Tired as I am. Let's go to bed.'
'In the middle of the morning?'
'I'm a woman for all hours.'
'I'm not sure if I'm up to it.'
'You will be.'
And he was.

15
Ladies in Retirement

As soon as I dressed I kissed him on the forehead and said goodbye.

'Where are you off to?'

'An exorcism. How does that sound?'

'Crazy.'

'That's the thing with you rational folk, you dismiss everything you can't grasp as nonsense. On balance I think I'd rather be thought of as irrational. Tell your mother we're birds of a feather.'

Tilly had returned to the kibbutz shortly after breakfast. I tried to 'phone her, but nobody knew where she was or at least no one was willing to contact her. I decided to take a taxi in the hope that she would still be there. Conan offered to come with me, but I reminded him of his determination not to get mixed up in my family's quarrels. 'In any case,' I added, 'if there's a stranger to the scene the exorcism may not work.'

It was a large kibbutz and I had some difficulty in finding my way around. The office was closed and no one seemed to know exactly where Tilly was staying or how she might be found.

'Try the tannoy in the dining-hall,' someone suggested. I didn't know if he was being serious, and I was going to do just that, when I had the bright idea of asking for Katanchik. Everybody knew Katanchik, and I found him in a deck-chair outside his house with Tilly stretched out on the lawn at his feet.

'Ah, have you come back to see me?' said Katanchik. 'I thought you would. Once a woman sets eyes on me, she can't get me out of her system.' He engulfed me in an embrace.

'I rather think the trouble is, she can't get me out of her system,' said Tilly.

Katanchik left us alone after a minute and I said to her: 'I suppose I owe you an apology.'

'You don't, you know, or an explanation – though I think the others in the hotel could have done with one. To be honest you left me feeling worried. Conan's a delight, but I can't see how you're going to settle down in marriage while you've still got these incestuous feelings for your father. I dare say it's a phase which most daughters go through, but it looks as if you're never going to grow out of yours. You should have married Callum, he was so much like your father in appearance and build and he was very fond of you.'

'Did he tell you that?'

'You lived together, didn't you?'

'That's one of the things which frightened me about you, Tilly: you know everything about everybody, and nobody knows anything about you.'

'What is there you don't know?'

'Where did you spring from suddenly when you became our governess, where did you vanish to?'

'Didn't my father tell you everything?'

'He was a sweet old man, but not very coherent.'

'What about Amy? I should perhaps tell you that I bumped into her at Grace's wedding, but she recoiled as if she had seen a ghost. I can't believe that she, of all people, could have kept anything to herself.'

'She might have told me everything if I hadn't mentioned I was your step-daughter –'

'And did that shut her up?'

'She became tearful.'

'I can't imagine it. She's as hard as nails, they all are, especially her brothers. I can't say my own are much better, but they were dim. And that was the thing. I was my father's pride and joy and, once it became clear that there was nothing to expect from my brothers, all his hopes rested on me. He hoped I would go to university, he hoped that I would become a doctor, but then I fell in love with Amy's brother. I was still at school at the time. We were married when I was eighteen and were separated before I was twenty. I don't suppose you know this, but only the man can initiate a *get*, a divorce, in Jewish law and he refused to do so. Father thought he might be holding out for money, but it wasn't even that. It was pure malice.'

'But you don't need a Jewish divorce to remarry –'

'Not in a civil ceremony, but supposing I wanted to marry in synagogue? And as luck would have it, I fell in love again with someone very religious, and once he saw I didn't have a *get* and would never get one, he wouldn't have anything more to do with me.'

'So what did you do?'

'What could I do? I stormed, I raged, I went berserk. When that didn't get me anywhere I lay down and hoped to die, and I nearly did. I discovered that life is a voluntary thing and if you want to give up the ghost, it's entirely within your power to do so; but then I turned and saw father beside me and felt I had to survive if only for him, but I couldn't, not as my old self. I wanted a new start among new people. I went to Australia for a while, but hated it, and worked my passage back as a governess to an English family, but I wasn't happy with them or with anyone else. They were fairly generous to me, but I was always kept slightly distant. I really wanted to graft myself on to a new family, and it can't be done in England, and as you know I didn't even succeed with your family.'

'You didn't succeed? We adored you.'

'As a governess, but once I became your father's wife I sensed resentment on every side. You never forgave my presumption, but in a way I was happy at "West Wynds", or at least happier than I had been anywhere else.'

'Do you remember one night you were crying?'

'Which particular night? I cried so often.'

'I remember only that one night, we all heard you. I thought your heart would break –'

'It must have been the day I got a letter from David's

mother – David was the man I had hoped to marry – saying he was dangerously ill and urging me to visit him. I couldn't bring myself to do it. I was afraid if I went back again I would never escape. And as it happens I wouldn't have got back in time – he died that night, poor boy. And that was the past I'd kept hidden, partly out of the fear that if I came to speak of it it might somehow catch up with me. I'm surprised that I should have been able to come out with it now. I suppose I think that at my age I'm safe.'

'Don't talk about your age. I wish I felt as young as you look. You talk about father and Callum being alike. You and Sophie are alike in that you're both ageless.'

'Sophie is so rich that even time treats her with deference. I spend days over the mirror and fortunes at the hairdresser in a vain effort to convince myself that I'm not past it. But look at these hands, aren't they the hands of an old woman?' They were mottled with brown spots, and I almost recoiled as she stretched out her fingers towards me. 'I had so hoped that we might become friends, you, your sisters and I, and especially you, for you were the one I liked the most, if only because you were the least precious and pampered, but you all kept your distance. In a way I understood it. Children always resent anyone taking their mother's place.'

'Why did you marry father?'

'Because I loved him, does that surprise you? And even so I hesitated because I could see there was little room in his affection for anyone outside his family, but I thought once you were grown up and had left home, things would change, but they didn't, partly because you were slow to grow up, and even slower to leave home. Ironically enough, the only one to leave with alacrity was Josh. But you stayed, after which I felt there was nothing to keep me at "West Wynds".'

At that moment the 'phone rang and we both froze. We had only heard it faintly, but we felt it somehow concerned us. Someone inside picked up the receiver and a minute later Katanchik emerged. He was ashen-faced and shaken, and his moustache, which normally bristled with confidence and looked as if it had a life of its own, flopped over his mouth, and it took him some time to find his voice.

Father had had a stroke.

The drive back to Haifa seemed the longest of my life.

Katanchik tried to reassure us that there were strokes and strokes and that he knew people who had not only been able to resume normal life after a stroke, but had found new energies.

'Half the people I know have had strokes. So maybe they can't use an arm or a leg, but you'll be surprised what you can manage without. As long as you've got spirit, and your father's got spirit. Plenty.'

Father was asleep when we arrived, and the doctor reassured us that the stroke had been 'a comparatively mild one'.

It didn't seem all that mild when I saw father the next day. He had lost the use of an eye, and of his right arm and his right leg. Later he said he 'felt like a piece of baggage'. His speech was slightly impaired.

Josh, who had flown back from honeymoon when he heard the news, tried to persuade him to remain in Israel and make his home in the kibbutz.

'It's all found,' he said, 'you'd have a small place of your own. It wouldn't be Roscoe House or even "West Wynds", but you'd be comfortable and you could help in looking after the gardens – or a job of that sort.' Father had always liked pottering about the garden and he had been fascinated by the exotic blooms he found in the kibbutz, so that he was not entirely averse to the idea.

'Would I have to give over all my possessions to the kibbutz?' he asked.

'Nothing of the sort. You wouldn't be a full member, but you would have a grace and favour residence. And perhaps in the summer when it gets too hot, you could stay with Vesta. You'd have the best of both worlds. I've just been in England,' he added, 'it's cold, wet and miserable. You'll be much happier here.'

'I won't be much use to you in the garden with one arm

and one leg.'

'A good gardener needs the right touch, not brute stamina. Everything here's mechanized. Look, try it. If you don't like it, Vesta will always be happy to have you back.'

He promised to think about it, but at the insistence of Sophie he moved to her villa in Caesarea to convalesce and Tilly stayed behind to help look after him.

I returned to London brimming with resentment, quite convinced that fate had it in for me, either through benign ways, such as Josh's wedding, which had taken the wind out of my sails and had forced me to delay my own wedding plans, or malign ways, such as father's stroke. What next? Would I succumb to general paralysis? Would Conan have a heart attack? Would the Thames overflow and overwhelm London? Would the third world war break out? I approached the few weeks left before our wedding more in trepidation than hope and almost resigned to the thought that it would never take place.

Our first task was to find a home. Conan had a tiny flat in a hideous rabbit-warren of a block near Sloane Square station, which seemed to be largely occupied by the ill-kempt, ill-kept women of ageing debauchees, which I was content to suffer for occasional nights, but I had no intention of beginning married life there. Vesta kindly offered to put the flat vacated by father at our disposal, which was rather more like it, but we had both decided we wanted a place of our own and we rushed around all over the home counties in our bid to find one. The very effort, at least, had the effect of clearing my mind a little of the weight of foreboding.

Both Conan and I stemmed from well-to-do households, both of us were trained as economists and, if pushed, we might have been prepared to take over the Treasury in the belief that we would not have made too bad a job at running the nation's finances, but we had no idea how to run our own affairs.

We had decided we wanted to live within reasonable reach of London, not too near his mother, possibly with a half-acre of garden, and six or seven, perhaps eight rooms, for we each wanted our own private studies, we hoped to have two or three children, we would probably need living-in help, and we wanted sufficient space to accommodate visiting friends. But when we came to look at actual properties, we discovered for the first time in our lives that we were among the poor. Conan earned a good salary, but he was in the habit of spending everything he earned and had no capital, and I too was by now almost penniless. We lowered our sights and began to examine smaller properties in less attractive situations, and finally settled for the ground floor of a Victorian terrace house in an inner London suburb. When Rocky returned to London and saw it, she thought we were mad.

'The place itself has possibilities, but what sort of neighbours are you going to have?'

'Poor ones,' I said.

'Exactly, and have you thought what sort of friends your children are going to make? You are going to have children, aren't you?'

As a matter of fact I had more than a suspicion that I was already in the family way, but I wasn't going to let her be the first to know. I said, 'Well, if we do, it won't do them any harm to mix with the sort of people among whom they're going to spend their lives.'

'But Conan's father left a fortune.'

'To his mother.'

'She doesn't need it. She could live on brandy fumes and stale bread.'

'You tell her that.'

'I'll lend you the money for something better,' but we had already borrowed money from Conan's mother for the down-payment, and from a building society for the mortgage, and we did not want to add to our indebtedness. We wanted the furniture and furnishings to be in keeping with the character of the house and I spent weeks looking round antique shops and salerooms. Vesta was extremely helpful and gave us a large mahogany dining-room table with twelve chairs, and a roll-top writing-desk.

We had decided on the date of our wedding, but I had purposely left the form of the wedding ceremony in abeyance and, out of consideration for father's feelings, I asked Conan if he would mind if we married in synagogue.

'Would I have to become a Jew first?'

'Of course.'

'Then the answer's no. I might have contemplated the possibility of adopting your religion if I suspected for a moment that you were yourself religious, but you're not. I'm not even sure that your father is, but he happened to chance upon an ancestor who was, and you're asking me to become a Jew not out of my own honest convictions, not out of yours, not even for your father's sake, but for the sake of what-do-you-call-him.'

'The Admor of Plotsk.'

'Well it's asking a lot, isn't it?'

It was, and we married in a registry office and had the reception at Roscoe House.

Father's absence cast a shadow over the event, but there was a sizeable contingent from Israel, including Sophie and Grace, Josh and Joss and even Katanchik, who, as far as I could remember, I hadn't even invited, but who almost assumed the role of surrogate father and insisted on taking a place by my side every time the photographer assembled us for a family photo.

'Your father is fine,' he kept reassuring me. 'He has settled down on the kibbutz as if he was born there. He is happy – a new man.' He almost suggested that the stroke had done him good.

We had not arranged for a band but, at the instigation of Katanchik, Josh managed to get hold of an accordian and Katanchik inveigled us – and even Conan's mother – into a *hora*, which we danced on the lawn, to the distress of the gardener, who stood in a corner tearing his hair and who later told Vesta that three hundred years of work had been undone in an afternoon.

I was slightly apprehensive as to how Stevie would treat the event, for by chance – and I promised her it was only by chance – our wedding day happened to fall on what she called her annual black day, namely her birthday. But she arrived all smiles in something white, silken and billowy, too billowy, I thought, for someone of her build.

The first thing she said to me, after falling upon me with kisses and tears, was, 'I suppose you've heard about poor Grace?'

I looked towards Grace who was in the company of a strikingly handsome man in a morning-coat and who did not look in any sense poor, but I suspected that I knew what she meant. She was without Otto. She had been without Otto at Josh's wedding. I knew that he was extremely busy, but I had also noticed that she rarely mentioned him in conversation.

'Her marriage has cracked up,' she whispered darkly. 'She couldn't have been married for more than five years.'

'She's been married for more than ten.'

'In which case one would have thought they'd have learned to live together. I mean one daren't ask people about their spouse these days, for one gets an embarrassed silence and the inevitable, "but didn't you know?". I really don't know why people bother. Might as well just live together. Makes separations so much cheaper and less traumatic. As it is, about the only people who get anything out of marriage these days are the lawyers. When I was your age, which wasn't *such* a long time ago, I wanted –'

I excused myself, for Tilly appeared just at that moment, wearing vaguely the same sort of outfit that Stevie wore, but with the height to carry it, and the same hat she had worn in Israel. She was one of the very few women I knew who looked good in hats. I rushed towards her and grasped her in an embrace which sent her hat flying and almost unsettled her coiffure. I couldn't understand how I could have viewed that dear and magnificent woman with such resentment all those years. She had helped father settle in at the kibbutz and had only just returned.

She was rather less sanguine about him than Katanchik. 'He's beginning to get around and is trying to make himself useful in the garden,' she said, 'but quite a number of the people have their parents living on the kibbutz, some of them elderly and religious. He spends much of his time with them, which worries me, for old age is contagious and so is religion.'

As we were talking, Grace came towards us and, for someone whose marriage was supposed to be in pieces, she seemed to be remarkably cheerful and composed, but what Stevie had told me was unfortunately true. I was upset that Grace hadn't told me about the break-up herself.

'I don't know how these things get around, for I haven't spoken to Stevie. You'd have been the first to know, but this is hardly the occasion to talk about broken marriages.'

'I'm truly sorry,' I said.

'I'm not, I'm much the happier for it. The whole situation was becoming impossible.'

I wanted to know more about it, but it was difficult to talk to her while there were guests bearing down upon me from all directions, but later, as people began to disperse, I took her aside, and she told me the whole story. There wasn't all that much to tell.

'When a scientist rises above a certain level he becomes a nomad,' she said, 'reading papers here, attending conferences there, now in one country as visiting professor, now in another on sabbatical, now in a third to compare notes with colleagues. At first I enjoyed it, because I liked travel and we went all over North America and Europe. But it soon became a chore and, in any case, once Callum and Amos were born, it was also impractical and I remained at home, while he shuttled around. I didn't mind this either, for several of the wives on the campus were in the same position and I made some good friends.'

'Then what caused the break?'

'Well, he wasn't with us even when he was with us, if you know what I mean. His mind was always on his work. You know I don't think I'd have minded so much if it had been another woman, for it would have suggested a streak of humanity, but he had no mind for anything but his work.

At meals we might all be talking about some small calamity which befell one of the children at school, but the conversation flowed around him, and as soon as the meal was over he'd dash back to his lab – we were virtually living on top of the shop. After a while – a long while as a matter of fact – I could stand it no longer, and we agreed to separate. He's taken on a visiting professorship in California, which makes it all the easier.'

Her news made me slightly apprehensive about myself. I regarded Grace as a sort of supernumerary sister, and of the five of us, two had already suffered broken marriages. Conan was involved in a great deal of travel and, in fact, when we first began looking around for a house we had tried to find something within easy reach of Heathrow.

We left that evening on the overnight train to Calais, and I asked Conan if he would have to travel as often as he had done before we were married.

'It's part of my job,' he said. 'We've got offices in Brussels and Amsterdam and I'm their European man.'

'Will you always be their European man?'

'Not necessarily. We've also got offices in Singapore, Hong Kong and Tokyo. One can't commute to these places, but I could be based there for a time. In any case I like travel, don't you?'

'I did.'

'Come, my dear. You're not that old and blasé. These journeys are like a breath of fresh air to me. I find England stale and claustrophobic.'

'What happens when the baby comes?'

'Babies are portable, and when they get older one can always dump them in boarding school. It's one of the reasons why international companies prefer to take on English people. Americans and Europeans tend to cart their entire household wherever they go.'

My spirits sank lower and lower as he continued, and by the time he finished I was in tears.

What a way to start a honeymoon!

Someone once wrote that to prepare for the worst is almost to invite it, and for a time my melancholy conviction that our marriage wouldn't work almost made it unworkable. I could see Conan being another Otto, hopping off here, there and everywhere three times a week and twice on Sundays, but in fact a few months after we married he was promoted to the planning division of the company which kept him in London most of the time. In any case, after our daughter, Helen, was born, he was disinclined to leave home at all, and I gradually accustomed myself to the fact that I was married, and happily married at that, and that I would stay married, and as one set of forebodings faded I began to discount others which beset me from time to time.

Stevie was a frequent visitor. She hadn't taken to Conan, nor Conan to her. She had good legs, but the mini skirt had come somewhat late to appeal to a woman of her age. It took her some time to inch her hem up to her knees, but once she had done so she liked the effect, and her hems stayed there long after the fashion had passed. Conan said she looked 'like a whore who has come out of retirement'. She overheard him and I was mortified, but I think she was rather taken with the description. It may have even given her new confidence, for one afternoon as we were having tea, she leaned forward and whispered that she had done 'something naughty. At my age too,' she added with a giggle. 'I had almost forgotten what it was like. You know, it's rather nice.'

'Anyone I know?' I asked.

'Shouldn't think so,' she said, digging her teeth into a cucumber sandwich. 'As a matter of fact, it wasn't even anyone that I know, but he was *very* experienced and *very* strong. He was foreign, Turkish, I think. Englishmen aren't very good at that sort of thing, are they?' Which was perhaps a tactless question to put to the pregnant wife of an Englishman.

'They're good enough to do the job.'

'Oh, you're talking about *functional* sex. Almost anyone is good enough for that. I'm talking about sex as a pleasure in its own right.'

'You had better be careful.'

'What do you mean?'

'Strangers can do strange things.'

'He did some *very* strange things, but they were a joy.'

'Will you be seeing him again?'

'It doesn't depend on me, but I do hope I will.'

She used to drop in two or three times a week and when several days passed and I didn't see her or hear from her, I began to worry and 'phoned her. There was no reply. That was in the afternoon. I tried again in the evening and couldn't get through at all: the line was out of order. I was by then too large to get behind the steering wheel of our modest vehicle and I asked Conan to drive me over.

'What for? Don't you see enough of the old cow?'

'I'm worried about her.'

'Do you think she's been raped?'

'Yes, as a matter of fact, but if you don't want to drive, I'll take a taxi.'

At which he put on his jacket and we drove over. When we got to the block of flats, we found several police cars outside and a small crowd on the pavement. We pushed through the crowds with difficulty, but once in the building we were stopped by the police. Who did I want to see?

'My aunt,' I said, 'Miss Courlander.' At which they exchanged glances and we were asked to wait while he went to see his superior. A grey-haired figure eventually emerged in a baggy brown suit.

'I'm sorry,' he said, 'I've got some bad news for you.' Stevie had been strangled and her room ransacked.

I nearly miscarried and was seriously ill for a time. Rocky came to look after me and Vesta flew to Israel to break the news to father.

I wouldn't have imagined anyone less likely to come to a tragic and violent end. Stevie had been the sun, the moon and the stars of our childhood – at least my childhood. Vesta had been able to establish some sort of relationship with mother, but I hadn't. Grandma had been a cold and distant little woman, grandmotherly in appearance, but not in temperament, and Tilly, too firm and officious to be easily approachable, so Stevie had meant everything to me. I found her warm, high-spirited and beautiful, and the house seemed to light up when she entered. She would have made a marvellous housewife and mother and, although she had had a good education and was a skilled linguist, I didn't think she was really cut out for a career. The war, I suspect, must have disrupted her life and put her on the wrong course, but I blamed Nick even more than the war. She could have married a dozen times, but she had set her heart on the Nick type and would not settle for anyone else.

Over a week passed before the police released the body for the funeral. There was a large crowd – it hadn't occurred to me she had so many friends – and I noticed many people I had seen her with at some time in the past, but whose names I couldn't remember. But one person, tall, white-haired, distinguished-looking, I recognized immediately – Nick. He arrived together with Tilly.

The funeral took place in the Golders Green crematorium on a cold, blustery, winter's day, with flecks of snow in the hedges and slush on the ground, and it reminded me strangely of the day poor mummy died thirty-five years earlier.

I had come in Vesta's Rolls, very much against the advice of my doctor, and remained in the car while everybody else went into the chapel.

They emerged half an hour later, chatting cheerfully and exchanging goodbyes, as if the fact that Stevie had gone up in smoke had relieved them of their burden of grief.

Nick noticed me in the car and put his head through the window. His eyes were sagging and watery, his nose was red, his breath smelt.

'How goes it?'

'I'll survive.'

'You're a big girl. How far are you gone?'

'Too far. By my calculations I'm in my fourteenth month. I should get a rebate on the next one.'

'You're very pale.'

'I'll be all right.'

Just then I felt as if I'd sprung a leak and asked him faintly to call Vesta. He didn't, but went to Robin instead, got the car keys and drove me straight to the hospital. Two days later I gave birth to a son. The boy, whom we called Willie, was fine, but I remained poorly for a number of weeks and Vesta took me to Roscoe House to convalesce. Robin was away, Conan had to remain in London, and Vida and Rocky came down to join us, so did Grace, for she had returned to England and her children were now at boarding-school. We were again a house of women, and I looked back on those few weeks as among the happiest in my life. I wasn't in pain or discomfort, but merely felt weak and would often sink into a cosy torpor. It was reassuring on opening my eyes to find the baby beside me and my sisters around me.

'Seeing Ducks with the infant makes me want to start again,' said Grace.

'What?' I said, '*sans* husband?'

'It's been done before,' said Rocky.

'But I've left it a bit late.'

'It's never too late,' said Vesta. 'Tilly had Josh when she was nearly forty-five.'

'Josh was a miracle child and Tilly was a miracle mother,' I reminded her.

'You know I do think babies are making a comeback,' said Vida.

'They've never fallen entirely into disuse,' said Grace.

'Yes, but they were something which only the working class had in any number. I think they're coming up market.'

'It's not that babies are coming up market,' said Grace, 'but that people are coming down market. Babies are about the only thing they can afford.'

All the talk of babies must have wearied Rocky, for she left after a few days.

'I do wish she would remarry,' said Vesta. 'I don't really think she's cut out for the role of eternal *femme fatale*, no woman is.'

'Why doesn't she have kids at least?' said Grace. 'She screws often enough.'

'She doesn't like to distend her uterus,' I said.

'I don't suppose she feels obliged to,' said Vida. 'As a family we've done our bit to keep the species going.'

'*You* certainly have,' I said. She had five children, Vesta had four, I had two and Josh one, but only one, Josh's son, Yigal, was a Courlander. I had vaguely thought of double-barrelling my name, but on reflection felt that Maitland–Courlander would have been too much of a mouthful. Josh had perpetuated the line and I felt fairly confident that the Courlanders were here to stay.

0641 01 853349 01 S   (IC=1)
BERMANT, CHAIM   04/30/84
THE HOUSE OF WOMEN
(3) C1983 FIC. BER

BER Bermant, Chaim
     The house of women

12.95

DATE

LONGWOOD DATE DUE 7 23
LONGWOOD DATE DUE 06 90
LONGWOOD DATE DUE 4 89
M 18
JY 31 881
LONGWOOD DATE DUE 8 16 90

Longwood
MIDDLE ISLAND PUBLIC LIBRARY
© THE BAKER & TAYLOR CO.